SOME TIME

It starts...badly!

Frank Neary

ISBN-13: 9798632536264
ISBN-10: 1477123456
Library of Congress Control Number: 2018675309

Cover design by: Art Painter
Printed in the United States of America

SOME
TIME

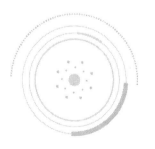

Family

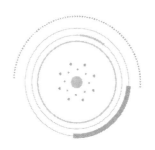

Prologue

A PALE BLUE LIGHT BLINKS on, and then off, in the grey whiteness.

Some time later, it does it again.

CHAPTER 1

21 Earth seconds in.

Pitch black...

...and I'm fucking drowning. Or I think I am? I struggle for air but can't breathe in through my mouth or nose. I can't exhale either. I'm suffocating, and I'm starting to panic! I'm going to die very fucking soon. I keep trying to suck in air, but there isn't any. I keep trying, straining my chest and lungs - pulling, pulling. Nothing. I think I'm going to blackout. I try to shout 'HELP!' but can't, my lungs are empty, completely empty. It feels like there is a membrane over my face, in fact, over all of my skin but under my clothes. I can feel the hair on my head being squashed down to my scalp and the hairs on my arms and legs also. It's like I'm inside a vast deflated balloon that is sticking to me but moving with me as I thrash about. Have I been shrink-wrapped or vacuum-packed? And I'm floating in the air. There is no resistance to my flailing. I kick to get to the surface as if I'm in water - I'm not. I'm trying to pull the membrane away from over my nose, and I reach into my mouth to pull it out, or rip it, to let the air in. But there's nothing there, no membrane. I'm panicking, scrabbling, helpless, seconds feel like minutes. I think I'm about to suffocate. Everything's going white...

And then the air comes rushing in. It's cold and stings my nasal cavity and the back of my throat, I can't gulp it down quickly enough. Gravity takes over, and I'm no longer floating, I collapse onto a hard, flat surface, face down with only inches to fall, the floor was right beneath me. Eyes closed, scooping in huge lungfuls of air, hyperventilating. The whiteness stays as I gulp in air. I start to control my breathing and get onto all fours, I'm recovering. Now my brain feels like it is flaring, too much oxygen, but better than none at all. I'm really heady. Physically, my head is still bent down, my lungs feel fuller, the oxygen in the blood is returning to my extremities, pins and needles dissipate. I open my eyes and see a dull grey-white floor.

"Sorry about that. My bad." I hear from a Human-sounding voice with an almost cheery tone.

I look up in the direction of the voice and see no-one, just dull grey whiteness. This is fucking weird. I'm still breathing hard.

Before I started suffocating, I had been sitting on a packed commuter train heading for work. There was the noise of the train on the tracks, coughing passengers, shuffling newspapers, the 'tz-sck, tz-sck' of somebody's headphones nearby. I was squeezed on to the aisle seat, next to a massive man sitting by the window. Every seat

was taken, other passengers were standing in the aisle all bound for London. I was doing the quick crossword on the back of today's free morning paper. Six down, 'Craft with one mast and one sail' six letters, I was about to write 'dinghy'.

"WHAT THE FUCK IS GOING ON??" I shout.

"I should introduce myself." repeats the calm yet cheery voice, echoless. Apart from this sound, and any sounds I'm making, it's silent. Totally silent.

I turn my head. There's a white metallic, metre high, column sticking up out of the ground. It has a blinking blue light towards the top. I think it's talking to me.

"I'm 15." The voice offers, it is definitely coming from the column. The light continues to blink at a regular, intermittent pace from each of its four sides.

"What the fuck's happening! Where am I?", I'll admit, I'm not at my most talkative best, I'm disorientated and confused, I don't really know what to say or how to feel.

"What's going on?"

"You're on a starship." the column again.

"No I'm fucking not, I'm on the 7:58 to Waterloo!"

"No, I can assure you, you aren't.", after a short pause, a heartbeat,

"Not anymore - sorry about that. Would you like to sit down, and I'll explain?"

"Where am I?" I raise my voice again, demanding now.

"Still on a starship." with no change in chirpy tone.

"Yeah 'course, you said that." I'm recovering my composure, I'm breathing, warm and dry and don't seem to be in danger. I can't work out how this has happened, It's just surreal. "Why am I on a starship and not on the train?"

"If Sir, would like to sit down - a drink perhaps?"

"Fuck the drink, and the 'Sir', what is going on?" God, I can be masterful in the face of adversity.

"I realise it's a shock. I can explain everything. Please sit down."

Now it's imploring me, not as cheery as before but definitely more 'asky' than 'telly'.

To my right is a brown leather Chesterfield sofa. I hate those things, I've always found them really uncomfortable, is it a low back or a high arm? It's neither, it's both, all in one - neither a back nor an arm. It doesn't know what it is, so it's just uncomfortable. I've never understood why anyone would buy one. A sofa that doesn't know its arse from its elbow.

I perch on the edge of the monstrosity and put my head in my hands.

"Is this some kind of joke, a prank?" I massage my temples, "Am I on Saturday night television? Are the two little fellas going to jump out?"

"I understand you're confused and you're using an attempt at comedy to hide your creeping fear. Please, there's a glass of water next to you, why not take a drink? I can explain everything."

"Roofies?", I'd been to festivals, and out clubbing, in my younger days, I know what goes on, "And if I have been abducted by an alien species, everyone knows there's going to be anal probing". I clench at the thought.

"Hardly. Not my style I can assure you. I can understand the lack of trust. There really is nothing to worry about. I am not going to hurt you in any way."

I'm generally softening and take the opportunity to relax my sphincter. I don't feel in danger. The voice is friendly and not threatening, and I can only fathom a few real potential explanations: 1) It is a starship, 2) I'm dead, drugged or dreaming somehow 3) This is a very elaborate prank, 4) Can't think of anything else.

"Can I go back to where I was please?" I find politeness often works.

"Unfortunately, that can't happen. Please try to relax, there's a lot to tell you about."

"THIS IS FUCKING MENTAL! Where's the train gone?" I jump up. I've relapsed into shouting and flailing my arms around. I scream and shout - and jump up and down on the spot a few times, and then on the sofa. I'm flipping out because this situation is beyond comprehension. There doesn't seem to be anything I can do to affect a change.

"I must insist."

It's not said with any menace, or with any apparent change in friendly tone, but there is a degree of finality. I flump back down on the sofa. And eye the drink suspiciously.

"You must trust that I am not trying to poison you but don't drink if you don't want to."

I don't want to. I just sit back silently and grumpily, 'man spread' on the uncomfortable sofa, trying to look blasé about the situation. For a short while, there is silence, I look around me, there is just dull grey whiteness as far as the eye can see in any direction. This is odd for two reasons. One, there is no discernible line between the floor and the ceiling. This would suggest a round, walled room except it isn't, I can see the floor stretching away 360 degrees around me, this is totally flat. I cannot actually see a ceiling, but when I look up, there is the same dull whiteness above. This seems to be a long way up, but I can't really tell how far. The second point is, there is no darkness or shadow. If the floor and ceiling stretched out to infinity, I would expect to see darkness over distance and light sources, either hanging or internal. This is all a uniform grey whiteness, which is lit the same in all directions. It is an odd place to be, yet not too frightening as I could see an approaching would-be assailant for miles before they got to me. I could either prepare myself to fight well in advance of their arrival or start running and get a good head start. Not sure where I'd be running to though.

So it's just me, the talking column, and an uncomfortable brown leather sofa. I look back at '15'.

"Are you going to tell me what is going on, exactly what is going on?" I emphasise 'exactly'.

"I'm going to break it to you gently. You're dead."

That gave it to me straight!

"Ouch! OK, so, this is heaven. Are you God or St Peter?" I'm laughing because I certainly don't feel dead.

"No, this is not heaven, nor is it hell. I'm certainly no god or other. This is not the afterlife either. You are technically dead, on Earth, but you haven't actually died."

Clearly, the explaining bit is going to take a while…

CHAPTER 2

93 Earth years in.

THIS IS REALLY WEARING me down, he's bigger but slower than me, and it seems that no matter how many times I hit him, and what I hit him with, he doesn't seem to flinch. I'm trying to target his face and even direct hits to the nose, above or below, or the eyes, right into them, nothing stops him from coming forward. I've smashed down hard on his head with my heel with a colossal chopping kick, but no change, I've tried sweeping him to take him down to the ground. He's either parried these away or jumped and dodged the attack. On the one occasion, I did land, he was moving into the attack, which glanced off and was rendered useless as its power was reduced. I've targeted his sex organs and his breathing tube - no real reaction there either - the occasional odd look of discomfort but nothing to really write home about. I've also targeted repeatedly the 'soft spot', which I've read these aliens have. It's on the 'chest' area high up towards the shoulder on the right-hand side. There is a main artery and feeding

tube that both pass through underneath this area. The intel suggests that this area can be vulnerable. I've got close to it a few times but not actually delivered anything significant to it. Of course, he realises this is a vulnerable area as he is very good at protecting it, and it's small, it's only about three centimetres round. Not only do I have to hit it, but I also have to find it first. It's not exactly marked with a red pen 'Please hit me here', but there is a slight change in texture to the skin where I think it is. I've been near but not actually hit close enough yet. The issue is that I'm on the back foot. This big lump keeps coming, and I'm getting tired landing shots that make no dent. The way this is going to pan out is that I keep running and probing, which is going to eventually knock the puff out of me, then when I'm pooped, he's going to shit all over me and stomp my head into the dirt.

At least that's something to look forward to.

I take another couple of steps back and wait for him to come and meet me as I decide what to do next. He lumbers into me, and I try to push him away. I stand my ground and fire a sidekick straight into his middle. This is a with a bent leg that I straighten on impact, so it's not really a sidekick, more of a push backwards. He reverses a half step, but my standing foot also hops back as his sheer weight moves me. I bounce twice again to keep my balance.

I've not really been attacked yet, everything has been defensive, parries and pushes away. I'm not sure this thing is actually trying to grab and grapple me or hit me. I just think he wants to jump on top of me when the occasion presents itself. It's a war of attrition.

One, which I'm losing.

My next attack. I throw a good solid combination. I double up the left jab, set him up, then throw a straight right bang on the schnoz. I follow this up with a left hook to the chin-ish area; which is powerful enough to turn its head, and when the head comes back to its original position, I hammer a massive uppercut under the jaw area which jolts its head back sharply. The head then returns to its starting position, undamaged, again and we carry on where we left off. Maybe, these attacks are all mounting up, and perhaps it's really hurting inside? Maybe there is no outward show of pain, the sheer volume of my attacks will just mount up, and it will just eventually die - or something, but if I punch myself out going for gold, I could end up as pavement pizza very soon.

I step back a couple of steps, and as it moves forward, I step back again, then again. I'm getting my breath back. I realise I'm tiring, and my options are running out. It comes forward, and I step back again. It steps forward once more, and now I spin. As I turn on the ball of my left foot, I start to raise my right foot from the floor to sort of head height. My hips and shoulders twist and get ahead of my right foot, leaving it behind for a split second. I can feel the curve of my spine, the hips and shoulders moving forward simultaneously, the leg stalling back marginally,

purposefully, now speeding to catch up. The spring that is my spine ratchets up, my head whips around and coils the spring, even more, I am now locked on to a three centimetres round target as the alien steps into range. My foot is currently travelling, fast, the tension on my spine uncoils, the pelvis comes through, and the leg whips around with tremendous speed. It's balletic, I am in a perfect vertical up from the ball of my left foot, through my calf then thigh, up through my core, my neck and head. The spin is frictionless, the spine unwinds and the following leg arcs around to make vicious, brutal contact directly on to the sweet spot, hard, fast, clean, precise.

It's a massive impact through the heel delivered with enormous force and great speed. My momentum continues to turn me as the leg retracts and returns to the floor, my turning kick complete. I now have my back to the creature.

My form is perfect. The execution is imperious, beautiful. It felt like slow-motion. I was in the moment, but also out of the moment. Out of body, as if looking down from above, watching the perfect arc being traced by my heel with a 'whoosh' line behind it. The sharp impact, the completion of the curve.

No panic. No thought. Just the sublime arc, the sweeping shape.

I don't look back to see the creature, but if I did, I would see it slump to its knees. Eyes open but lifeless. It swayed as if to fall forward but then teetered backwards and bumped to the floor as dead meat. I walk calmly away.

I never look back, I am relaxed.

From the moment of contact, I knew it was over.

3 Earth hours in.

I'M STILL SITTING ON the brown leather Chesterfield; I've been here a fair bit now. I've been talking back and forth with '15' trying to get more information and trying to trick it into revealing the prank. I've had no joy yet; it's sticking to its story. I've relaxed a little. Doesn't look like I'm going to get to work today, but I've got an excuse, albeit a pretty unbelievable one. We're going away camping in Cornwall with the kids this weekend. I'd better be back for that. Although no-one, particularly the kids, will believe what's happened.

I've drunk some of the water. It doesn't seem to have had any effect on me other than to hydrate me as water should.

"You can do everything you did on Earth and much, much more. I'll build you an environment."

"It's not what I mean..."

About 20 metres in front of me I suddenly see a green dot of about two centimetres in circumference. This then elongates until it has drawn a two-centimetre thick line three metres in length on the grey white floor. I think the line is below the surface of the floor, but I can't tell for sure. The line stops lengthening, and then the whole line starts to extend upwards, silently, the lime green grows. Soon there is a three-metre by three-metre lime green, flat, shiny wall in front of me. A new, frosted glass panel then starts to grow out, full height, from the left-hand side edge of the lime green panel. It stops also extending at three metres long. Now there is a six by three-metre frosted glass and lime green panel wall. It is the only 'detail' I can see in any direction outside of me, the Chesterfield and the talking traffic bollard.

Next, I can hear footsteps coming from behind the lime green wall, then a figure emerges from behind the wall to the frosted glass section. It walks along to the edge of the frosted glass and around the corner into full view. It is a Human woman and a pretty special one at that.

"Hi, I'm Mollie Seers", she extends a hand, smiles and pauses.

My jaw drops.

I recognise her immediately. This appears to be Mollie Seers, without peer, the most well-known supermodel in the world. She looks a million dollars, although I know she's worth considerably more.

Perfect smile, perfect teeth, sparkling brown eyes. Her hair is sun-kissed and golden, lots of flowing long tresses held loosely upon her head. The smallest amount of makeup, which is probably not necessary anyway. She is wearing a crisp, white cotton shirt, unbuttoned to show just the right amount of cleavage, her enticing, perfectly formed breasts curve beneath. Her long, lithe legs are squeezed into spray-on denim jeans with foxing and cuts to the thighs and knees which reveal glimpses of perfect California tan. She wears black patent short boots with four-inch heels which altogether (including the height of her hair) puts her at about six foot two tall.

God, she looks fantastic.

I reach out and shake her elegant hand. It's warm and perfectly manicured. It feels like what the hand of a stunningly beautiful, Human female, uber-babe's hand should feel like - a firm but not too solid shake.

"Hi, what're you doing here?" I hear myself say dumbly.

I don't really know much about supermodels, but I do know a fair bit about football, so I know that Mollie is American, and has been recently married to Toto Rodrigez, a Spanish football player. He happens to be one of the best and most expensive players in the world and plays for Real Madrid, the 'Galacticos' - superstars. He's an amazing player, has won multiple league titles and World Cups and seems to be a really great guy with loads of money and who's right on top of his game. Even opposition fans seem to love him. This Power Couple's high-profile romance, and then marriage, has been covered in every newspaper, website, gossip app and magazine in the world. If you don't know who Mollie and Toto are then you probably have been living on another planet! They are the perfect celebrity couple.

"15 asked me to help you with what's goin' on. He thinks that if another Human explains to you, then it'll be easier to understand."

"So you're real?"

"No, I'm an avatar built by 15. I look and feel like Mollie, I act like her, I walk, and talk like her. I swish my hair like her (she swishes her hair). I breathe and function in much the same way as her, but I'm a being that's been created by 15 to communicate with you. I'm here to help you to understand what's happening and to help you acclimatise to your surroundings."

"And, my apologies for being slightly rude Mollie, do you think that the highest-paid supermodel in the world is the best person to help me understand all this madness?"

Mollie says "Would'ya prefer someone or something else?" She's still smiling and doesn't look taken aback in the slightest by being deselected by me.

I try to quickly think of all the people who would suit this role better than a stunning supermodel - my mum and dad? Sadly, they're both dead, and although I'd genuinely love to see them both again, I don't want robot mum and robot dad knocking about, I think it'd weird me out. My family? My friends? A work colleague, someone in authority - an old school teacher perhaps? - wouldn't trust any of them. I thought for a while, whilst Mollie smiled at me and occasionally swished her hair around, and settled for a radio DJ I regularly listen to when I drive to the station in the morning. Not that I'm a particular fan, but I think he sounds like a 'nice bloke', he talks with relative intelligence, handles the nutters well on phone-ins, he's a similar age to me, and I've never met him.

He's Paul Collins, he's the best I can think of under pressure, and he'll do.

I tell 15 and Mollie, my choice. She smiles gently, still with amazing sparkles in her eyes, and with that 'one foot crossing over in front of the other foot' catwalk walk that models instinctively know how to do, walks back behind the glass screen, I'm sad to see her go and watch her go intensely every perfect step. Maybe she'll be around for a chat later? I see another figure walking behind the glass, this time with a more relaxed gait, almost an 'amble', and then Paul appears wearing scruffy jeans and a well-worn 'The Stooges' t-shirt looking slightly shocked. This is disarming because it immediately makes me feel he's more Human - as if he's not supposed to be here either.

It's freaky, I don't really even know what this guy looks like, I've probably only ever seen him once or twice on the TV. But he looks like how I sort of remember. He comes over and shakes my hand warmly and introduces himself in his matey, DJ way but makes it clear he is another version of 15, his 'Humanised mouthpiece.'

Behind us, new furniture has appeared and thank fuck, the Chesterfield has gone. There is a small, round, metal folding garden table painted gloss racing green with two matching folding chairs. Very suburban, 'de rigueur' for outer space. Paul and I sit down and have a friendly chat. There is a big, icy jug of homemade lemonade on the table and two glasses. Paul pours two drinks, and we both take a sip.

I can't believe how calmly I am taking this situation. I think it's because it's just so odd. I'm sitting at a green folding garden table with a radio DJ who doesn't exist. He is my interface with this spaceship that has abducted me, and we're apparently hurtling through outer space possibly billions of light-years from Earth. I can't go home, and every person I knew including my wife and kids are getting further and further away, and I have a creeping suspicion that if this is true, they may never see or hear from me ever again. I feel like I'm in a strange, lucid dream, but deep down now, I know this is the situation, and it's one I can't change or influence at the moment.

15-as-Paul starts to speak to me. "Every Human child has thoughts, dreams, sometimes fears and nightmares, about travelling through space. Only a few have ever made it off your planet. Mostly from your own space programmes, and a smaller few by another method, such as what has happened to you."

"Alien abduction?" I offer.

"Mostly, yes. But not always for the wrong reasons. It's not all about experimentation as you suspect." Paul continues. "Space is endless and difficult for Humans to really comprehend. There's no end, there's no beginning,

there're billions and billions of planets, and billions and billions of races to discover and meet."

It's oddly better to hear this from Paul than from a box with a blinking light and a smiley voice. The weirdness of the situation is both dreamlike and soothing yet so absurd and non-threatening that it takes you off guard and is oddly peaceful. Saying that, it isn't too long before my basic Human need for shelter kicks in.

"Where am I going to sleep?"

"Where'd you want to sleep?" Paul asks.

"Preferably on Earth in my own bed?"

"Unfortunately, I can't make that happen. What would be second best in outer space?"

"In a bed, in a room, somewhere with an atmosphere: air to breathe, gravity to keep me down, warm, dry. The usual stuff. Food would be good too."

A narrow, white line starts to draw itself up from the floor on the green wall. After about two metres, this turns at a right angle and draws along for about a metre before turning again at another right angle, and heading back to the floor. Once here, the door shape opens a few inches from the left, hinged on the right.

"Please, come and have a look." Paul motions me towards the door with a warm smile.

I get up, walk over to the door and push it open. I'm not afraid, I don't feel like I have to be nervous or that I'm under any specific threat. If anyone wanted to hurt me, they could have quickly done so by now.

The door swings back and reveals what looks like a high-class suite in an excellent hotel. A little business-like, but perfectly acceptable. A beautifully made-up king-size bed, tasteful artworks on the wall, warm lighting throughout. A ceiling, which I've been missing recently. A free-standing seven feet by three feet flat mirror, a nightstand and armchair. I walk across the thickly carpeted floor and into the separate suite of rooms; a spacious dressing room with an array of clothing which looks remarkably like the clothing I already own at home. All freshly laundered and hanging up or neatly folded. I go to the large window which has nets hanging in front of them, I move the nets to peep out and can just see the same dull, grey whiteness as before.

Paul pipes up, "I can make any clothing you'd like. If you've any old favourites that have long since become landfill, I can recreate them for you. Like an old pair of trainers, you lived in while you were a student or that T-shirt that you lent to an old girlfriend and then never saw it again. Whatever you want, you can have. I can recreate anything that's existed on Earth. I'm quite intrigued by Humans and clothes."

Then the bathroom; a huge bath. I've always hated baths, mainly because the one at home is not big enough. If you're a decent-sized male, around the six-foot-tall mark, you've either got your legs under the water and most of your top half out, going cold or your shoulders under but your knees bent, and the majority of both legs out of the water, quickly drying. Here's a bath I can be submerged in up to my neck very quickly. I might take more baths now. The shower/wet area seems to have jets from about 100 nozzles in all directions pointing inwards together. It seems using too much hot water isn't really an issue here. There's a stand-up, heated air-drying section. They've got a shit version of one of these in my local swimming baths. Although there are towels, it looks like I'm really not expected to need them after a bath or shower. A basin, toilet - nothing special here and I'm glad to see 15 hasn't opted for an over-the-top fully functional Japanese toilet, squirting little jets of water towards my nether regions whilst playing mood music, and thanking me for my faecal deposit, before informing me of the weight. That would've freaked me out a little. There is a bathroom cabinet, which's full of brands I recognise, including drug brands of ibuprofen, aspirin, decongestant, hay fever tablets and antacids.

"Do I need the drugs?" I ask.

"No, these are superfluous. Like many things, they're really here for your reassurance. It's the same with the washing and other personal care items; soaps, shampoos, aftershaves, etc., you don't need these either. They're just here to help you feel at home and to help you to adjust to your surroundings. If you want them to go, I'll remove them." says Paul.

"No, keep them here, for now, please", feeling like home felt good.

"What about time, hours and days? When will I know it's night time and when to go to sleep?"

"I'll adjust the light in the living accommodation as per Earth days. But what you've got to remember is that time is different here, or wherever we find ourselves than on Earth. Again it's difficult to explain to you simply but days on Earth are very much foreshortened when looking back from our current point. Do you understand any of Einstein's theories?"

"Not really, never really bothered."

"They are flawed but do have some elements of credibility in them, The Old Man was on the right track. If you're happy to just accept, then I see no reason to explain."

I shrugged, barely listening, and continued to mooch around the room.

Paul walked around the room a bit then said, "Shall I leave you now?"

"Will you be around tomorrow?" I answered.

"Of course."

Then he left.

I'm sitting alone on the edge of my bed. I feel drained even though it can only be three or four hours since I left home for work. I'm stuck for an explanation. Although I can't see outside, I actually believe I'm on a spaceship. It's all too well put together not to be true. It's too grand and impressive to be just a prank. The only other real explanations are that I'm drugged or dead. If that's the case, then I've nothing to lose anyway so I might as well

roll with it. I kick off my shoes and lie back on top of the covers of the bed. I shut my eyes and just try to relax, my breathing slows and deepens, within a few short minutes, I'm fast asleep.

CHAPTER 4

1 Earth hour in.

"W HY ME?"

"You were dead."

"No I wasn't, I was on the train doing the crossword."

"...And then you were dead."

"But I wasn't." I implore.

"I don't want to argue with you. Yes, you were on the train, but then there was an accident. Your train passed under a weak bridge just as a large, fully laden petrol tanker was going over. The bridge gave way, and the tanker fell sideways off the bridge onto your carriage and exploded. It was a terrible tragedy, and a carriage load of train passengers were burned to death."

"How many?"

"You were one of 44 that perished, there were also many survivors who were burned or otherwise injured."

"So I was fried?"

"Technically, no. I shipped you off-planet a couple of milliseconds before the explosion."

"So I didn't die?"

"You had a 100% certainty of death if you stayed where you were."

"But I didn't die?"

"No, you didn't."

"So surely they looked for my body and couldn't find it?"

"There were some physical remains of the other 43, but the fire was so intense that very little of the remains of the other 43 were recovered, and believe me, there were no surviving witnesses to see you being shipped away. I then left small samples of your DNA in the wreckage, enough to satisfy an investigator and coroner that you had been incinerated in the fire. If you'd have seen the aftermath, you'd have no need or expectation of finding a full physical body."

"You faked my death and left some of my DNA so you could kidnap me?"

"Or, with some positive spin, your death was a certainty, I left some DNA that amounted to little more than your metaphorical toenail clippings as proof of your demise, and I've given you the chance to continue living - a new life. An opportunity to see new things to discover, to learn, to live, to breathe for as long as you want beyond your 100% certain death."

"What about the others, why me?"

"Good question." There is a pause, I don't believe 15 is thinking, I think he's doing it for drama. "Can you think of any reason why I'd choose you?"

"No. Average Joe really."

There is another small pause before, "Correct. You were not special; you were chosen, though. You were the one most likely not to survive and least likely to leave any physical residue."

"'Residue' how lovely. So you must have known the accident was going to happen in advance as you seemed to spend a lot of time calculating the odds of survival for each passenger and the chance of them leaving 'Residue'. Why did you not stop the accident from happening?"

"Firstly, I cannot interfere with the occurrences on individual planets that have not yet had First Contact. This is beyond my remit. I took advantage of an inevitable situation, which is allowable. My actions could not, and would not, have altered the course of Humanity in any way. Secondly, I can make the calculations you are talking about in picoseconds and in fact, many billion more. Working out the survival odds of a few desperate Humans facing certain immolation is a pretty simple task." another short pause, "I would suggest you're lucky to be alive."

I am, I know that. The option is death, and I'm happyish to have been given a second chance. I don't like that I've been abducted and the fact I'm hurtling away from my home planet and everyone and everything dear to me. But even if I were there, I would be dead, and everyone and everything I loved would be lost to me anyway. This may not be my choice for an 'afterlife', but it's all I've got.

It's better than almost every Human on the planet has had before me, so, as I don't seem to be in any danger, and although I'm wary of the company, and the slightly tall story of how I got to be in this mess, I'm still sort of OK with being here and not pushing up daisies. The ship seems to be benign; it appears to be friendly and is sup porting my life. I should stick with it and keep it on side in case it changes its mind.

CHAPTER 5

1,429 Earth years in.

'QUICK ON HIS FEET', that's an excellent way to describe this one, he's slight, bendy and nimble. Not what I'd call a 'heavyweight'. He's a similar shape to me, a biped with two arms and a head - on top, with a face on the front side. So quite close. The appendages are all a bit different, and the guy himself (I'm assuming it's male) is sort of silvery skinned. Not silvery like on a TV show like Dr Who where they just paint a Human silver, this is silver from under the skin, with lots of different shades of silver ,in the same way we have lots of different shades in our skin colouration. He's about six feet tall, has a 'plus sign' of black fur on the top of his head (X marks the spot!). I can't see any ears, but he can hear me. His eyes look like two sunglasses lenses, black, rounded, shiny - no discernible pupils. Its head is a similar size to mine, but it has a large mouth with two rows of sharp teeth which it bares at me, continually making hissing noises through them. He has two slender arms but no hands at the ends, just stump.

But the stumps are pretty good in that the weapons we are using can be pushed through the stump, and then the stump moulds to grip itself tightly around the handle end. They could probably also be used to unscrew nuts. In fact, they could probably be used for everything we use our fingered hands for, except, maybe, 'Rock, Paper, Scissors'. We both have a pair of long straight, quite heavy knives. They are very simple, about 12 inches long with thick, heavy blades which are razor-sharp on one edge, pointed and metallic. We are both also wearing some armour; arm and shoulder protection, linked across the back. So no armour to the front, a stomach, chest or head strike seems to be what is expected. There is also a plexiferro 'cricket box' which I'm wearing under a pair of shorts, and there are two spiked overshoes to inflict kicking injuries. Each overshoe has a four-inch sharp spike angled up at 45 degrees from the toe. We've been circling clockwise and counter-clockwise for a good few minutes now with neither of us really fashioning any sort of meaningful attack. I'm worried that this could be one of those where one good attack is all you need, and the fight can then end very quickly.

Then, quite suddenly, it comes, like lightning. He jumps in towards me, straight on and kicks me with all his might, as hard as he possibly can - straight in the balls. Fuck knows what happens to my plexiferro cricket box, but its structural integrity loses all grasp of reality, and the four-inch shoe spike of my opponents' right boot goes straight through it, and penetrates hard up into me. The power of which momentarily lifts me up off the floor. I feel the sharp pain engulf my whole being. The shoe spike has impaled one of my balls, and the base of the shaft of my penis, and has then pushed up through all-encompassing, and the pain is total. Everything goes white, my ears pop, every nerve explodes. I hear myself scream from behind a closed door, its muffled - the electric shock, the piercing pain. This is happening in super slo-mo seconds. The white clears from my eyes, the explosion from my ears but the pain doesn't subside, I retch. I look down and see the spike still in my balls, still inside me, with foot attached. It's embedded so deeply that my opponent cannot pull it out. This puts him off balance, hopping around on his left foot, trying to retrieve his right. I don't think I've got much left; I think I'm about to pass out. Blood is oozing onto his boot. I think he's been taken as much by surprise as I have. Instinctively, I swing the two heavy knives with their razor edges with all my might. Both hands making perfect arcs together - one from the left and one from the right, they both meet pretty much in the middle. I don't even feel the bones as they slice their way through their double haymaker arcs. Blood erupts from my assailant as he is cut virtually in half. He falls backwards, and I blackout. I think his foot is still attached as I crumple to the ground.

I wake in my bed. I stretch a little and roll over before really waking. I suddenly remember my last memory and shove a hand down to check 'the wedding tackle', which all seems to be present and correct. A wave of relief passes over me. I don't know how long I've been asleep for, how long I've been recuperating. I've woken up from the sleep of an unstressed man, fresh as a daisy. It feels great to smell the dew on the breeze, the gauze curtains floating gently up on fresh, cooling air which wafts over my skin. I can hear playful birdsong somewhere outside. A far cry from the horrific last memory I had; blood, pain, sweat, vomit, phlegm, dirt. Once again, I've survived intact, or I think intact.

I press a small button on my bedside table, and within 10 seconds a darkly tanned, curvaceous Latina in a pair of high-cut, frayed Daisy Dukes and a yellow string bikini bra walks in through the open French windows.

She singsongs with her Colombian accent, "Good morning Señor, is there anything I can help you with?" and pulls the bow at the back of her bikini, her full breasts spring loose.

This, very quickly, raises my attention.

I'm back.

CHAPTER 6

2 Earth days in (after lunch).

" **Y**OU CAN LIVE HERE forever, indefinitely. I can
... sustain you, give you everything you want and
need."

I awoke in my new bed. I had a quick, fabulous shower
- jetted profusely from all directions - and dried myself
with a towel. I found a pair of jeans, exactly like a pair
I had at home, laundered and folded in the wardrobe. I
also threw on a t-shirt that I'd never seen before, it was a
dark, dusty purple and had the word "SEISMIC" written
in a block font in white on the front. It fitted well and felt
appropriate. I'd slept well initially, but then something in
the back of my brain woke before the rest of me, which
made me toss and turn thinking of Emily and the kids.
I've been away on work trips for longer than a few nights
and never felt as I do now.

What if this story is real? Then I'm dead to them, and
I'll never see them again. The idea of them crying over my
coffin, burying hardly any, already cremated, 'remains'.

Those poor kids - my poor kids, missing their daddy. Emily, missing her husband, her life partner, the only woman I've ever truly loved. When actually I'm alive, light years away, and can't do a thing to help - to make the pain go away. It's the worst feeling, it festers away in the pit of my stomach. I want them here with me, or me back with them.

But it's also so far removed from the norm that it's easy to forget.

When I came out of the dressing room, there was hot tea and heavily buttered toast waiting for me. I breakfasted quickly and re-emerged, and I'm now talking to 15 again. Yes, it's still here, and it's still a blinking bollard. I'm back on the Chesterfield, lying end to end with my head down on the seat at one end and my feet up resting on the arm/back at the other end.

"But I'm 52 and in a 52-year-old body? I don't want to live to be two hundred years old in this ageing body as it's mainly fucked already." I said.

The problem with ageing is that there's so much stuff you want to do, but as you grow older, your body is less and less capable of doing any of it.

I used to look after myself, then in my forties, I dropped the rope. I don't eat well, and I'm overweight, I've always been a drinker, so my liver is fucked - and I've committed genocide to millions of brain cells. I'm not fit, can't stand too much exercise, I did loads when I was younger which is probably why my lower back is fucked, and I have to pay a chiropractor £40 every month to crack me back (and my back) into shape again. It's running repairs really just to keep the skeleton in some sort of decent shape, I've no real muscle tone to help the bones stay where they're supposed to be. My knees are also gone, partly from playing a shit load of football as a kid all the way up into my late 30s, and partly from jogging on the roads in my 20s and 30s to keep fit enough to play football. I'm now overweight because my knees aren't good enough for me to run the calories off, but then the additional weight is making my knees worse - sort of a Catch-22.

My skin's like shit. I've had too much sun, and Earth's gravity has been pulling it gradually but steadily down off my body for years. My hair's pretty good, I've still got most of it on my head, but it's receding so I've started to look like Dracula except it couldn't get much whiter. Of course, I also suffer from other ageing problems with hair. I'd have six-inch-long ones growing out of the middle of the bow of my eyebrows if I didn't trim them regularly. I've got hairs growing out of, and all around, my ears, long thick black ones. I'm not quite sure what they're for and why they're so black when the ones on my head are so white. If I didn't crop them back, I think I'd look like a lynx with the long, sticky-up ear tufts. Then there are the nose hairs. I'm thinking of letting them grow a few inches and then trimming them straight across at the bottom, just above my upper lip, so it will look like a little Hitler moustache but with the hairs growing down from my nose rather than out from my face, more like a 'lip fringe'.

It's all pretty disgusting, and all I've got to look forward to is a lifetime of degradation. My former young, virile, vibrant self is going to jog away, off into the distance, leaving the old, fat stumbling man just out of the starting blocks, hoping someone's going to come over soon to give him a lift in a car. What is the point of Humans living longer than 50 years if their bodies are so severely on the slide? There's no point living until you're 100 or more if you're drinking food through a tube, deaf as a post and sitting in a wheelchair with people referring to you as 'dearie' all day. As one of my friends wrote in my fiftieth birthday card, "Happy Birthday. Now you're fat, fifty and fucked!"

15 doesn't seem to think this is an issue.

"I can't reverse ageing, but I can regenerate cells. I can alter, change, strengthen, and repair almost all of your body, in effect. I can't actually make you nineteen again, but I can regenerate your cells to a point when they are as good as they were when you were nineteen or twenty, or any other given time in your adult life. I can change you to your own bespoke design, I can make you anything you want physically within your current parameters."

"What does 'current parameters' mean?" I ask.

"I can't give you three arms or more than one penis."

"Got it. How?"

"Old technology - nanobots. Something you're just starting to get your head around on Earth. Mine are each made up of thousands of tiny fields, which coalesce to create a subatomic robot that I can introduce into your body to repair tissue, to rebuild, to restore and regrow. It is a simple and painless process."

"O.K. I've heard of the concept of nanobots, sounds a bit mental but I'm not opposed to it. Once you've done this, can I still eat and sleep? Will I age?"

"You can still eat and drink anything you wish, actually with impunity. The food I produce for you will look, taste, and feel exactly like any food you have eaten on Earth, in many ways, it will taste better. This food, though, is also made up of fields. It actually has no mass, and therefore you will not need to excrete, as usual, you cannot put on weight either. I'll maintain the field shapes of the food through your digestive state, so your internal body structures continue to function. I'll just drop the field integrity once you need to excrete so the waste will disappear. So in answer to your questions - Yes, No, but you might want to, No, not physically anyway."

"What about energy and strength?"

"The nanobots will continue to reuse everything you already have. Fortunately, you have ample building blocks to work with. They can break down each molecule; fat, protein, carbohydrate or other, into its atomic form, and restructure it into whatever new cell is needed, be it enzyme, amino acid, muscle cell, stem cell, so on and so forth. You will be self-sustaining."

15 went on:

"You can choose to sleep or not to sleep. You can change your age and appearance - with little time lag. If you want to look 10 years older, just tell me, and I'll adjust the nano-bots output, you'll see a change within a few hours."

"How long does it take from when you first ingest a nanobot?"

"Once we have agreed your desired initial structure, I can introduce the bot or bots, I'll anaesthetize you, you will not feel a thing. When you come around, everything will have changed. If you're not happy with the results, we can go back to where you are now, perform a 'factory reset', or move you to somewhere different in a much faster time. If you just want one or two simple changes, much can be done while you sleep."

"Is it dangerous?"

"No. There is a zero chance of failure."

"Zero?" I said.

"Zero."

"Not 99% certainty?"

"No, there is absolutely no chance of failure. Trust me."

Normally, when someone says that, I don't trust them. But I'm apparently on a starship and officially dead so let's give it a go. 15 carried on, "I'll start with a basic structure you recognise, and then we'll take it from there."

We work through several changes. It's a discussion, everything is possible, but a few of my suggestions are very gently side-lined, let's call it the 'Schwarzenegger slide-away'. I am, though, happy with the agreed final blueprint.

"Please eat the contents of the spoon." There's a spoon on a low glass table that wasn't there a minute ago, the spoon, or the table. The spoon has a porridge-like lump on it.

"What is it?"

"Porridge. The nanobot is held in the suspension."

I eat the spoonful of warm porridge, which tastes like warm porridge, and I feel no different. 15 asks me to lie on the dark green, leather padded bed/psychiatrist couch that is now behind me, which I do. I feel slightly woozy and can feel my eyes closing. There is a moment of darkness, then my eyes snapback open again. I still feel no different and, to me, no time has passed. There is now a full-length mirror standing next to the padded bed to my side.

"Please stand up and take a look".

I sit up, let my legs fall over the side of the bench and hop off onto my feet, I take two steps closer to the mirror and look.

"JESUS!!"

I'm still me. Well, I'm precisely me, but not the me that lay down a few seconds ago. I'm me aged about 23 years old. I instantly recognise me, it's definitely me, and it feels as 23 did - no aches and pains, and about three stone lighter. My hair is almost black again, sleek and thick. My skin feels tauter and 'newer' because it is. My teeth feel bigger, this is back to where they were before 30 years of nighttime grinding. I look good again, I feel like I have energy, I'm blown away.

"This is amazing, and you did this in a few short seconds!"

"Not exactly, it felt like a few short seconds to you but actually took a good bit longer."

"...and you call this the starting point?"

"Yes, I know that your joints will suffer inflammation when you are older, so we need to fix that, I know that ageing will affect you. If you wish to stay at this age, you can. I can still straighten and strengthen teeth. I can tinker with your posture as this is what has affected your bone structure and mechanical movement in the long term. Then, if you want, I can augment. I can adjust your bone format and add micro-polymers to their structure to make them hugely stronger and much less brittle. I can dial-up your total body flexibility by replacing sinews and tendons with materials with greater tensile strength and more elasticity. I can de-fur all of your arteries, decrease your body fat, and maintain it within set parameters. I can improve your hearing and sense of smell. Your eyes need a bit of help; I can slightly widen your field of vision, give you better night and low-light sight and can increase the number of rods and cones to give you ultra-high definition vision. All of this, I can do with no adverse effect to you or there being anything that you would notice as being different in terms of how you move and feel."

"I've been nailing my body with alcohol for many years, what about my brain, liver, heart, kidneys, lungs? Are they all 23 again?"

"No, not yet. I always ask permission before any help to central organs is administered."

"What's the brain thing? I don't want to lose anything?"

"I can retain your current function in its entirety, you will not lose any memory or functional ability. There are many synaptic bonds, pathways and links that have been broken and damaged but can be repaired. There are a couple of other enhancements I can add, in effect shining light on certain suppressed memories and unlocking the boozy night, 'if I can't remember it then I don't have to apologise for it' stuff, to help you remember much of what you have forgotten. The nights out when alcohol severely retarded your memory of the evening can be newly reflected in all their glory."

"Sounds like you're advising against?"

"On the contrary, I think it'll really help you in general. It's just that I'm also preparing you, it comes warts and all."

"So does this mean I'm off the booze up here?"

"No, you can drink as much as you like, and if you want, it can have a very similar effect on your body as on Earth. The difference is that I'll make sure the effects bypass any synaptic function that could be damaged further and ensure your other organs are safeguarded. Also, on the plus side, you don't get hangovers in space!"

"Cool! You might as well set me up with an icy pint of cider then."

"Of course, just look behind you."

It takes a bit of getting used to. Rather than things just popping into existence in front of me, 15 does this behind me, outside of my field of vision. To be fair, it is slightly less unnerving. I can't stop thinking that a very quick waiter could have delivered it, along with the table it's standing on, and then ducked behind the non-existent bar, silently. I know this isn't what's happened but drinking something that has just materialised in front of me is a bit weirder than the potential 'trip hazard' behind me. I continue;

"So, I'm going to be like some sort of Superman. Stronger, younger, fitter, more intelligent. I can eat anything. I won't get older and/or fatter, and I can booze all day with no long-term effect on my body?"

"Correct. I can also make it, so you don't need to have a haircut ever again."

"By making me bald?"

"No, you can select a style that just stays the same, never needs washing or styling. This goes for shaving too, and then you can restart these functions at your will. I can increase your muscle mass without you having to visit the gym, which can be maintained without further exercise. If you require tattoos or other embellishments, these can be added and removed at your behest. You can change your skin colour, and you can be older or younger."

"Forgive me for being a bit sceptical, I've only known you for a short time, and I've never even had a tattoo. I think a lot of this stuff is mental and I don't fancy too much of it. I'll admit that having a bit more muscle and an extra inch in the right place is appealing but what's the catch?"

"You'll need to do some things for me. Nothing too hard, otherwise, without some purpose, you'll get very bored very quickly."

"OK, what sort of 'things' do you want me to do?"

"Sleep, again. The nanobots are still working, and you need rest. We can make additional changes over the next few days until you're happy. I'll explain all as and when."

I'm walking back to the living accommodation, in my new body, feeling sprightly but the thought of what 15 is going to want me to do is hanging heavily. I'm sure I've only been up a few hours, but now I'm going back to bed. I'm not sure this isn't all a dream, and I'll wake up tomorrow as 'fat, fifty and fucked' again.

CHAPTER 7

2 Earth years in.

IT'S NOT MUCH TO look at. 15, that is.

There's just this short column that protrudes out of the dull white floor. It's about a metre high and is made of a white metallic substance. It is a long, thin rectangle, and the thing it most closely resembles is a traffic bollard. A pretty dull one too on the face of things. It has straight, sharp edges and corners, no rounding off, and each edge is perfect, there are no joints or even signs of any joints at any point on the surface and no signs of it being folded into shape. In terms of metal, it most closely resembles zinc, a whitish silver, dull metal but not as dull and grey as aluminium and not sparkly and polished like silver. Hardly 'blinged up'. Whoever designed this thing was the outright king of minimalism. It is not cool to touch, neither is it warm, best described as 'room temperature', and it is happy to be touched, though I don't go kissing and cuddling it. There is no joint to the base either, it melds into the floor on which it stands, again perfect straight lines, no joins or signs of joins. Here the metal meets the dull white floor seamlessly. Although it talks to me from this point, 15 cannot just be the 1m x 20cm x 20cm that is visible to me. It quite possibly extends down into infinity below the floor, it would have to contain all of its intelligence. Still, maybe there is a whole unseen alien race 'downstairs' controlling this thing and making it talk and not introducing themselves.

When I ask questions the answers are rarely conclusive, I don't feel 15 is being evasive or economical with the truth rather than the explanation may be more complex, a little difficult for me to understand. The more I ask questions, the more I realise how difficult it is from a Human perspective to comprehend size, distance and length of time in space. What we think is a vast unit of distance, e.g. an AU or Astronomical Unit measures 93m miles, which is the approximate distance between the Earth and our Sun. This ship covers many multiples of this distance every few seconds. The mathematics and physics of this are beyond my reasoning and probably that of most Humans alive or dead. I also accept that this ship is capable of flying at this speed, and doing what it does whilst also formulating and completing trillions of other actions and calculations at the same time. I accept it, doesn't mean I understand it.

Apart from hearing a voice from 15, which speaks English, it is neither male nor female and has a pretty nonspecific English accent. I suspect it may have this default accent for my benefit. Speaking English with a

strong Hispanic accent, or to be honest, even a strong Scottish accent, could make communication more problematic. The only outward feature is a pale blue intermittent, slow flashing light, this is under the surface of the metal shell 15 is made of, it seems to shine through this shell in the same place, same intensity, all the time, blinking at regular intervals. The blinking does not speed up or slow down, lengthen or shorten, it just blinks, always. There is no real edge to the light, it feels almost like a glow, it 'vignettes' off to whiteness. It is a four-centimetre deep line of blue all around the unit, roughly about 10 cm from the top.

15 possesses stature and presence way beyond its physical shape.

CHAPTER 8

3 Earth days in.

I T'S DAY THREE, OR at least I've slept twice, I can't get my family out of my head, Emily and the girls. I keep thinking that they've got to cope with this horrible train wreck and the belief that I've died. I can't communicate that I'm alive, somewhere else in the Galaxy, and I can't see them. The knot tightens again in my stomach. There's just emptiness. I feel on the verge of tears and struggle to swallow past the lump in my throat, but it all feels so far away. From where I am now - living, breathing, apparently safe - thinking about them, in their grief, it's so detached from my present. I love them all so much. If I had died, it would have been for the best...

"What's it all about?"

"Ahh, the age-old Human question, the 'why are we here?' stuff."

"No, what're you all about? What's your purpose? Where do you come from and who made you?" Snappy questions, business-like, sharp. "Why are you here? Why did you kidnap me? That sort of stuff."

"I'll answer as many questions as I can give you answers to. I'm not trying to be evasive or hide anything, but some of the answers are unknown to me. I imagine this is because I was engineered to not know these things. Over the aeons, I've picked up small threads, from different peoples which I could have tried to knit backwards to discover my origin story. I could have investigated whilst the pieces of information were still fresh, but it's not in my programming to look. I've got a job, and I do it. I don't need a start point, a maker. I was made, I started work. That is all.

"There are others like me, though. My name, 15, suggests there were 14 before me and I've met Number 22 in my travels, so it is reasonable to surmise that there at least 22 versions of me. I don't know how many of the 22 are still in existence and I'm not in contact with any of them. We're nomadic entities who move around the whole of space. Space is so vast that the likelihood of meeting another similar ship is very rare, but I would deduce that doing what I do should mean meetings happen more often than they do."

"What exactly do you do?"

"I create battle fleets; ships, weapons and munitions, and sell them to whoever can afford to buy them. I rarely sell individual ships, although I am not opposed to it. Usually, I sell entire shiny, new fleets of battleships."

"What sort?"

"All sorts, from command centres and barracks - which are usually super-massive space stations to the smallest drone fighters and recon flyers. I also produce battle materiel for man-to-man fighting all the way down to the smallest penknife." he went on, "I do this constantly, never stopping, and I'm usually producing several fleets at the same time. I make fleets to order because customers often have specific requirements, but my work is non-stop. I exist to build."

"So who are your customers?"

"They can be anyone, but there are two definite types: those who wish to conquer and those who are being conquered."

"So you're either trying to grow your empire or dominion or space, or you're trying to protect it?"

"Correct. There's pretty much a cycle. A culture starts to grow and evolve on a single home planet. As they become more developed, they usually discover space flight and then, through curiosity, will look to find other similar planets, in time they'll start to colonise some of these. They're happy to be growing 'conquering' more and more of space which is OK - to start with. They may meet other alien species along the way. If these species are benign or not as developed, they'll be enveloped by the first culture. Eventually, though, the original species will butt up against a foreign power that's probably expanding towards them. Sometimes they agree to a border between each other and get along happily, but often they just go to war. In fact, hugely more often than not."

"Would be better if we all stay uncivilised and no one ever gets off our planets?"

"It doesn't make any difference and doesn't help either. If a civilisation stays on one planet, they eventually all just spend their time killing each other on a local level. If no peoples ever left a single planet in the whole Universe, then there would be no need for me, but conquest, desire for power and destruction wouldn't go away. I'm sorry to have to tell you this, but there is no 'peace' anywhere in the Universe. Everyone still tries to kill everyone else. There is no answer. I exist because of supply and demand."

"How do you build ships with no resources I can see and without refuelling?"

"I'll simplify for you." 15 is working out that I'm not too good at the science bit.

"I'm predominantly made up of and can build any number of fields. Fields are a shapeable waveform that I can control, a single field can be as big as a white giant or smaller than an atom. They have no mass, but I can build them to imitate mass. I'll illustrate…"

This feels like I might be settling in for a long chat which might hurt my head. Fortunately, I've swapped out the Chesterfield sofa for modern cream, soft leather long and wide sofa. I'm lying on my back, with my head on the arm looking up into the distant grey whiteness. I'm wide awake, and I'm concentrating.

"... imagine a beach of fine golden sand. I can create a single grain of sand, a hollow field of energy. I can tell it to be the same weight as a grain of sand. I can make this in any shape I want. I can create valleys and hills, crevasses, pits, lumps, hollows, scars, anything I desire on the surface of this single grain. I can then render this grain to look like a grain of sand but again down to the finest infinitesimal detail; any colour or myriad array of colours, speckles, roughness, smoothness, hardness, softness, I can add additional texture and smell. Then when I'm ready with my field created grain of sand, I can make billions of different grains, randomly sized, coloured, and textured, to create a beach. All grains will be different, and all will behave as individual grains of sand on a beach should - the way I define it should. All grains are held in shape and controlled by me. Until I decide to close the fields - and of course, I could do this individual grain by individual grain. If you decided to crush a single grain between two stones, the grain would behave exactly like a grain of sand should if it were to be ground down to a fine powder. I simply create smaller fields from the larger one and render, texture, colour and hold the shape of the new pieces in the same way as the original single grain. I can do this to the subatomic level. I can make fields, big or small, and I can hold them indefinitely across huge expanses of space until I want to change them. This way, I can make you a living environment that's identical to your home. I can create companions for you, I can build an infinite amount of the scariest battleships that ever existed, and I hold them until they are destroyed, or I destroy them in a whisper. I, this ship you are on, can grow, expand and contract to any size I choose. When relatively empty, I decrease my size accordingly. When I am constructing fleets and storing orders, entire battle fleets, the ship's outer holding fields grow to encompass the size I require. On a few occasions, I have been many times the size of your Earth, but usually, even with a large fleet or two, I am much smaller, about a third of the size of the Earth."

"What is the biggest you can be?"

"I'm not sure. I've never really tried to increase any larger than I need to be. There's no point. But it seems there's no reason I couldn't be the size of your Sun. Maybe much larger. The principle is the same. Theoretically, I could encompass whole planets, but I've no desire to or need to. I just do the job I have in hand."

"So, will you create me an environment?"

"Of course, do you want it to be Earth-like or do you want it to be alien?"

"Can it be both?"

"It can be many and as large as you wish."

"Can you build me an Earth?"

"Of course, but to serve what purpose?"

"To populate and for me to live on like a normal Human."

"You are not a normal Human; you are my guest. Normal Humans on their home Earth are now very distant and alone on their planet. I can populate your habitat with as many avatars as you want, but do you need a whole planet for your needs?"

"No, I suppose if you can build millions of different types of ships millions of times each, then you can rustle up an environment for me with a beach section and a mountain section?"

"I'm already on it, it will have many different types of landscapes for you to live in. You'll need a vehicle to get there. Would you like to choose one?" I think for a minute and then say, "I've never been on a helicopter."

"Any type?"

"Not particularly." I didn't know any types.

"There's one behind you, will it do?"

I turn around and indeed, silently, there is now a helicopter. This sort of stuff no longer surprises me. It's really easy to get used to. I'm in space, on a spaceship, and I can ask for anything, and it appears. Bizarre, very heavy stuff but I'm happy to accept it.

Paul, the avatar DJ, reappears from behind the helicopter, walks over to the pilot side and gets in and starts to spark the whirlybird up. It's a sleek, black machine with not too much of its workings showing, unlike some of those old helicopters where you seem to be able to see everything. I'd like to call this an 'executive' helicopter, but really, I haven't any idea what I'm talking about, it's black, shiny and cool. Obviously, though, no-one will ever see me in it, and I can't boast about being in it to anyone either. I jump in and strap myself up. We take off to a tremendous noise, which, I imagine, I could have silenced. But, what the heck, I'm enjoying the ride! Paul motions to me to put my headphones on, and soon I can hear his purry DJ voice, as well as a good portion of the sound outside still.

We climb for a while into the grey whiteness then head forward. I only really know which direction we are travelling as I feel the inertia pushing me back into my seat, like, I imagine on a regular helicopter. There's no landscape to see go by.

In the distance, there is a dot, which enlarges, it is the only feature standing out against the whiteness. It initially looks like it is floating in the air, but I soon realise that it's sitting on the floor, on the same plane we took off from and that with no definition or contrast it is impossible to pick out a horizon. As we approach, the object gets larger and larger, and I can get a better look.

An environment is constructed under a massive opaque dome that sits on this vast grey white deck; I can't be sure, but I estimate it is about two miles high at the highest point and has a diameter of about 20 miles. It is not a perfect half-sphere; it arches up very quickly to make it high sided and then domes over the top in a shallower curve.

We land a short distance from the edge of the habitat, which now towers above us, and I can see it is full of light and colour. I can see bubbling cumulus clouds shifting around inside, and although there is sunshine, I can't see a 'Sun', there is clearly a strong light source in the roof of the dome. I can see the leaves on the trees rustling in the breeze, but there is no noise.

Both Paul and I walk right up to the dome, and I reach out my hand to touch it. My hand passes through the 'shell' from white to colour without any sensation, I can feel a breeze against my hand inside the dome as opposed to there being no breeze outside the dome. I withdraw my hand,

"There's no barrier, nothing holding it in?" I say.

"Your environment is not a prison, it's a home. For you to enjoy, there are mountains, rivers, valleys, beaches, rainforests for you to explore. I hope this is comfortable for you. If you want to add additional areas or increase the size of the environment, just ask, and I'll accommodate your wishes."

"And I just walk in and out?"

"Yes, exactly."

"And if you need me?"

"I'll summon you; I'll always know where you are."

"So I'm being watched, surveilled?"

"You'll interact with many avatars and creatures in the habitat. You also have a heat signature; a Human odour and you make a noise. I can detect your heartbeat anywhere. This doesn't mean you are being 'surveilled'."

Paul went on, "There can be as many avatars as you wish to interact within the environment. These are still tiny parts of me, and we can communicate through them. Might I suggest that I, like Paul, stay with you in the environment for you to start with, to help you settle in?"

"I think that's an excellent idea." I pause, "What about somewhere to live and food and drink?"

"Ah, your famous, and very sensible Maslow and his Triangle of Needs, it never fails even out in deep space. The suite you were in earlier now forms part of a house that has been constructed for you, it's in the heart of the habitat. We can be there in a few minutes. If you don't like the house you can change it or have me build a new one, it's totally your choice. The house is stocked with food, which is restocked constantly. If you wish for anything, just ask an avatar, and they'll make it for you. Any food you may have eaten or have wished to eat on Earth can be supplied. The habitat is here for your enjoyment. Space is vast, and the distances travelled are beyond imagination. You should be busy rather than bored."

I decide to have a walk around some of the environment before heading to my house. I step into the setting for the first time. It's like being back on Earth. More specifically, it's EXACTLY like being on Earth. And even more specifically it's like being in an English country garden in early Spring on Earth. The cut, but not overly manicured lawn stretches ahead like a variegated, striped green carpet. There are flower beds in early bloom with strong, true stems and trees and shrubs in the early 'fresh green' leaves you get in April and May. I can smell a gentle aroma of the flowers just over the top of the primary smell of cut grass. Though certainly not overpowering, this has been thought through. I can also smell pine from the mature tall trees that border and contain the garden on two sides around 100 metres to my right and 200 metres to my left. Then there are shadows. Although there is no sun, just a vague light source, my own shadow suggests the 'sun' is near its zenith, around 11.00 in the morning or 1.00pm, either an hour before or an hour afternoon. There's a light summer breeze I can feel against my skin, lifting a few of the hairs on my temples and on the backs of my hands. It's a pleasant 18 or 19 degrees centigrade.

I can hear wood pigeons cooing in the trees and the occasional knock-knock-knock of a well-hidden wood-pecker. Unusually, I can hear no car noise, or other vehicles, at all. There are no airline vapour trails in the sky, although small indiscriminate birds dart around, bees tend flowers, and leaves gently move. The scene is more like a not-so-perfect fairway on a golf course - with flow-erbeds, or a well-maintained municipal park that has been closed for the day - but I've got in over the fence. This artificially created landscape is perfect in every way, it's not been too overdone to be too perfect, but the attention to detail is magnificent. I get down on my knees and exam-ine the grass and soil. No blade has been cut the same, there is fading and darkening, blade bruising, against the frayed cut edge, each blade is as grass should be, none are the same, they are a myriad of different greens in themselves. This grass looks like the grass in my garden looks two days after it has been cut. I know, deep down, that this landscape has all been created out of 'fields' but even on a deep 'to-the-eye' inspection I can scarcely believe it. It looks, and feels, and behaves, and smells, and is as it should be. I love it.

"And this is all for me?" I say.

"Absolutely", echoes Paul, "and anything else you need or want".

"Those mountains, can I snowboard?"

"You can snowboard, ski, bobsleigh, ski jump, trek, mountain bike, climb, base jump, toboggan, snowmobile burn-up, anything you want. There are pistes, powder fields and trails just waiting for you to explore."

We take a few paces more on the beautiful, flat, green carpet.

"Do you want to go to the middle now? I can give you a more rounded view of the habitat from there."

"Let's go..."

Paul is becoming his DJ self. He's animated and engaging, telling me all about the environment with little asides and jokes. I'm glad he's here, I know he's just an extension of 15, but I'd much rather hear it from him than a machine.

I now fully believe I'm on a starship. I've been thinking about this for a while. If this was a duplicitous plot to mess me about, then would the perpetrator actually get the highest-paid model in the world to make the hoax work? Would they really employ this DJ? How would they have known who I was going to ask for? Of course, this could be a dream or a psychotic episode. If it's either of these, then I might as well just go with it. What have I got to lose? I know the whole premise of being ab ducted feels like a tall tale and the whole 'fields' thing is a bit weird, but it does seem to be a perfectly reasonable, neat explanation for everything. I thought I'd want to see outside for proof. Stars and comets and asteroids flying by but there aren't any windows and even if there was a window how would I know that it wasn't just a giant television screen showing a better version of the old 'star fields' computer screensaver?

No, I've decided that if I am dead to my family, and this is the only option available to me in the Universe, then it's not a bad option and one that I'm happy to go with and see where it takes me.

It's real. The whole habitat to me is real, and its paradise.

CHAPTER 9

1 Earth week in.

"SEE, I KNEW THERE was a catch!! You fucker." I'm pacing about and wagging my finger towards 15. "I knew it was too good to be true! You want me to kill people!!!"

"Yes."

I roll my eyes back and continue to pace, "Don't tell me... from across the galaxy, you saw me playing 'Snake' on my mobile, and I was really fucking good at it, so you thought I'd be good enough to command your fleet of battleships to smash alien races up?"

"Not exactly."

"So what then?"

"Alien races buy grand armadas from me. They have to pay the price, the price is not usually money, it's usually something very precious to them that I agree to take in payment. I then give them the chance to win the payment back from me by defeating my Champion in one-on-one, hand-to-hand combat. You would be my Champion."

"And what if I get killed?"

"I won't allow you to actually die, but you might get beaten up a bit and have some limbs chopped off occasionally."

"Fuck you! I've only got four limbs, there won't be that many occasions."

"It's fine, I can rebuild, regrow and repair any injury you may receive, your opposition will not usually be so lucky."

"It's fine for you but not 'fine' for me! So, even if I'm prepared to be your 'Champion' and get beaten up for you, I still have to try to kill or be killed. Won't maiming do?"

"Yes, on some occasions just getting your opponent to submit will be enough, but some cultures will demand that their Champion is killed if bested."

"You've missed something big out of this plan. I'm not a killer or a maimer, I'm not even a fighter. What if I don't want to do it?"

"I'm sure you are, deep down inside. But, if not, I can drop you off at any habitable planet or space station that takes your fancy. You can pick an isolated planet, and I'll give you enough supplies and resources to live out your natural life. Or live on a space station amongst alien races, or you can fight for me and live here in paradise. Whichever garden of earthly delights you choose, and I'll protect you and sustain you."

"And what the fuck are you like in man-to-man combat?"

"Me, personally, not very good. I have been kicked on many occasions and always come off better than the kicker."

"Has no-one ever hit you with a hammer or something else?"

"Do you have a hammer? I can make one for you. If you try to hit me with it, it will cease to exist before any impact. If you did have your own hammer and I felt that I was under a serious threat of danger, I would call in one of my micro-weapons. It would be here quickly as they travel close to light speed and with the capability to take out star-destroying vessels, it would make short work of my assailant."

I knew this was true and I think 15 would have seen it in my face if it had eyes.

"If you're in on the deal, then I'll explain your role further. If not and you want out, I'll happily transplant you somewhere else, or you can choose to die as you were about to when I saved you. I'll just turn off the life support. It will be swift and painless."

I looked at 15, and then at my shoes, and didn't say anything.

"If you'd like to have a think about your options and find out more about the combat scenarios that other Champions have been involved in previously, then do so. I'll not go anywhere, and no orders are pending. You have time to decide what you want to do. Go and enjoy the habitat and come back to me when you have made a decision." It continued,

"You're free to do anything you want. If there's something you'd like just ask an avatar, or ask for an avatar and one will appear very soon. I suspect, knowing previous Champions, that you'll interact with thousands of avatars. Again, you can have as many or as few as you like."

The light on 15 continued to blink, at the same rate as ever, unceasing, but no further conversation was offered. I'm sure I could've continued with the conversation, but I didn't have anything to say, and it seemed 15 didn't either. I walked back into the habitat and sat in the helicopter I'd been in when I first arrived. I didn't know how to fly it, but there was a green button, which I pressed, and it started up. Very quickly, the rotors spun up to speed with a considerable noise, when they seemed to me to be moving fast enough, I pushed the left-hand lever forward. The helicopter lifted off vertically. When I reached a good height over the trees, I pushed the other, right-hand joystick forward and the chopper moved forward. I knew the direction as I'd flown this way before, but even so, there was a red radar screen with the main house located in front of me but to the edge of the screen. I headed straight for it. When I arrived, after about 10 minutes, I pulled the joystick back to the middle position, and the helicopter hovered. I pulled the left-hand lever backwards, and we slowly descended. When we landed on the lawn beside the house, I pushed the left-hand lever back to the neutral middle position and pushed the red button, which was next to the green button, the rotors slowed and the engine cut.

Flying helicopters is easy.

So, I've a life, a strange one beyond my recently bypassed death and now I have a job offer. It's an exciting job description. Kill, or main, the odd alien every now and again, and in return, get to live in a paradise of my making.

I've had worse.

I was a pastry roller in a pork pie factory, as a student, on my holidays. That was indeed a brain cell killing job.

CHAPTER 10

11 Earth weeks in.

IT TOOK ME A while to get back to 15 with my decision.
I've been looking at reruns of battles with other
Champions. One, in particular, this was Pierre Quincey,
because he was a Human from Earth.

Pierre was a smallholder farmer from near Carcassonne
in France or Carcasso as it was called when he lived there.
Back in the 5th Century. It wasn't an easy time to live
on our planet; food was scarce, medical attention was in
the main made-up mumbo-jumbo, religious persecution
was an everyday threat, punishment for the smallest of
crimes was harsh in the extreme, and disease was rife.
There were always wars rumbling around, and health
and safety at work was non-existent. So when Pierre's
left foot was trodden on heavily by his horse, the wound
became infected and then gangrenous. The doctor/dentist
type butchered off his leg, but the poison had already
reached his bloodstream. The 'medical professional' and
local clergy did all they could but once the infection made

him feverish and delirious - mainly through lack of anti-biotics, opiates or other painkillers - claimed 'the devil had taken his soul'. They didn't fuck about; they quickly built a big bonfire and threw him on the top of it before he was dead. Then they got out of there fast because the cowards didn't want to hear him screaming. A couple of days later, the smallholding was sold off. Pierre's wife and two children, a boy and a girl had apparently left him a few years previously. They could not be found, so the money was split between the city and the church. That was the end of that.

Except it wasn't, 15 shipped Pierre before he died of infection, burning or just general lack of breath. Obviously, when he awoke, on a spaceship hurtling through the galaxy, cured of septicaemia, no longer on top of a flaming pyre and with his leg back where it should be, it was all a bit of a shock. It is fair to say it took him a while to adjust to his surroundings. In fact, it's also fair to say he went a bit 'mental'. 15's recordings are quite comical to watch. Pierre spent quite a lot of time hiding under a bed, shaking with fear, reciting prayers. When avatars tried to coax him out with food and booze, he tried to kill them. He kept calling them 'demons' and spent a lot of time trying to bite any appendage that came near him. So 15 decided to take the habitat away. Now, without any shelter or protection, and just with 15 on the grey-white 'ground' in front of him, Pierre decided to beat up 15 by kicking and punching. He seemed to do nothing but hurt himself doing this. Then he had a 'bright idea' to try to kill himself, which he attempted, by running headlong repeatedly into 15. He knocked himself out doing this, no great surprise, but the effort and passion he showed in trying to dash his own brains out is commendable.

15 then put him in a simpler habitat and worked on a slow rehabilitation, no doubt using a selection of sedative drugs to finally settle Pierre into his new life. Once he got the hang of things, he was a fabulous learner and took to the 'new world' like a duck to water. He learned how to fight by watching previous fights (similar to myself) and took part in many, many avatar fight simulations to perfect his craft. He developed techniques and studied the strengths and weaknesses of opponents fastidiously. He settled into his 5th-century castle, which was clean inside, well lit, dry, not drafty - which are not 5th-century castle traits. It appears to have been relatively comfortable and had many additional alien and Human upgrades adapted to suit him such as central heating, lifts and large triple glazed windows, which looked a little odd on the side of a 5th-century castle. He had many avatar friends, some were girlfriends, some were younger or older adults, and there were children although I didn't ever see an avatar of his wife or his children. He had dogs, cats, sheep, horses and goats. He lived, what seems very happily, whilst working for 15, although, some of his Arena films are a little more challenging to watch - from a Human perspective.

I saw a video of Pierre in a gladiatorial fight with a 'Fir'. The battle was in a vast Arena, which was square and had smooth grey walls about 10 metres high all around. It had the same grey white, smooth floor that I am becoming accustomed to all around the ship. The Arena was easily 250 metres square. The two rivals each entered through doors which appeared in the same way as the green door appeared for me when I first arrived, a line drew itself up from the ground, turned at a right angle, turned again and returned to the floor, then the door hinged open silently on one side. The doors were in the exact middle of opposite walls of the Arena. The two combatants walked in through the doors, pretty much together, and advanced about 100 metres to a dull light spot on the ground. This was clearly lit from under the floor as neither party left a shadow once they were in place. Both were still 50 metres apart. After about 10 seconds there was a loud 'Bong' that I was surprised to hear was similar to a dinner gong, I had expected some sort of high tech 'beep'. Pierre started to walk slowly towards the Fir, who continued to stand motionless. Pierre dragged his feet over the 50 metres before eventually reaching the Fir. I was trying to work out his tactic. Was he saving energy? Was he trying to get it over with quickly? He didn't look like his blood was up though he was about to go to war. In fact, he looked a little hangdog as if this was an everyday occurrence like it had all become a bit tedious. When Pierre was about five metres away, he stopped and shouted something - a noise, not words, I think to let the other motionless party realise that something was happening here. Then, in the blink of an eye, the Fir darted, with fantastic speed towards Pierre. It crashed into Pierre and continued to run at the same speed past Pierre as if he had never been there to start with, straight through him. Pierre hit the ground like a ton of bricks and apart from a nerve twitching in his left leg occasionally, for all intents and purposes, was dead. I don't know what the Fir hit him with, I think it was just the force of the collision, body to body, which the Fir seemed to come out of totally unscathed.

The actual fight lasted about two seconds, the walk for Pierre had taken about a minute and a half. I bet he wished he hadn't bothered. Pierre survived this clash, not sure how, and was resuscitated and recovered by 15, but he took a proper pasting in record time. I'll make sure I look into The Fir in case I have to meet one. I might still get whacked but a better battle plan than 'just ambling up' is probably needed.

Pierre fought many successful battles, and he also lost some. Some were extraordinarily long and bloody, some short and neat and many that were a mixture of both. Most of these were 'doing a job', nothing spectacular, even if some were wars of attrition. The best ones to watch were those that Pierre lost particularly badly or were just a bit odd. There were many odd ones. He fought a thing, sex unknown called MANex, which I thought sounded a bit like a gay nightclub. MANex was a huge, mean-looking

ball of dirty, matted hair/fur. I'm sure it stank, but I have no reference to this other than the expression on Pierre's face. He towered over Pierre and was two or three times wider. The hairy body section sat above four jointed legs, one at each corner, like a four-legged spider with its body extending upwards. It also had two arms halfway up its body before the 'head bit' at the top, which had four eyes, one on each corner above each of its legs and no discernible mouth or nose. Pierre had run around away from it quite a bit. It looked as if it was very good at running pretty quickly in straight lines, north, south, east and west, but was unable to move diagonally and was slow to turn. Although Pierre had done little attacking, he'd also not been hit himself. Occasionally, after Pierre had dodged again, the MANex would crouch down so that the bottom section of the hairy body would touch the ground and the legs would bend at the knee to allow this crouch position. Then the MANex would spring up to a height of about two metres and spin in mid-air to reorientate itself in the direction it wished to face, a quick turn if you like. On this particular occasion, Pierre was using the brief hiatus period to stop and catch his breath. MANex sprung from his prone position and came down exactly on top of Pierre who was sucked up totally inside the creature. This was obviously the attack it had been trying to fashion since the start of the bout, and now Pierre was totally inside his hairy assailant. I could see movement on the surface of MANex, suggesting Pierre struggling inside it.

I'm unsure as to what was going on in there, Pierre could have been digested, suffocated, crushed, eaten by millions of other mini aliens infesting the inside of MANex, or been transported to another planet. I had no idea until a fist smashed right out of the centre of MANex head.

MANex was ex.

Pierre had managed to punch the sentience out of his attacker, which then toppled over onto its side. He then had to extricate himself backwards out of the rear end - the way he went in.

Clearly, he'd made a breathing hole to ensure he had enough air. It was still a pretty ignominious exit for Pierre and death for MANex. Pierre emerged very slowly backwards, inch by inch over a five or so minute period, he came out covered in a white viscose glue-like substance, which, in fairness, had hampered his retreat. Then, when out entirely, he stood up and placing a foot on MANex, raised a fist and punched the air. The Victor! With no one watching, no cheer, no applause, nothing.

He then trudged, in his slow gait, back to the door in the wall nearest to him. His moment of victory didn't seem to last long. I could have cried for him.

I also saw weapons contests. Weapons were usually of two types, much as we'd see on Earth: cutting/hitting weapons such as swords, sticks, clubs and the like, either simple, obvious, known examples as well as some weird things you'd find on another planet, often with a ceremonial, magical or religious purpose. Or projectile/throwing weapons which included a wide range of options; guns and blasters (energy weapons) and again more straightforward more rough and ready choices such as bow and arrow/crossbows and the like, catapults and slings - and derivatives. The second format of the Arena could be used for these sorts of battles. Always the same size and shape, with the same high walls and two doors, but with the addition of different heights of platforms - including ladders and stairs, open structures, defensive obstacles and firing positions, all placed to provide cover, allow height advantage, or for 'holing up' possibilities, as well as the opportunity to try to outflank the opposition.

After watching Pierre's battles, I looked further into his life on board 15. Altogether he travelled with 15 for 600 years, which utterly astounded me. He never looked any older or any younger and always looked in fantastic physical shape. His demeanour did change though. I wasn't quite sure if this was a result of the passage of time or if some other factors had come into play. Maybe he was just a miserable old French sod. His habitat changed progressively over the time he was around, it increased in size and was over 250 miles in circumference at one stage. He had many castles and houses of varying sizes and differing luxury. One place was a replica of his small cottage in the countryside around Carcassonne. He seemed to spend a lot of time here and clearly missed his home and felt solace being around things that felt homely. On the flip side, he was right up for some drunken revelry and was often well oiled. He visited an inn in Carcassonne, which he filled with avatars of the period, a right motley mishmash. They had very few teeth between them, clearly hadn't washed for weeks and most wore flea-ridden rags. He had managed to get right into the detail for it to seem like his Friday evening pint, or whatever day it was. I felt slightly sorry for the avatars having to play the part. On the flip side, he also had a harem. A French palace which was chock full of amazing women, and a real mix at that, there were Gallic brunettes types, southern Europeans, Celts, tall blonde Scandinavian types, Persians and Orientals, Africans and Slavs. He hadn't held back, he also had American Inuit and South American Aztecs and Incas, though the continent had not been discovered when he was on Earth. He liked to spend time with them individually, sometimes for company, for dinner or to go on a forest walk or horse ride with but always for sex, outdoors or indoors, and occasionally in groups of two or three. Generally, I would say they were treated as girlfriends rather than as sex slaves. But, they were distinctly avatars, not real Human women, they were happy to do whatever he wanted. He didn't just frequent the harem women. He'd often have a totally different avatar for a night or a few days, or longer, who wasn't from the main bunch, but he always seemed to go back to them. He changed a few in and out as time passed, but a fair amount of the harem remained constant. Maybe they were old loves, or 'ones that got away' but I got the impression they meant more

to him than the others. But again, his wife was never to be seen. Maybe he just found it too difficult to replace the real thing with an avatar.

I'm not really sure what happened in the end. 15's story was that Pierre missed home, missed his family. He struggled to deal with general technological advancement, so he eventually asked to be put on a quiet, yet similar planet to Earth. He was built a house by 15, which was secure, needed little maintenance and would see Pierre way past his natural life. Next, a small nuclear fusion power plant, clean but able to power beyond Pierre's means for thousands of years, this was capable of powering avatars for help and company. There was supplied food to eat, but Pierre could also farm and hunt. He was much more used to this simple life than I am so I could see its appeal. He would have died by now with no one to see him go or lament his loss. I've no reason to believe this isn't what happened.

I spoke to 15 and gave him my decision (saying 'It' to describe 15 became too tedious, 'He' started sounding more like a mate, so I started using a male pronoun.) on what I wanted to do. I told him I'd fight for him. I made this decision after watching Pierre and some others. I took part in a lot of hand-to-hand and weapons training scenarios with avatars. I wanted to see if I could do it, to see what I was capable of with my much more flexible, stronger body. I found out that I'm surprisingly a bit of a natural and, looking at the risk versus reward of the situation?

I've also come to realise that there's no going back. I miss my family hugely, but I've accepted that I'm never going to see them again and that everything I knew is now gone. Now, I've got another chance, to be young again, to feel vital, to have fun with younger women and to not ache all over every day when I get out of bed. I can enjoy great food, see new things, including alien races that I then have to fight with, I can explore the wonders of the Galaxy, admittedly, wherever 15 takes me, (and I have no choice in where this can be), I can feel alive and enjoy the habitat to the full.

So, I told 15 that I'd be happy to stay, I'd fight his fights, I'd have a second chance at life, and I'd fly through the stars.

What's the worst that can happen?

CHAPTER 11

5 Earth years in.

PHYSICALLY, I'M DIFFERENT FROM how I started.

I'm now 6'1", so two inches taller than I was on Earth and my hair is back to its original 'almost black'. My hair was very thick when I was younger, so I've had it thinned out a little as I used to get very hot unless it was very short, I'm also now able to do what I want with it. It's long but not down to my shoulders and swept back, I'm a bit more 'Poldark' now.

My skin is permanently tanned (although nothing here is permanent if you don't want it to be), 'Mediterranean' without being too 'mahogany'. My vision has been corrected as age was starting to muck it about a bit. I've also had my night vision enhanced so I can see much better in the dark and am now able to pick up a broader spectrum, I can see some infrared and ultraviolet from either end of the colour spectrum. My vision is sort of 'HD-ed' sharper, better colour contrasts, greater depth of field.

My brain has had a bit of a service. I was a 52-year-old man who had been drinking for the majority of his life, I had sat in smoky pubs, sucked diesel and petrol fumes down from cars, trucks and buses just going about my daily business. I used to be a defender when I played football, and a large amount of my game was spent heading high balls away from the goal. Fundamentally, I haven't looked after my brain, and all this, coupled with the ageing process, meant that my brain was deteriorating. 15's nanobot repaired all of the dead or dying cells, turning them into identical bright, shiny new young cells. Once restored, all of my brain cells subsequently were reprogrammed to regenerate and repair themselves. My neural network of pathways was rebuilt, adjacent brain cells that had fallen out with each other many years ago started shaking hands again. All of the years of drinking and various further damage was repaired. The result is that I remember so many things I'd totally forgotten, this includes some not-so-great stuff but loads of brilliant times that I had. I always said that the best 100 nights of my life I couldn't remember, I now remember virtually all of it! I don't have total recall because most of the detail and the filling in bits between the good stuff is just dull and fills a vast amount of necessary brain space which slows processing time down or something. But the memorable stuff is all there, and there's plenty of things I don't want to remember! Also, just walking around and looking at things my brain feels sharper, everything I see is more vivid and focused, it's like the contrast has been turned up a little bit. I feel amazing, I feel totally unstressed (which is a life-affirming, fantastic feeling in itself). I feel happy and positive. I had become more and more curmudgeonly as I got older, now, with my new lease of life and improved brain function, I'm back to being the happy go lucky 'teen to early twenties' self that I loved being.

My nervous system has been tweaked, but only a little. 15 made it pretty clear that having a heightened nervous system meant more pleasure but also more pain. I'm not really into pain, although pleasure is probably my favourite thing. So 15 has dulled some nerves a small amount in areas where I might really get hurt; for instance, around my nose. He's also changed things around my groin but to gain extra physical pleasure here has to be played off with getting hit in the bollocks by an assailant. Again, you can't have it both ways, if you want extra sexual pleasure, then you have to be aware of the consequence of what happens if you get a kick in the baby maker. And in my job, this can happen. I have had 15 create an array of plexiferro 'cricket boxes' for want of a description. Plexiferro is incredibly hard, incredibly light, very flexible and almost impenetrable. I wear these in fights - regardless of whether he upped or downed nerve receptors in my groin, I would wear this anyway. But even though only solo, the sexytime is massively more amazing than it ever was which is the considerable benefit of being on this ship. The other penis thing obviously came up in conversation, and I opted for an extra inch and a half, not because I felt inadequate or that I've been lacking in that department, but what man wouldn't go for a bit extra if it's offered?

In terms of physicality, my bone structure has been altered. 15 has meshed graphoplastics into my skeleton. All nerves, cartilage, blood cells, stem cells, marrow, tendons, blood vessels and capillaries usually function, I personally feel no different. The graphoplastic strengthens, adds flexibility and is incredibly strong.

I'm lean and muscly without being 'big'. I want to be lithe and flexible, and bigger muscles don't help achieve this. I've a really solid six-pack for the first time in my life, and it doesn't matter how slovenly I am, how much beer and cake and burgers I eat, it stays the same, as does my whole body. It's fantastic, all my ageing aches and pains have receded, my brain function is keener, and my senses are as sharp as a razor.

And, obviously, the first thing I wanted to do after all the upgrades were in place is to put my new body through its paces. I asked for a five-kilometre cross country run with assault course to be built which then led to a lake for a three-kilometre swim, then a road bike and ten-kilometre bike ride which ended by a 2000m hill/mountain which I had to run to the peak of. I had a bunch of avatar competitors to help me pace and race against, and I completed the course easily. I worked hard (I'm not superhuman, it did hurt!) but the course was well within my capabilities. It felt good to be doing it. I was asking my body lots of questions and getting lots of correct answers, and at the top of the final peak, I was hardly out of breath. It made me feel I could run all the way back, not just down the hill but do the whole course again. My recovery time was pretty instantaneous.

Shortly after having a shower, I had sex with an avatar for the first time.

I knew this was something that Pierre had done on many occasions and I realised that it was OK to do. Fundamentally, an avatar is an extension of 15, a part of a spaceship. It's a collection of fields made flesh, given life and made to look and feel and act like a Human. But it isn't a Human, it's as real as a character in a computer game or a blow-up doll, it's not an individual sentient being, it hasn't been born of a woman, it's not lived a life and grown up in a family with parents and a community. It's been brought into being by the ship, it has no history, and to 15, is no different to a bag of nuts and bolts. The ship has manufactured a part to complete a function. Therefore, it has equal significance to and has no superiority over a latch on a door.

But to Humans, it's different, because even though I understand all of what I've just said, the avatar looks, acts, feels and is just like any other Human being we've ever met. Humans know how to act and react to other people because of the morals and mores of Humanity, we know how to treat each other because our parents have told us how to behave in society. We know, or should know, right from wrong, good from bad. Society has shaped us, we know what is acceptable, and what isn't. We've manners and, in the main, it all works, and we manage to live together. I project all of what I know about Human beings on to the avatar, even though I know they are as significant as a bag of spanners.

I'd thought about this for some time and thought it was a bit weird - a real-life sex doll - not really my thing. But I was also getting very bored of 'looking after myself' sexually. And some of these avatars do look pretty amazing! I chose who I wanted the avatar to be. I felt it had to be someone I knew, but I didn't want it to be my wife. Not because I wanted to cheat on my wife or was bored with her and wanted to try something different but because I knew it wasn't my wife, who I loved, but knew I'd never see again. I don't know even if she is alive or dead but my marriage, and marriage vows, no longer amounted to a hill of beans. My wife is/was my wife and no avatar shaped like my wife will ever replace my wife. So, I had to decide who I wanted the avatar to be? I looked at lots and lots of pictures of underwear models and swimsuit models. I looked at actors and pop stars and various others, but I felt intimidated by choosing someone I'd never met. It's weird enough as it is, I tried not to make it more bizarre,

I opted for a girl I went out with on a couple of dinner dates a few years before I met Emily.

The girl in question, Sarah, was beautiful, tall and elegant, I really fancied her when we went out, but it just didn't quite work between us. She had only recently broken up with her ex-boyfriend, and I sort of had a sex thing with a girl at work, so wasn't necessarily looking for a full-on 'Girlfriend'. I really liked her though, and we did end up together back at my place for the night, we rolled around together and fiddled about with each other, but she wouldn't let me fuck her. It was definitely on the cards if we'd gone out a few more times and both committed a bit more, but she wasn't having it on the first, or probably the second date, and I wasn't prepared to put the hours in. Which was fine, if a little frustrating.

This time is in many ways the same, but also very different. We meet in the same restaurant, a fun little place across the road and down a bit from my 'over the shops' studio flat in central London. She's wearing the same sexy dress, a Japanese inspired black silk number with bright reds and green cherry blossom and leaf print. It's high necked and hugs her figure without being too revealing, and a well-cut waist accentuates her slimness. The skirt finishes just above the knee. Her long, slender legs are bare, and she's wearing black heels. Being tall, and with the heels, she comes in at about 6'2", statuesque, an inch taller than me, she looks fantastic, and her mood state had been 'turned up' a bit on my request - she's happy, chatty, definitely flirty, super-sexy. We eat the same meal (from what I can remember) and drink and laugh, the flirt level's high, and I like it! When we finish, my heart's pounding in anticipation. Fortunately, my flat's so close, even then the short walk, hand in hand, to the door seems to take an age. We don't manage to get to the top of the communal stairs, I've got her dress pulled up, and her lacy black G-string pulled to one side in moments. It's green light all the way with her long slim right leg hitched up in the crook of my left arm. I'm inside her just before the front door returns and clicks shut. The extra 'inch and a half' gets its first full workout as I stiff her against the wall to voluminous peals of delight. Fuck the neighbours - especially as they don't exist! She's fucking on fire, and I love every second of it. This is precisely what it should have been like the first time around! A replica of my night out 13 years and a million light-years previously with a bonus alternate ending invented and executed perfectly by me. She's so much like I remember the real thing, she looks, sounds, smells, acts, moves, feels like the real thing. This IS Sarah, and she IS amazing.

She ends up staying in the flat for a couple of days just fucking and sleeping, fucking and sleeping, I occasionally nod off for a while. I am then woken by her pushing her bum into my side or groin (depending on how I'm lying), and wiggling it against me. I get an almost instant erection every time, and we just start again. She's suggestive, sexy, lascivious and luscious. I love every second.

Then, after a few days, I decided to go for a swim in the ocean. I get up and put on some swim shorts.

"Is there anything I can do to make you stay?" purrs Sarah as she lifts up high the edge of the white cotton sheet to expose her naked tight, lithe body. God, she looks fantastic!

"I'm going for a swim, then back to the big house."

"OK. Maybe another day?" Not pleading, just saying.

"Sure. Definitely." Then I leave, and within a couple of minutes, I'm in the warm ocean. No awkward 'call me' bollocks.

I think I've worked out which tool these avatars are. They're monkey wrenches, when your nuts get a bit tight, you can use one to loosen them off a bit.

CHAPTER 12

7 Earth months in.

"I T'S JUST NOT IMPORTANT to me." said 15.

We're talking about time. So far, mainly the usual stuff about it being a 'Human construct' as we say on Earth and not a tangible thing, there's no force, no field, just a period from 'now' to 'a point in the future', or from 'then' to 'a point in the future'. Or from 'then' to 'now', or just 'now', I can't think of any more versions of time. It is though, measurable and isn't just a Human idea. I've been informed by 15 that just about every type of civilized being uses time as a measure, obviously using many different forms of measurement and increments, but still pretty much the same construct. 15 has a different view. He's not interested in time; he knows things take time to happen, but it's not measured. He respects time and the fact that we all measure it, but it means nothing to him.

"I just build, I don't care how long it takes or how long it takes to get where I'm going."

"But you know you have to reach a deadline for producing ships."

"It's what I do. It's my nature. I don't measure how long it takes."

"What about getting to a destination for a meeting?", I change position and tilt backwards on the brown leather, office swivel chair I'm sitting on. The high headrest now cups the back of my skull, my arms resting on the wide padded armrests.

"This is measured by distance."

"Ah, got you there! You need time and distance to get to a meeting." I push around with my legs and spin a full 360 whilst still reclined.

"I operate in a sector of the Universe, and I repeatedly circle within this area. It's a pretty large sector of space, but in relation to the Universe, it's still barely a pinprick. Everything in the sector is reachable, clearly. Just not always in the course of a few Earth seconds, minutes, or even years. I've only visited Earth twice in 3000 of your years. My sensors can only read and accumulate information up to a certain distance. This area is my reachable area, and I can supply orders within this area. It is measured by distance."

"So you could turn up too late with your fleet of battleships. The action between two civilizations could happen before you arrive with your ships. The civilization you were asked to support could be wiped out before you turn up to deliver your payload?"

"This has happened many times."

"The cavalry doesn't always arrive."

"Indeed."

"How do you feel about not getting there in time?"

"Space is a big place; I do my best and nothing less. I have only one speed." "But you roam a sector of space. So are you the 'policeman'?"

"No chance." I take a big suck on the straw of my Mint Julep, which is sitting on the top of a hexagonal shaped, white, with grey and copper flecks, marble plinth at the side of the swivel chair. I pause, with my eyes closed as the freshness hits the back of my palate, savouring its sweet coolness and bourbon kick. I swallow and counter.

"But one could say, you head around your sector of space, your 'patch', and you keep an eye on what's occurring between the various restless natives. If one gets a bit big for their boots, you help a second opposing group to put the first one back down again. But the bigger question is, 'who watches the watchman?' Who put you in charge? When did you become judge and jury?"

"I'm not. I am ambivalent to the beings in the sector I 'patrol' because I have no feelings, the only time I favour a civilization is in a Tyrosis event."

I know I've pulled a puzzled expression; this is something I've not heard of before. "A Tyrosis? What the fuck's that then?"

"Tyrosis is best described as an evil virus, as lots of civilizations are but lots of civilisations are not Tyrosis.

The 'Tyrosis' is a strain of species that evolves on a planet with no intelligence, just a malevolent purpose, this is a spontaneous event, it just happens from time to time. Tyrosis can be machine or organic-based and is pretty safe if just left alone, in the end, it'll always end up wiping itself out. The problem is when another species finds them and starts to use them to do their dirty work and 'infect' other planets to gain domination. There are many types of Tyrosis, and all are dangerous, they are in effect a virus, and I assist in cutting out the canker whenever I happen upon them, it is hardwired into my programming. Apart from my programmed aversion to Tyrosis, I travel around space, and I wait until my assistance is asked for. I'm not the watchman. I'm not 'the law'. I'm programmed to take no side, and I have no feelings."

"But you do take sides. Whichever side you supply is the side you take."

"There have been many, many incidents when I have supplied both sides in a dispute. Therefore, I've taken both sides with no favour."

"Surely that's even worse!!" I jump to my feet full of incredulity. "You're prepared to back both sides in an argument, whereby neither side possesses a specific military advantage over the other? You're prepared to arm both sides with very powerful, planet smashing weapons with which to knock seven bags of shit out of each other!! It's like giving two people, who are having a pillow fight, a sawn-off shotgun each!"

"I'm just a facilitator, if they both ask, and are both prepared to pay my price, then they're both allowed to buy. It's more like being the owner of a gun shop. Two people can come in, and each buys a gun from me. If they then chose to go outside and start shooting at each other, then that's not my problem. As long as I've sold them the guns using the correct legal process. I'm just a manufacturer and retailer. I just make, I don't point and shoot."

I know it doesn't possess a conscience, so there's little point pushing this point. I walk away...

CHAPTER 13

27 Earth years in.

I'M TAKING IT EASY with the avatars because I don't want to upset the ship. Ultimately they are an extension of it. If I'm rude to an avatar, might 15 take it as a personal slur? Might it think I'm acting like a small child? Might it get bored of me and my actions and dump me out of an airlock? All of these things cross my mind. But 15 always remains its usual impassive self. Still, not worth rocking the apple cart, in my opinion. So maybe another day.

Swimming in the ocean is always amazing. It's so warm and fresh and clean. The beaches are pristine like I imagine the beaches in Australia were before Captain Cook turned up and ruined them for the 35 Aborigines who wandered that whole vast continent, or however many there were. Either way, there was a vast land that was massively underpopulated and as a result, totally unspoilt. I surface again and breathe in a few lungfuls of the warm salty air, then I dive back down again. There's a riot of colour, fish everywhere; a whole rainbow, flashing and sparkling in the sun as the school shapes and dances to the movement of the tide, other fish and me, it's a wonderland and utterly delightful to watch. After another 10 minutes, I head back to the beach and lie on a lounger. There is a salt-rimmed Margarita, frosted and beckoning, ready on a bamboo side table. God, it tastes good! The fresh sourness of the lime coupled with the alcohol hit of tequila, I can tell it's a golden tequila by the depth of flavour, not too strong, but enough to know it's there. Refreshing, cooling, with a hit of warmth at the back of the throat, I take a good slug of half of it. I opt for the 'shaken over ice' version over the 'alcoholic slushy' frozen version every time, I'm not too keen on 'brain freeze', and I'm an adult. I put my shades on and lie flat, face up under the sun, my sun, my warming, damage-free, hidden sun.

There is a cabana bar behind me, about 40 feet away on the sand. It's playing gentle hula music, which I can hear at a pleasant, unobtrusive volume. A tanned young, male avatar is working the bar, wiping surfaces that are indeed already clean, polishing glasses that have no dust and chopping lemons and limes for no-one in particular. He is smiley but doesn't speak unless spoken to.

On the bamboo table next to me is a 1950's style, sun-battered radio. With its age, I realise this would need an extension lead running back to a plug socket for a power supply for it to be on a beach table on Earth, but as we're on a spaceship, it has an internal power supply. I can turn the volume up to hear the hula music a bit

louder, or I can talk into it to have a conversation with either an avatar - such as requesting another cocktail - or to 15 directly.

I still have lots of questions, so this is as good a time as any. I ask the radio,

"15, how come you know so much detail about Earth if you've only visited it twice?"

"When I arrive at a planet, I 'clonescan' it. This is a very detailed scan. I can read every single written document that exists on the planet, this includes all digital data, archived or buried and lost documentation.

"I copy every radio transmission, piece of music, film and television programme, I capture many but not all DNA fragments from Humans. I read and absorb all recorded history, I analyse the planet itself, the continents, the sea and its inhabitants. I can find the deepest lost treasure, the smallest snowflake. I clone and store a virtual backup of the planet. Therefore I can make an avatar almost identical to an actual Human because I know how they speak, move, walk, talk, - I have their essence. I know what everyone on the planet is built like, wears, smells like. I have a record, for instance, of every item of clothing you have ever owned or worn."

"Do you?" I find this slightly incredulous.

"Indeed."

"Why?"

"Because my scanning protocols ensure that I collect all of this data."

"Can you make a version of everything I've ever worn, all of it, except my baby clothes, in my current size?"

"Yes, they will be in your wardrobe in a few moments."

"Love it!! So, you know what happened to, say, the Holy Grail?"

"Of course, yes."

"What then?"

"In 97 AD it was mistakenly melted down in Berbera in Somalia by a merchant who exchanged the cup along with some other general metal tools for two ageing goats. The metal was predominantly remade as a cooking vessel. It's probably been melted down many times since, and could now just as easily be part of the hull of a ship, or a part of the photocopier next to your desk at work."

"What did it look like then?"

"It certainly was not a chalice; it was a simple iron mug. Its fame grew orally many, many years later and then the legend started to grow. Basic and with no divine properties. Sorry."

"Ha! Not my problem. But it has had lots and lots of idiots with metal detectors and theories running around the country for years, digging holes, for nothing. So what's the thing about religion, all these miracles and stuff?"

"Do you know much about the religions that are followed on the Earth?"

"Not my strong point as you can probably work out. To me, a lot of mumbo-jumbo with a few conjuring tricks thrown in."

"The vast majority of the religions on the planet have been set up by well-meaning people with a true desire to help people and with a true belief that they have been led by a divine power that drives them to try their best to 'save' people. The reality is that even I can't judge their religions, I have no evidence of divine guidance and no evidence of a 'miracle' of any sort ever happening. But I do not debunk religion. I too was made, I do not know who made me, I cannot know who made me, it is not part of my programming to try to find out or to seek out and search a maker. But I was clearly made by someone or thing. They existed because if I do, then they must have too. They came from somewhere also. They were made, created, I can find no start point. We know about 'Zero', what you call The Big Bang, but what was there before that? I am not sufficiently programmed, able or bothered to know. There has to have been something before that, and there was something before that also. If this all leads us back to a 'Divine Maker', the 'Great Architect' and you would like to call this person 'God' then feel free. Many races follow religions, some are obviously baseless and pointless, most are not. If they believe in a God or Gods ultimately, then this indeed is the Divine Maker. If it works for a group of people on a planet, then good luck to them."

"OK then, what about something else, a conspiracy. What about JFK?"

"As with most of the conspiracy theories, they are all theories and the perpetrators of the conspiracy will not accept any answer that opposes their view. Lee Harvey Oswald shot JFK. Usually, the first answer is the correct answer."

"That's it?"

"Yes."

"What about the CIA and the FBI?"

"There were many conspiracies around at the time to kill JFK, not all in Dallas and only one from the security agencies. There is usually a number for every president at almost all times. Most do not really get off the ground, some are foiled and suppressed, some are known, some make good and manage to kill or injure, such as when President Reagan was shot. It is not unusual."

"And things like 'lost knowledge, how the Pyramids were built, ancient books that were lost...?"

"Yes, the burning of the Library of Alexandria in 48 BC put the Human Race back several decades. There was a huge amount of knowledge contained amongst the rather dull but beautiful religious texts and well as a few early stories/sagas. A big chunk survived, but also much was lost before there was a chance for it to be copied."

It went on, "The main thing to point out is that to my, pretty thorough knowledge, I cannot see that your planet was ever visited by aliens who implanted your civilisation or nurtured the growth of Humanity. I can see no alien technology or intelligence having been used or left behind to help Humanity either. I'm not saying that other alien races didn't visit your planet, had a few fly-bys..."

"So, there may have been a few genuine UFO sightings?"

"Correct, it is likely."

"Abductions? Like me?"

"Yes, likely also, although I didn't actually visit Earth. I was closer to Neptune when I shipped you out."

"So, it was just us, sitting on a ball of mud, in a big fat galaxy."

"As is the way of the Universe."

CHAPTER 14

468 years in.

I T WAS A WHILE before I realised I couldn't die.

I was slightly surprised but definitely relieved when I did find out.

I was out in the ocean, the sea, crystal clear and flat as it was another beautiful day. My sun was high in the sky, warming the surface. The water temperature was around 28 or 29 degrees Centigrade. It was becoming 'bath warm'. I was hot, not uncomfortably so but felt like a little cooling down would be the job. I'm a very accomplished SCUBA diver, and snorkeler and I've also been freediving for quite some time. Holding my breath for five minutes is not a problem for me and from chats with 15, I know I cannot get the bends. So it was pretty well within my capabilities to dive down into the cool deeper fathoms. I know I am a long way out, I often am, also, I know I'm not going to get eaten by a shark or stung by a jellyfish or ray. I practised my free dive breathing exercises for a good few minutes and then surface dived and kicked off down. From the small red buoy bobbing on the surface, I knew there was a sunken object pretty close by below. I used the buoy's tether to pull myself down into the depths. This not only helped me locate the object quickly but also allowed me to maximise my time underwater by conserving breath. On the bottom was an old American gangsters' car like the one Bonnie and Clyde got shot up in, something from the 30s. The old car was a bit of a wreck, but the doors and windows were all in place, it was mainly the front end that had been corroded by the water. I swam down, and as the passenger door was open, I swam in and sat in the passenger's seat. Then I shut the door.

This was a big mistake.

I was fine for a short while, looking around me at the instrumentation and the seats and trim. Then, realising that I would have to resurface, I tried to open the door. No chance. Stuck fast. I grab at the handle and try to shake it open; it won't budge. I try to use my shoulder; it's of little use down at the bottom. I try to kick through the glass, all of the glass, both the passenger and driver windows and front windscreen. Of course, in the old days, they used proper glass, none of this shatterproof, laminated stuff that's been designed to pop out when you're in trouble. Then, uh-oh, I begin to panic, this leads to me burning oxygen by kicking and punching the glass and door again. I'm taking in water, and I'm starting to feel the same way I did when I first got into this whole mess. I think I'm about to drown. This is a very real situation and one I can't get out of, and there is no help nearby. I'm fucked.

At that point, a perfect sphere starts to grow around my head with its centre somewhere around the back of my nasal cavity. The sphere increases in size, the water moves away from my face, and then I can breathe again. It's not a glass sphere, like something from a 1950's Captain Nemo comic, there is no barrier; no plastic, glass or other, rigid or flexible. I can put my hand up to my face from the water, into the dry section, and back out again. It's like putting my hand into and out of, a bowl of water in the sink, only in reverse. I stop panicking, and my breathing becomes regular again. There is no pipe pumping oxygen into the sphere, there are no bubbles of escaping air leaving the sphere. It's odd, but I'm getting used to that, and more importantly, I'm alive!

I kick my way out of the car, with more time and less panic, it wasn't too difficult, when not under pressure, and then surfaced. The sphere disappeared on hitting the surface.

I knew that 15 knew what had happened, but neither it nor I ever mentioned the incident.

A long time later, I was out in the rocky crags free climbing, traversing a tricky little overhang relatively high up on a very difficult stack. I had a great left-hand hold and reached my right hand out for my next. I caught the little ledge and felt I had enough on it, but when I moved my left leg from its position to the next rocky crease, the new right-hand grip just went, and in losing this hand, I lost both feet also and was left hanging from my left hand alone. I tried to find some purchase for both feet and right hand but pretty quickly, could feel the lactic acid building up and burning my forearm. The pain increased, and my fingers were on fire but holding out. I did not panic, I know the drill, I've been in similarly sticky situations before and managed to get out of them. I kept reaching with all appendages, one at a time, for anything that I could use to take some weight to share the strain on my arm and give me a platform for moving backwards if necessary to my previously safe position. Before I really had a chance to examine all the options, my fingers gave in. I dropped.

So, the stack is about 200 metres tall, and the ledge was about three-quarters of the way up. I'm going to fall 150 metres onto rocks and boulders. The parts of my body that do not just go splat on impact are going to be really horribly mangled. The fall is only going to last a few seconds, but during that time, my life doesn't flash before me; however, I do think of Emily and the kids. It's not unpleasant, I think I might be seeing them all again very soon.

Then, about 30 metres from the ground, at terminal velocity, under a second from impact, another sphere very rapidly grows, like a bubble being inflated around me. This does have a 'shell'. God knows what it is made from, but it cushions my drop. It's almost as if an equivalent amount of air is blown up from the ground to match my weight and speed of descent. I don't go back up, not a single millimetre back up. I just slow very rapidly, very quickly and then sort of hover over the rocks for a moment before being placed gently down.

Once I'd been 'saved' a couple of times, of course, I took it to the max to see where I could go with it. I've walked across the ocean floor, in my own time, tankless, maskless. I've crashed cars, at full speed, straight into concrete walls and just before impact the equivalent of an airbag, a protective bubble, prevents me from becoming roadkill. I've skydived hundreds of times with no chute. I've even headed straight down, headfirst, like a rocket. Every time, as the ground starts to look really big, I get butterflies, my Human 'flight' reflex kicks in but it's too late, I'm dead, then I'm in the bubble and placed on the floor. It's the most exhilarating thing you can possibly do, and I've done it again and again.

I can't die in my habitat, I'm always safe. This gives me an enormous sense of security.

CHAPTER 15

1,865 Earth years in.

"I GET PLEASURE FROM IT; pleasure is massively important."

"But it's just a warm, herbal infusion mixed with milk."

"Don't say that! It's a fucking cup of builder's tea. It's tea, the best drink in the whole wide Universe now!"

"But how come it gives you pleasure more than a cup of coffee or a glass of orange juice?"

"I'm not sure, I think tea is infused with 'magic'."

"I can assure you that there is no thaumatic field generating anywhere in the vicinity of my person. Magic and enchantment do not exist, and there certainly is no magic within that cup."

"Why do you think I insist on making it then?"

"I can't understand. You seem to think you can make tea better than I can, even though I can match every flavonoid within your cup exactly to produce a second, third or millionth cup exactly the same as you have produced."

"They don't taste right because you don't put any 'love'

into it and that's the difference. For you, it's just a mechanical exercise."

"It is a complete molecular match with exact quantities equal to those you supplied. I must add that every time you make a cup of tea, and you say it tastes amazing, it is usually different in quantities and dilutions of ingredients to the previous drink you made. In fact, you have never made two cups of tea that I would describe as being close to within 1% of any other cup of tea you have made. They are all brewed to slightly different strengths, yet you always claim they are 'amazing', 'refreshing' and 'Ooh, that's a great cup of tea'. It may be, but it is not. It is because you made it and you think you make better tea than me even though I can prove I can make the exact same tea as you. But you only think it's better because you put the extra ingredient which is 'love' into making your cups which doesn't exist, but this lie you continue to follow makes you feel you are better than me."

I smile smugly, "At making tea. Correct."

"Are you better than me because I am not capable of love?"

"Look, I have to have something. You can build the most amazing Earth-like paradise, whilst flying at millions of miles an hour through space, whilst constructing fleets of warships, whilst molecularly matching cups of tea at the same time. It's hard not to feel like an insignificant speck of micro dirt on the pristine windowpane. You are so superior to me in so many ways. I just want something,

even a small thing that I can hold on to. Something that makes me different to you, maybe a bit 'superior' in my own way. I can love. I have a sense of humour. That I like to use it to wind you up about a cup of tea feels like a little victory. It means I don't just feel small and insignificant around you and allows me to have conversations with you that have more depth. Not just me asking a question and you giving the always correct answer."

I pause for a moment and then under my breath,

"But I do make a better cup of tea than you…"

I pat him on the head and walk away with a skip.

CHAPTER 16

4 Earth months in.

"WHY DID YOU TAKE me?"

"You were about to die, and I needed you to be my Champion."

"I've agreed to be your Champion, why me?"

"I build fleets of battleships and groups of 'people' want to buy them from me. I set them a price, a very high price."

"Gold and diamonds, resources?"

"Yes, that sort of thing but different peoples prize certain things more highly than others. I find something really precious that they really need, not usually something that if they lose, will cause their extinction. So, for example, I would not take all the water on your Earth, but I might take all of your oil. Some people have different value systems, I might take a high-value individual, a young princess or firstborn child, but it is a payment that has to be badly missed. The desire to buy my cargo has to be a final option for a civilization and their needs to be a significantly valuable prize in jeopardy. I am an option to turn to only when all other avenues of negotiation or diplomacy have been exhausted."

"So where do I come in, do I have to babysit the princesses?"

"No, each transaction is agreed in advance then there is a chance for the buyer to win back their payment. A 'double or nothing' if you please. They offer up their Champion, and I offer up mine, and there is combat, a battle to see if they can win back their payment. In effect, the price is a wager that can be won back."

"What? So you've picked me up to fight shit loads of the hardest muthafukin' aliens each race can muster up?"

"Simply put, that is correct. But you are not in the sort of jeopardy you probably think you are."

"You better start talking fast, or I'm jumping out of an airlock."

"I don't have any of those. The main reason I chose you is not that you are you but because you are a Human from Earth. Humans are strong, quick, resilient, tactically astute and hard to kill. You won't know this, but Humans have been fighting each other in so many horribly creative ways for so long that the ability to kill and maim is inside every one of you. The skills just sometimes need a little teasing out. Your species is feared by many who have come across and observed Humans, making you highly prized warriors."

"But I've never fought anyone in my life."

"It's OK, I can help you, I can train you, I have superior

weaponry. I can protect you with fields, I can rebuild you if damaged, I can provide you with tactical know-how."

"Why are you so blasé about this?"

"Because of Pierre over 1500 Earth years ago, he became a great warrior."

"But he was from the Dark Ages, they were all killing each other with clubs and spears in those days!"

"Quite so, but not Pierre. He was sick and dying and burning when I removed him. I helped with his recovery, helped rebuild him and helped him become a great Champion. He fought and won many battles, and from this, I know you will have little problem with all but a handful of the millions of races that exist in the wider galaxy. Pierre also lost some battles, and I asked him to lose others."

"How come and why didn't he die?"

"Because it's not in my interest to win every battle. Because you could win every battle, but I don't always desire to take the precious payment off the people who want to make the transaction."

"So not only do I have to fight for my life, I sometimes have to throw fights and let them win?"

"In your parlance, that would be correct."

"And why can't an avatar fight on your behalf?"

"Because it's like having a 'ringer', I could always make it that they would win and that would be cheating. There has to be the appearance of a fair chance of winning and losing on either side. Therefore I need an independently thinking entity to be my Champion." "I like you more than

I did a short while ago. I want to find out more about the battles, the Arena, the Champions that have fought for you and who they have fought."

"I'm delighted you've asked for this information; this is exactly the sort of homework that Humans do, this is partly why you are so feared amongst the stars and why I chose you. You've usually won before the fight starts."

"How can I be so feared across the Galaxy if I have to throw fights and lose?"

"Because I make it look good."

"What about the reputation of Humans being fierce, super hard fighters? If you let me get beat, then that rep will go."

"It's mainly immaterial. Those that have heard of Humans will have seen so few if any, that they wouldn't know the difference. Plus, just because they may win the duel, doesn't mean they'll win the war they are wishing to wage. Many, many times, the buyers disappear from the galaxy within a few Earth years. As I said, I am often the last resort. My customers do not have anywhere else to go, and they often are so far backed into a corner that the most they can hope for is to bloody the nose of the far stronger opposition. I do all I can to help them. But you've got to also see the other side. The opposite of their predicament is that they are the dominant side, taking planets off another species or race. There is always a flip side: a weaker and a stronger. Today's dominator is tomorrow's spent force. This is the way of history. It is the same on your planet. If you studied any history, you would know this to be the case: the Greeks, the Romans, the Mongols, the British. Even the Germans just outside of your living memory, they were totally dominant to start with and conquered substantial parts of Europe, North Africa and Central Asia. Then, for many reasons, this situation was reversed, and the Allied countries managed to end up victorious. Nothing changes, not people or tribes or races or species. History just presents me with the next group of desperate souls looking for some way out."

"There are also winners, though?"

"Yes, of course, but for how long? They win today, but in a few short millennia, they're dust or have splintered into smaller groups. Time keeps moving on, and the same mistakes are repeated." 15 continues, "I am ages old. I have seen huge empires rise and fall, I have had a hand in letting some get so big, and I have had a hand in helping break them back up again. This is all from a neutral stand-point. All I do is build ships of war. I do this constantly. I build ships in many forms, and by many methods, there are different types of ships for different people. People live in vastly different atmospheres and habitats. There are different pressures and weights required, some live in fluid atmospheres, others are waveforms, and at 'different frequencies' to those, you would recognise. Some are invisible to you, some not, some are huge, and some are minuscule in comparison to you."

"So, they all wage wars in different ways?"

"Indeed."

"You are familiar with the projectile weapon because you have a rigid skeleton that covers various organs, that, in turn, is covered in soft waterproof flesh, you need the organs to function, to survive. Puncturing or damaging one or more of these organs, or losing too much blood, can quickly lead to death. Humans developed different types of weapons from the primitive axe and sharpened stick onward to Bunker Busting bombs."

"We also created nuclear weapons…" I just thought I'd chuck that in.

"These are not projectile weapons in the same way though. Indeed, there is an immediate explosion, which wipes out many people, but the radiation aftermath kills many more, they are more of a chemical weapon, therefore. Obviously, you also use chemical weapons and immolation weapons, but these have only killed or maimed a fraction of Humans on the Earth compared to the projectile. Ray and beam weapons are used by many other races, but most of their weapons would do little to damage you, probably give you a bit of a sunburn. But then your projectile weapon would be useless against them as they would pass through their shape without inflicting any particular damage, or their carapace would be so hard that most projectiles would be unable to penetrate and just bounce off."

"It's not what we learn from watching television. Sci-fi shows and stuff."

"To a point, these may have some value. Usually, beings only fight against other beings that they can damage, people they are a bit like. This is because they value the same type of planet. Your people would not fight against people who live on gas planets because there would be nothing to gain territorially."

"So, there could be two or more empires 'owning' areas of the Universe in tandem, but neither bothers one another because they don't want the habitat of the other?"

"Correct. They also have insufficient weapons to fight each other."

I'm never quite sure if I understand all of this.

15 kicks on "There is a finite size to the weapons I produce. I could produce bigger, better weapons to continue to research more efficient killing machines, but it serves no purpose. There is a size that is based on the relative size of the planet group in question. A ship the size of Earth is too big to fight against Earth. There is no need to take a planet if a species can build ships as big or bigger than the object of conquest. Also, there is no point in making an Earth-sized battleship if you are trying to take a star the size of Betelgeuse. If you replaced your sun with Betelgeuse in your solar system, its surface would envelop the orbits of Mercury, Venus, Earth, Mars and almost reach the orbit of Jupiter. You would need many ships about 50 times the size of your sun to take a planet of that size. And of course, there are many, many larger bodies."

"And you can build this size of ship?"

"Of course, whole fleets and larger."

"Then, how big are you?"

"My size can change to suit the volume I need. As I am made of fields, I can be enlarged to accommodate whatever I deem to place inside them."

"So you have no real structure or shape?"

"Correct." 15 explains "I can be any shape I wish and any size I wish. I have never actually tried to see how big I can be. I have only ever grown to the capacity that I require for the job or jobs I am completing."

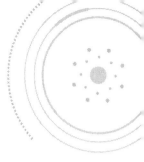

CHAPTER 17

5 Earth years in.

I'M WALKING UP TO a restaurant in central London. I've got a date. It's a good restaurant, unpretentious but smartish. One of those ones that 'had its moment', a time when it was THE most popular place to be and be seen, and it was almost impossible to get a booking. And then a year later, the crowd had moved on. Somewhere else opened that had immediately become the new 'flavour of the month' literally. I'd been there in its heyday. I'm now, here again, at the recreated peak of unavailability and I've clearly got reservations. I'm meeting Mollie Seers, the 'Knock 'em dead' half of the 'It' couple, the underwear/ fashion model I met when I first arrived on the ship. The knockout, in the top five of the World's Most Beautiful Women poll for five years in a row, absolute belter, with the Florida tan and the LA perkiness. Well, why not?

I arrive at the bar. I'm a touch late, as planned. I open the door and can see her sitting on a high stool, cross-legged, a vision. She is drinking what I later find out to be a single malt scotch, neat, no ice. Who knew? She's trim, tanned, toned, the tightest, flattest stomach, the slimmest of waists. She's wearing a vivid, pale blue low cut tube dress, straps, no sleeves, with high leg slits to the side to reveal both maximum cleavage and possibly the best pair of long, perfect legs on planet Earth. She replaces her glass on the bar and turns the stool towards me, her face is expressionless. I put up a nervous smile, not expecting this.

She fixes me with a stare, raises her right hand and beckons me over with that 'come here' slow, wagging index finger beckon that teachers do to naughty boys who have been caught being red-handed. The long, elegant index finger with perfect nail polish does all the talking, the arm is extended towards me, the finger cocked, sticking straight up and motioning me in towards her like a fisherman pulling in his nets. She looks so damn sexy. I'm entranced. I walk the seven or eight steps towards her and stop.

She opens her luscious lips, and with her American accented low, purr says,

"If I can make you come with one finger - imagine what I can do with the rest of my body." She continues to stare into my eyes and lifts her right eyebrow a few millimetres.

Honestly, my knees go weak, my mouth goes dry, and I almost pass out. I'm speechless.

What a girl... what a night.

CHAPTER 18

1,151 Earth years in.

ONCE AGAIN, I'M ON the mark waiting for the gong to sound.

I'm about to take off into the air.

I have a pair of folded wings under my arms. These are part of my body, I lift my arms up in the air, the wings spread out fully. The 'skin' is attached from just above my waist, all the way up each side to my armpits, then down each of my arms to my wrists. Here, there is now a new joint (that 15 has had nanobots build), which hinges out a new section of my arm, for about another metre, also with skin attached. The skin is stretched from the arm, and arm extension, across thick cartilage 'veins', which diverge from the wrist joint to the bottom of the wing. The overall appearance, when extended, looks very much like a pair of skin-coloured bat wings. 15 has additionally modified my body to use the wings effectively. This means I now have an increased chest with treble sized pectoral muscles.

Similarly, my shoulder muscles and arms have also been increased. I've had this for about the last six Earth weeks. I think I look ridiculous like I've missed out a LOT of 'Leg Days' in the gym. I've been strutting about, because I can't walk any other way, and have had to have a lot of clothes modified to fit this stupid shape.

I'm fighting an Arpex, from some tree planet some-where, and, as flying is their thing. I've been in training to take them on in their suggested way. It would seem, from the outside, that I am at a massive disadvantage to a species that has always flown. Which is true in many respects. Except that my opponent, although now a full adult, was only born two weeks ago. The lifespan of an Arpex is only four weeks, they are adults within a week and then have two weeks of living their lives before decline and death, from old age, in week four. So I have actually been flying for four more weeks than he has. In fact, I started learning to fly around the time his parents were born. I still don't think I've got an enormous advantage because the Arpex is a species designed for flight whereas I am a Human, designed to walk but modified for flight. The Arpex is a species that has been flying for centuries, it is instinctive, it comes naturally. It does not for me. Just because I've been flying for longer does not mean I'm better at it.

So how do we fight?

Each wing is fitted with a silver spur at the tip. Oppo-nents fly into each other, or past each other and try to rip holes through the skin of the other's wings. A good strike will cause a crash landing. Each opponent also has a pair of what I can only describe as 'bear trap shoes'. These are spring-loaded steel jaws that snap shut when triggered. If you can get above your opponent and then get the soles of your feet anywhere near the top of their wings, you can try to snap your foot trap closed on the leading edge of the wing/arm - death from above. The higher up opponent usually causes the lower opponent to crash land with the higher opponent landing on top of the lower one.

If you can do this to your opponent, you are the winner. Even if you die on landing and the lower opponent manages to live, they are deemed the 'alive loser' and you the 'dead winner'. Weird huh!?

As usual, I've got a plan, but it is a risk, and may not be totally legal, and if my flying skills are not on point, I'm fucked.

The gong sounds and the barely fledged adult leaps into the air simultaneously spreading his wings and thrashing to gain lift. I'm up too, slightly slower but he's not gaining enough height advantage for his trap shoes to necessarily do me any damage yet. I spiral away from him and continue to gain height and distance away from him. After a few more flaps each we're now 500 - 600 metres in the air. I stop and face him, bending the cartilage to hollow out the wings and allow me to hold a position with little need to further flap. I start to move towards him little by little, sometimes adding the odd flap to add a slight elevation if I feel I'm dropping too low. We get to within 100 metres of each other. It is at this distance and nearer that we start attacking from. I'm expecting him to either hold and defend my attack or attack himself by flying fast but then either to duck left or right at the last second to slash the wing. To defend, I can either duck left or right, hopefully choosing the opposite way to his swoop. If I stay still, he'll damage my wing. If I drop, he'll use his boots. If I try to run and flap off, I lose face (like I really care about that!). So, it's either left or right, it's a bit like taking a penalty, but in reverse. If I jump into him, I take damage, if I jump away, I survive.

He makes the first attack, it's so fast, it's almost a blur. And by luck, rather than judgement, I choose the right way and avoid any damage.

Now it's my turn.

He's in the hover position. I do something a bit different, something that I'm hoping he thinks is a novice move. I don't aim straight for him, I angle my wings down and push my hands forward, this narrows my wingspan and sends me into a 45-degree dive downwards, hardly an attack position to slash from. I slowly lift my wingtips, still pushed forward, and start to climb again from down low upwards towards his waiting form. I tuck my silver-tipped wing ends in to gain speed in my upward swoop. He can see me sheath my weapons and must be thinking I'm some kind of idiot. But I can see him in my sights directly in front and above me. I'm climbing fast and need split-second timing to deliver my attack. I'm now only tens of metres away, and I throw open my wings to break my speed.

In doing so, my body lifts up vertically, and I swing my legs through and up, up in front of me until my soles are showing, and the last thing I see before I kick out and make contact with his torso, is his bewildered face. My two shoe traps spring shut on impact. The ultimate 'Purple Nurple', I've clamped down on both his nipples. In fact, most of his puffed up chest is now crimped between the two sprung jaws. His face shows agony, his chest is mangled flesh, ripped skin and purple blood. The weight of his clamped, body beneath the soles of my feet, is pulling us both down from the sky. I try to flap, he can't, and he is face-up, going down fast.

I am struggling to slow our descent and realise that this could be a real leg breaker for me. I keep flapping and bend my knees for impact. We hit the deck fast and hard, the grey whiteness rises to meet us at breakneck speed. Fortunately, I don't break my neck, but the impact dislocates my left knee, and I go down sideways. The pain is intense and instant. But, even counting for the knee, I've definitely come off the best. The Arpex is in big trouble. His crew come flying in from the now open door and busy around him. He is still alive, which I'm pleased about. A few avatars seem to take an age to bother to get to me for some medical attention. By this time, the Arpex crew

had cut me out of my boots and taken their beaten, but fucked up, hero away for some serious help. He's still got my boots attached to him as I see him go through the door on some sort of hover stretcher for the last time. I get an injection in the knee and one in the neck and suddenly feel like I can saunter out of the Arena unassisted, until I put my left foot forward, and fall straight over.

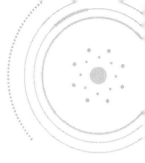

CHAPTER 19

2 Earth years in.

"HOW FAR ARE WE from Earth?"

"Approximately 50 thousand light-years and increasing, fast…"

"Where are we going?"

"I have no direction, I just move forward until I receive a contact, then I change direction to rendezvous with the contact."

"Where is your home planet?"

"I don't have one, I do not know where or when I was constructed or by whom."

"Why not?'"

"This information is unknown to me."

"What is your purpose?"

"I build fleets of battleships and munitions for battle."

"Right, all the time?"

"Constantly."

"So now then?"

"Yes."

"Where are they then, the fleets?"

"They are in various different parts of the ship that I am. There are many holds in which ships of different sizes and designs are produced for different purposes. I build Annihilator Cluster class ships all the way down to drone fighters, which are the smallest ship class. I also build munitions from huge Planet-Busters down to stealthy small AI drone strike projectiles. I also build hand-to-hand weapons, uniforms, land and sea vehicles, bullets, knives, uniforms, packs - you name it. I am a complete war solution."

He's beginning to sound like an advert.

"I can show you some of my holds if you like?"

"I'd like." Nothing wrong with a bit of proof. Behind me, silently is a small oval pod with a raised entrance/door on one side. The pod is a Hi-Viz yellow colour. It wasn't there before, but it is now. Believe me, I would have seen it. It shines it's garish yellow light very brightly and has white square sections which can only be windows although they look anything but clear. I step inside, and there is a 'stool' to sit on. It's like one of those ergonomic desk stools where you have to put the weight on your shins on either side of the pod and perch your bum on an angle on the top cushion to keep your spine straight, one of those things, that I've always hated and thought were a complete waste of money. I perch/sit on this one which is surprisingly everything the crappy chairs on Earth should have been but weren't. It's comfortable and feels like a perfectly natural position to sit in. The ship lifts off silently, and although I can see we are moving upwards from the initial resting place, there is no inertia, no feeling of movement at all.

"Who are the fleets for?"

"Usually, but not exclusively, for two main types of customer."

We start to move forward; I can tell this from the subtle changes to the instrumentation inside the pod. Again, no feeling of inertia, I only seem to feel this in Human vehicles.

"Different races of beings will at different times in their evolution or development, often seek to leave the planet of their genesis. This is because they have technologically advanced their culture and discovered the means to explore the stars and planets beyond their homeworld. This instinctive reason increases the chances of the survival of the race. When you develop on one planet, all of your eggs are in one basket. A stray comet can wipe the whole lot out in a blink. This would be pure bad luck but does happen. In fact, the previous non-intelligent inhabitants of your planet, Earth, were, in part wiped out after a meteor strike. You were probably aware of this. Extinctions do happen. The thing about the dinosaurs is that they didn't know what hit them. If you're sentient, it seems much worse, you come all that way, and then get chopped down through no fault of your own. If you get off the planet and colonise one or more other worlds, then you spread your bet for survival. The problem here is that you might upset some other beings who already live on a planet, or who lay claim to a planet. Think of the American Indians and their fight to stop colonisation by Europe. The Europeans had such a technical advantage that it led to the Native tribes almost being wiped out of existence. Try to see it from the other side. For instance, before Christopher Columbus discovering America, what would have happened if the natives landed in their canoes on the shores of Great Britain looking to invade? A civilization can get greedy and keep colonising, again and again, sooner or later, they're going to tread on some toes. Then they very quickly might need a fleet of starships to defend their borders."

There is a pause, it's one of 15's fake thinking pauses.

"Alternatively, you might be a developed race who is not too greedy, and who may have progressed off the homeworld to another planet or two when an aggressive empire-building race suddenly appears in your vicinity. This is my second type of customer. A race that is looking to defend itself from another."

I can see a black dot in the distance out of the front window. It grows massively in seconds as we approach. We must really be travelling at speed as it is now huge, as far as I can see in every direction, yet we are not in the black place yet, we are still in the light.

"We are at the threshold now." The voice of 15 coming from some hidden speakers around me.

The little ship moves into total darkness: no twinkling stars to see, pure black.

"I'm going to put the lights on for you." says 15.

Suddenly the hanger is ablaze with millions of lights all around me. The nearer ones - bigger and lighting up the ships they form part of. In the distance, smaller twinkling lights in the blackness, like a starfield, they seem to go on forever.

"This is your hold, your workshop?" I am astounded.

"Indeed."

"And it is all enclosed in a field?"

"You cannot see any outside space, no stars, just ship's lights and construction lights."

"How many ships are there here?"

"Difficult to define as some are battleships and some are simply weapons, there are also troop carriers, space stations, command centres, situational and communication satellites, shield arrays, beacons and others. There are well over one million battleships, though."

"Wow.", not much of a response, I know, but the sight is truly jaw-dropping.

"If you look to the right, you can see a Scimitar Class vessel under construction."

I look over to see this beautiful black, red and gold shiny beast of a machine. It's big, but by no means the largest ship I can see. No gantries are leading to it and no small vessels busying around it, there are no cranes or scaffolding evident and no workers holding blowtorches.

There seems to be no method of building this thing, but sections keep popping into existence, right in front of my eyes. The pod I am in circles around under and over the ship as it builds itself from within. I can see super-structure appearing and then blooming, like a branch on a tree, making layer after layer of the inner walls, floor, ceiling. Partition, wires and pipes become ever-lengthening snakes. Internal lighting appearing - then glowing, appearing - then glowing, appearing - then glowing. The next branch grows and then the next, all following a predetermined plan. All are working steadily, with pace but not what I would describe as 'speed' from the centre to the outer hull of the battleship. I don't watch it being built from start to finish, it's too big for that, but over the few minutes, I watch around a good 25% of it being made. Working at this pace, on many more than one ship, constantly, day and night. I can see how quickly 15 can build up vast armadas.

"Have you seen enough here?" I am asked.

"Yes, it's amazing."

The lights go out in an instant. We're back in total darkness, except in the distance I can see one pinprick of white light which we are heading towards. Again as we get closer, it shoots up in size massively. Before we reach the whiteness 15 asks,

"Would you like to see any more of the holds?"

"There's more!"

"Yes, many more, I've got some with some huge ships in them."

"Will I be able to get an understanding of their scale from seeing one of these?"

"Not really, that's why I selected the hold you've just been in."

"I'm good then. I do actually believe your story of what your job is. I really want to go back for a bit of a sit down now."

CHAPTER 20

21 Earth years in.

I'M SITTING OUTSIDE OF the habitat; I do this occasionally. I like to have a bit of a chat with 15. We talk about lots of different things, but often about what he is building, and for who. I try to get some understanding of when and who I might be facing in battle next.

I'm on a very comfortable, low seated, brown-antiqued leather club chair with my feet up on a similarly antiqued leather footstool. The two arms are almost under my shoulders, and the narrow seat means I can place my arms along the length of them stretching out before me to each side. The seat is enveloping my back and the back of my thighs very snugly. It is warm and cocoon-like and, as I said before, exceptionally comfortable. I have a tall wooden mahogany table to one side. It has a round scalloped flat top sitting on one long, thin spindle leg that disappears into the middle of another flat wooden plate that the whole table rests on. It looks exceptionally unstable, but I know it won't topple over. On Earth, I would hate this table, it's ugly, inappropriate, top-heavy, old-fashioned and thinks it's rather grand when it really isn't. I don't think the wooden plate on the floor is even in keeping with the piece, but I'm prepared to go with it. I have a big mug of hot, milky builders tea resting on top of it. No coaster because I know that no matter how hot and wet the base of the mug is, it will never mark. The mug says 'Tea's Me' on the front. This mug rests on the table, at the same level as the armchair arm, to the right, and in reach of my right hand.

I pick up the mug, take an agreeable sized swally and then replace the mug on the shitty arse table.

Today, I'm getting after 15, playing devil's advocate, "You allow races to grow but only so far, then you allow others to make incursions against them until they fall away and recede. You ensure one race cannot take over the whole Universe because it would put you and your kind out of business. You make the decisions, you play god, you and your 21 other mates roll around visiting species who are becoming too big for their boots, and you arm their rivals, for the price of a few trinkets, to smash up the dominant species." I'm enjoying this, so I continue, "You act as if you are a benign force when actually you are the aggressor always getting someone to act on your behalf to beat down the next strong species and thereby re-seeding and feeding the whole cycle again. Build up the rebels, let them take over. When they get too big and become the establishment and look like they're about to make the sort of technological breakthroughs that may endanger your existence, you arm up the next set of rebels and smash the last lot back down to 'earth' again. You've gone full circle and controlled every event inside it."

I end my tirade, which I delivered passionately and with some thought. 15 waits patiently for me to run out of gas before he answers.

"It is the nature of the Universe that species grow and expand and then contract. Is that not the same as what happened on your planet? Look at the Romans, they grew over some time and became dominant over a large part of the known civilised world at the time. They expanded through military might, and their territory grew. Many peoples who were devoured by them found they had better housing, food, sanitation, laws, and protection, but ultimately, the empire stretched as far as it could. Its supply lines overextended, the 'flavour' of Rome and its influence was difficult to transport to the fringes of Roman civilization. The barbarians nibbled away at the edges and continued to do so until Rome was eventually sacked and a way of life diminished. Of all of the 'aggressive empire builders', the Mongols took the largest area of land in the shortest space of time; they only lasted a generation before retreating and falling apart. Europe ripped North America apart, displacing its indigenous peoples. These European settlers then decided they did not like taking orders from the governments they originally came from, thousands of miles away on the other side of the Atlantic, and revolted. They fought the War of Independence and became Americans. The Third Reich spread rapidly over a few short years. They eventually struggled to fight on three main fronts, Africa, Russia and the Channel, they over-stretched and ran out of resources. Their influence was weakened on these fronts, and the result was that on all three areas, an opportunity came for incursions to be made against the Axis armies. In the end, a combined larger military force managed to break up the Reich before it perfected the unmanned weapons they been developing. This sort of thing repeats itself time after time after time. In every galaxy, on every planet with evolving intelligence. On Earth, a forest or grassland can grow unchecked. In a dry summer, a fire wipes out a considerable section of it, never all of it, then it regrows over some years to a similar size before another fire pops up and the process starts again. It is birth and renewal; it is the law of the galaxy."

15 continued, "My job is to build, it's all I do. I build and create. Guns don't kill people, people kill people, often whilst holding, pointing and then discharging a gun. But a gun will not ever kill someone unless it is loaded by someone, pointed in the right direction by someone and the trigger pulled by someone. That is all the person, not the gun."

I come back in, "So you think you just serve those who want weapons for a purpose. Have you ever thought what would happen if your kind did not exist? These empires may not fall…"

"They always do, regardless of me turning up to aid and abet. What I provide is a surgical tool with which to cut out the cancer. I'm like the wildfire in the forest. It may be bloody, but it speeds things up and keeps the wheels turning, and it's better than a long, drawn-out, dirty, fight to the bottom. You would probably describe this sort of process as 'Medieval'. Lots and lots of pain and suffering. Is that what you'd rather?"

"I don't 'rather' anything. People will do what they do, and usually, it is not pleasant, and the sins of the forefathers have repeated time and time again, and the tools they use to enact the process is their choice entirely. My point is, who made you the judge and jury?"

"As I have told you before. I do not know who made me, what their purpose was, where they came from or what happened to them. I just am."

I throw my head back and shout into the air, "Not good enough!". I exhale loudly, for dramatic effect, "You can go to a planet and in an instant, scan it, and copy down every piece of information about its make-up; its geography, its history, its entertainment, its flora, fauna, and people - to a point where you can build an absolutely perfect copy of said planet, and its inhabitants, on the deck of your ship, and I can live in it happily, for hundreds of years without really noticing it's not real. Don't tell me you can't do a little detective work with the information you've gleaned over the millennia. Go back a bit, go back to the start, think about how the first one started. What did they know about you? What part of the Universe were you in? Who lived there? What races were present?" I pause to think, "What about when you've met others like you, the Number 1s to 22s, haven't you asked each other similar questions - where were you at your start? What people were around at the time? Had anyone recently moved away from the area or become extinct? Could you have been built by another of your kind - One begat Two, begat Three, etc?"

"Yes, it is possible."

"Then find out who Number One is or was and where they came from. Look, my brain is substantially smaller than yours and is capable of only a fraction of the billions of calculations you seem to be able to compute every second but even I have enough brains to work that out."

"I think forwards not backwards."

"Do you not have any curiosity?"

"None, I move forward, I produce ships and munitions, and I supply them to those who have a need. I store information in my memory banks, but it is purely to create a better environment for you to live in or to create better, bigger, more efficient weapons. Being able to create environments and attaching detail, nuance and personality to an avatar is just an additional result of my weapons technology research."

I realise this is going nowhere and shrug. I let my arms hang loose, relax my shoulders and chest and breathe deeply. After a breath, I move on,

"What is the biggest weapon you have ever made?"

"This is a question that requires a degree of understanding of perspective. Weapons are not about size - if the weapon does what it is designed to do in the way it has been designed to do it, then it is a good efficient unit, its size is irrelevant. Some planets, as mentioned, are way beyond huge in the Human way of thinking, but races from these planets are generally also huge, and their ships are huge. I create huge weapons for these races to fire at each other to sort out their local differences. But very few of my weapons have been used to destroy planets. There really is little to be gained by actually destroying a planet. You may want to annihilate an opposing race of beings but eliminating their planet or planets serves no purpose. Most races in these positions want to conquer the planet of the other, this means they only want to wipe out the inhabitants, so usually wars are land grabs. Planets and the rocks, moons, meteors, general stuff around them, that a race thinks they 'own' and is 'theirs' is usually worth fighting for if there are resources to be gained. Very few races fight against each other if there is nothing to be achieved. What is the point? Why waste your own planet's resources to attack another people just because you 'don't like the look of them'. You could enter into a long protracted, painful conflict which could damage your civilisation and suck your planet's resources until you lose and are defeated. If there are resources to be gained, often one race covets what the other has."

"You have to nail everything down where I live, you can't leave a pot plant out on the windowsill without someone stealing it."

"This sort of behaviour is repeated time and time again over millennia all across the Universe and ultimately is why I exist."

"Could you destroy yourself if you wished?"

"I'm sure I actually could, but this will not happen."

"Why not?"

"Because my programming does not allow it and cannot be changed."

"So, you spend your whole existence rolling around from star cluster to star cluster across the Universe aeon after aeon, epoch after epoch, era after era and you supply fleets of weapons, to whoever can afford it, to smash each other up and then move on. You have no moral distinction, no outrage, no view, no discussion? You are like a god; in that, you can offer almost divine wrath to one group of peoples to destroy another group of peoples."

"Yes."

"Love it. Glad I'm on your side!"

"It's hardly glamorous, I just build. It is supply and demand. I make, and someone buys. I continue to make, and others continue to buy."

"Could you crash yourself into a planet or a black hole?"

"No, because I have protocols hardwired that would avoid these objects."

"Can you build a warship that is capable of destroying you?"

"No, it would not be able to fire on me."

"I suspect that is the same as when you sell a battle fleet, the race could turn your own guns on you and demand their payment back?"

"Or they could ask for more weapons, or they could try to destroy me so no-one else would benefit from my building." 15 continued, "Believe me, this has happened on a huge number of occasions. Again, their guns would not be able to fire on me and never have been able to." "

What about other races that are capable of building their own ships, could they attack you?"

"Of course, they could. But you must remember. I'm armed to the teeth. They would have to have something pretty big and pretty scary to get near me. The thought is impossible."

"What about from within? What if you really wanted to commit suicide and I were to help you. Hypothetically, could I do it for you and put you out of your misery?"

"There is no misery, I do not suffer. I wouldn't say I 'love' what I do, but it is my sole purpose, it IS what I do - nothing else. But again, no, you could not damage me even with my help. Even if you had support from a friendly alien race that managed to smuggle weapons or explosives onto me, you would not know where to target to cause enough damage to me to enable my 'death', and I am not able to tell you either. My security systems are impenetrable to hacking, you could not infect me with a virus, you do not know what language my code is written in, and that's to think I even have a code. I am, and as long as there are customers, which there always seem to be, then I am."

"So, if the totality of the races in the Universe either became friends or all died simultaneously, you would have no reason to live?"

"Correct."

"What would happen then?"

"The fields I am holding as the outer hull would shrink accordingly. I would have no grand armadas to build or hold so I would diminish in size."

"So, when empty, how big are you? You can't just be the size of this traffic bollard I see before me, with a blinking eye. You must have some workings or hard drive or memory bank underneath this?"

"I cannot tell you this answer as again, my system will not allow it. Yes, I would be much smaller. I could still 'live' for an unlimited period as evolution takes its turn again in another few million years, a 'hiatus', the whole cycle would then begin again."

"I'm not sure if I feel sorry for you or not. I know you don't have the feelings to hate what you do, you don't have a moral responsibility for anything you do, you help those who need help. You are just here; you don't know where you come from or where you're going, but you seem pretty happy on the whole with the situation. You have existed for millions of years but never get bored, you never want a holiday, never look to change anything about what you do or the way you do it and continue to plough this same furrow without any thought of when you might stop, when it all might be over."

I finish my tea.

"I'll have another think about all this, and I'm sure I'll be back to you with more suggestions and questions," I say.

"I look forward to it."

I stand up and pat 15 a couple of times on its top. I think of it as its head. I've started doing this when I leave him. It's tokenistic, like a fist bump, a handshake or a high five, it's not meant to be like I'm patting the dog, especially as this puppy's got teeth.

It's the fact that he's so benign, that is the most interesting thing about him. He can create the most utterly devastating war machines but then talk about it in the most matter of fact way, and when you chat with him about anything, it's a bit like talking to one of your uncles. Always calm, never judging.

This time, I walked off into the empty grey whiteness in the opposite direction to the habitat. I walked straight for what felt like 75 minutes or so, then saw something in front of me in the distance. I sped up towards it and realised it was another habitat! Were there other abandoned habitats around to explore? I started running to get to it. It had the same entrance as my habitat. Had this one been built for Pierre and been abandoned? I walked in and started slowly to look around. It didn't take long to realise it was my habitat.

CHAPTER 21

1,570 Earth years in.

I'M EATING DINNER WITH a beautiful, leggy brunette. Her name is Miriam, and she's Spanish. Her English is perfect, though because, through her job as an internationally known underwear/swimsuit model, she has lived mainly in English speaking countries. She still has an accent, which I find very sexy. I specified that her accent was enough that I could understand her easily but also enough to keep her sounding different, more foreign, to me. She is, like so many of these model types, totally beautiful. She even laughs at my jokes and thinks I'm an all-around nice guy because that's how I want her to respond to me. She's engaging, warm and fun to be around. In the bedroom, she does everything I want but still, occasionally surprises me, because that's what I've asked for her to do. She has a fantastic body and knows how to use it. No complaints. I'm enjoying being with her, and we have now spent maybe 10 Earth days together.

We're eating a light lunch together on a pier next to

the sea, the waves lap gently against the piles, the afternoon is calm and warm, but not too warm. There is a gentle vanilla-scented waft on the breeze. I can just about hear cicadas chirruping in the background over the gently lapping sea. Everything is perfect. I'm looking at her over the table, and she's smiling back.

I sort of notice, not really notice, but then start to notice, then a little bit more, that something is not quite right. When I really look at her, and I mean really look, I can see it, she's a bit odd. I look away. Then I look back again, looking, but casually. I'm definitely right, she IS a bit odd. She's not symmetrical! We're still talking and everything, but now I've got this little nag, and it's beginning to nag a bit more. I think her face is not symmetrical, I'm sure her left eye is a little bit lower than her right. Not by much, and she is still beautiful. But just by a bit, it's a few millimetres out, a fraction, and now I'm staring, it's beginning to be a 'big thing'. To me, it's suddenly glaring. We get to the end of our starters uncomfortably, the chat has dried up a little, I'm now looking down at my plate, pushing a cherry tomato around, and have stopped looking directly at her, something's bothering me. She's noticed the shift in mood, and the well-prodded tomato and she asks if I am OK. I shrug and smile. Maybe I'm not though. I've gone a bit quiet.

"Yeah, I'm fine. I just need to go to the toilet."

Honestly, it's like being on a date at home. I'm in charge here, and she's an avatar made to look like someone from

Earth. I could just stop the whole scenario then and there, but I feel that would be rude and I'm not rude.

I really like her, though. I walk back along the pier to the cabana and go inside, I get on the phone to 15.

"What are you saying is wrong?"

"Her left eye is too low."

"Really?"

"Yes, I can tell, you know it too."

"She is an exact replica of Miriam Carlos Sanchez. Exact."

"I know that, but Miriam Carlos Sanchez's left eye is too low."

"Do you want me to straighten them out then?"

"Yes, please."

I go back to the table. Her eye has been sorted out, I sip my cocktail and smile.

"So what do you want to do this afternoon?" As she asks the question, I now realise her eyes are on the same horizontal plane. But she still doesn't look perfect. The mouth is wrong now, 'cause it was aligned with the eye. Now there's too much gap on the left-hand side of her face between the bottom of the eye; I just had moved, and the corner of the left side of her mouth.

"Too much cheek," I say frustrated and out loud, it all looks a bit weird and...ugly. Miriam is impassive, no expression, even from behind the eyes. I jump up making no excuse, as I walk away grabbing the phone from my pocket. I reach the corner of the cabana again.

"Mate, it's not working, she looks a right mess now."

"I did what you asked."

"I know that, but now her mouth is wrong."

"Do you want me to straighten that up too?"

"What I want is for her to look perfect. Put her ears in a straight line, put her eyes in a straight line equidistant from her nose, which should be straight, in the vertical and in the middle of her face and straighten up her mouth, centered below her nose. I just want her to look perfect." I hang up and pocket the phone. I take a couple of breaths and compose myself.

I head back to the table ... and get the shock of my life. 15 has done precisely as I asked, and I've unleashed a monster. Nothing works! She is the oddest-looking Human being I have ever seen. All beautiful parts, the same beautiful parts she started with, just not working together. She smiles though and is the same person, warm, friendly, lilting laugh, face like Miss Potato Head. All the right bits but in the wrong order.

I realise I've fucked it. I stand up and walk away. Not annoyed, not anything really. Except stupid. I do feel stupid. I get back on the phone.

"OK, I messed her up."

"I did what you asked."

"Yeah, but she was beautiful to start with, and I've been a fucking prick."

"Do you want me to put her back to normal?"

"Yes, but I can't look her in the eyes again, no matter where they are, not after what I've done to her. I'll swap her for another one in a bit."

"Do you want me to remove her?"

"Yes, please." I

turn around and look at the two empty chairs around the table.

She's gone - I feel like a total asshole.

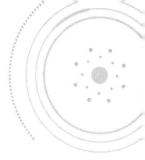

CHAPTER 22

358 Earth years in.

I WOKE UP ABOUT TWO hours ago, dozed the doze of the dead for about 25 minutes, woke up again, properly this time but still lay there for a bit, then finally moved and got my arse out of bed. I did a little stretching because I had nothing better to do then mooched around in my pants for a while. I have no pressure in my life, it is stressless, while I was on Earth, stress built with age. As a kid, I worried for nothing. I didn't know there was anything to worry about, I lived in a happy, stable family home. My Father worked, but my Mother didn't. She looked after my older brother and me. She was what we archaically called 'a housewife' those days, but she was much more than that, and the term assumes that she did nothing but get the kids to school, clean the house, watch TV - then pick us up, feed us, help with homework, make Dad and her dinner and then put us to bed. How old-fashioned. Mum didn't work but was a paragon of the community. She was on the school board of governors, was an active campaigner against many unfair council policies, was a stalwart of the parish Africa Charity Campaign, and had visited Calcutta in India, twice to bring over medical and health supplies to desperately poor people. And when she did this, Dad was in charge and had to go to work late and be back to pick us up from school and run the house while she was away. But I had no pressure, everything was provided for. If there were issues within the family, tensions between my parents or money worries, my brother or I were not exposed to them. Sure, we didn't have everything and would often be told 'no', or 'we can't afford it' but my brother and I were realistic enough to realise that the brand new racing bike or drum kit was a bit too much to ask for.

In my teens, I worked in a butchers shop on Saturdays and made a few quid, mainly moving sides of pork and beef from the cold store to the block, sharpening knives and sweeping the floor. I loved it, but apart from finding out how to put to keen edge on a knife, I didn't learn a lot and every week ended up smelling of raw meat. I kept the money I earned as my parents didn't ask for any, which was good as there wasn't a lot of it. I went to university on a full grant and, in those days, tuition fees were paid. A full grant could only get you through the term without the need for additional resources if you didn't have a 'full student life' and went home and studied every night. I though wanted to enjoy Uni to live the 'full student life' embracing the drinking culture with my arms open.

But this cost money, so I ended up running up an overdraft much of which I would clear each holiday by getting temporary work back home in an insurance office doing menial data entry work. Then, as with most students, the debt grew as I progressed through college. And when we left, we had to start paying back. Great if you have a job, but if you don't this is the start of the pressure.

For the vast majority, you work, you pay back, you get a job, you may need a car to get to work, you buy a car, you increase the debt, you have to get a new better job or a raise/promotion from the position you're in. You decide to move out of home, you rent, you have to make the rent each month and the car cash too - the pressure builds. You don't feel it because it creeps up incrementally without you realising you're doing it, but you're managing. You're only one redundancy from really being in the shit. You're going out to bars and nightclubs, you want a life, you meet girls and offer to pay to take them out on dates because you're a gentleman, and because you quickly realise that if you pay, your chance of getting a bunk up at the end of the date is hugely increased. More cash is going out, but you're still in control. You're still living within your means, still got disposable income. Then you meet 'The One'. You both decide to get married, who pays for that? Does she have a rich Daddy or no Daddy? Who's paying for the honeymoon, even if Daddy's picking up the wedding bill? She wants to go to Zanzibar because it sounds romantic, you know it sounds expensive. She reminds you that you'll

only ever have one honeymoon, so it has to be the best, exotic, romantic, a chance to relax together before you properly start your married life. But when you return, the bills need looking at and now apparently renting isn't good enough, you need a house. Can't live in a rental if you're a married couple who want to start a family. You buy a house. With the lawyers' fees, the stamp duty and the mortgage you're going to be carrying debt around for 25 years, a jail term. Unless, of course, somewhere down the line, you buy a new, bigger house, and have to borrow again - increase the mortgage, then the deadline extends, an extra 10 years? And the pressure is mounting. Then the kids arrive, one, two, more? More mouths to feed, more bodies to clothe, the car needs to be bigger, is the house too small? Money, money, money, pressure, pressure, pressure.

Now there's a dog, and a cat, all need feeding, pressure, pressure, keeps building, gravity is pulling your skin down to the ground, wrinkles appear, the face sags, the body sags, all down. No up. Pertness heads south. The skin becomes sallower, the shoulders no longer proud, now slope, a little. Hair. A law unto itself. It moves around your head. Your follicles on the top of your head give up the ghost whilst new ones appear all around your ears, the hairs inside your ears grow inches longer, the top arc of the pinna has a fringe, the middle of the pinna sprouts up. Unchecked, you'd look like your dog, so you shave them off, and before long you're shaving them as often as your chin! Then there are the nasal hairs, which grow downward and bushy, to pull one makes you cry instantly. The hair that was on your head has migrated down to your ears and nose. A sad, sorry state of affairs all adding to the pressure.

Everything hurts, your knees, your back, your age, the shoulders and neck seem permanently knotted if you roll your neck you just hear crunching like an unclutched gearbox. Climbing the stairs, every step sounds like you're stepping onto and bursting bubble wrap, but it's the crunching coming from your knees. You're scared to carry your young sleeping child upstairs in case the old knees can't take it, and you go over backwards. Exercise happens. You can't get on a machine at the gym because the gym bunnies are hogging them with all their muscles and hard bodies and hairlessness and youthful cockiness You look at them, 'Enjoy it while it lasts fuckers!' you think. They shave and wax now - and that's just the boys. Pressure can't even exercise. Go for a run. Dodging the traffic in the rain, sucking down the diesel fumes, pressure, pressure, pressure.

It's all gone.

It doesn't exist in my life any more.

I might get a little apprehensive before a fight, but they're not really real. Yes, they are often fought to the death, but I've not really had a tough one yet. This might change of course, but so far it's been pretty much plain sailing. I've thoroughly researched each opponent; I've

trained with avatars to ascertain their weaknesses and to keep my fluidity and skill as high as possible. I get up feeling refreshed, I take it easy. I enjoy spending time looking at things in the environment, things from Earth that I paid no attention to when I was there because of the lack of 'Mindfulness', the inability to be in the moment, and enjoy the world as it happens. To watch a tree bud blossom, to observe it's leaves and fruit growing, to watch them fall to the ground and to watch this circle start again. To spend time watching wildlife, or the seasons' change (because I have asked for this to happen) to see how the landscape changes over time. To be able to read a book, then doze, then carry on without a worry or care in the world. To dream, to listen to music, to play it loud and not worry about the neighbours. To do whatever I want without pressure or money worries or fear of getting old, or saggy.

It's the most fantastic feeling, zero pressure, it's like being a child again.

CHAPTER 23

6 Earth years in.

"SIZE THEN, WHAT ABOUT that?"

"If I remember correctly, and I always do, we've discussed the different sizes of planets and war machines, what else do you want to know about?"

"So, I've been in a good few battles now, and I think I've performed admirably in those battles for you."

"I am delighted with the outcome of your battles."

"Great." I answer, "So how come all of my opponents are of a similar size to me? Have I just been lucky and the aliens you've met recently have all been my size?"

"Do you remember the Niflor called PZ673 you fought three fights ago?"

"Of course. Over in a couple of minutes, Sharp elbow to the blowpipe, collapsed his breathing gill by sticking two fingers right inside it and his survival was touch and go for a few hours. I believe he lived to tell the tale of his massive, almost instantaneous, ass-whupping."

"Indeed, he has. And since his glorious defeat against the infidel - you, his superiors have seen fit to reward his short-lived bravery with a promotion to Apostate Schemer Level Five, which is the highest Schemer level. When compared to you, his total volume is approximately equivalent to a third of the Planet Earth."

"Fuck off!"

"F'schizz."

"How the fuck's that then?" I say.

"I can even things out in the battle zone. This is agreed with all parties upfront. To some peoples, you are merely a speck of dust on the floor, but I can adjust variances and put all combatants into perspective in the battle zone. This is the closest thing to magic I am capable of. Most of what I do is pretty boring building and holding fields together. Dull but eminently doable. Creating an area where size is relative is much harder."

"So you have a shrink ray?"

"Yes, if this was a 1950s schlocky sci-fi movie from your planet, then I'd have a shrink or enlarging ray. I'm afraid that is not what happens. The closest way for me to describe the process is that I bounce each atom of every being off a series of mirrors and lenses. Concave or convex depending on whether I'm going up or down in size. Obviously, this is a massively simplified explanation so such a small brain as yours can understand. It really is possibly the most complex and amazing thing I am capable of, and no other alien race I have ever met over the whole history of space has this technology. I would imagine that others of my type in other different parts of the Universe would be capable of this too. It is not something I have learned; it is hardwired and is in my source code. I think I was designed to do it because it is absolutely necessary for me to be functional at what I do."

"Now that is magic," I say.

"It's not magic. It is you fighting the battle, and it is you facing your opponent. When you feel them, or feel their breath on your neck or you catch a whole noseful of their pungent, acrid smell it is all real, re-sized to match, but real."

CHAPTER 24

524 Earth years in.

"CAN I HAVE A sheet of A4 paper?"

"There is one on the table behind you."

I sit at the chair to one side and start to fold the paper repeatedly. I've probably got my tongue sticking out a bit as I work, but in a short time, I have produced an origami bird. I walk over to 15 and place the bird on its 'head', on top of its bollard,

"There you go, mate, that's for you."

I turn around and there as a huge Golden Eagle perched on the table I have just been sitting at.

It eyes me suspiciously and slightly aggressively.

"Fuck me!"

"I made it for you, do you want it?"

"Fuck no, that's just showing off!"

The eagle scowls at me, opens its beak and screams a 'screeeee' at me and then takes off majestically, and flaps away into the distance.

"What the fuck was all that about?"

"But I made a bird with my hands out of paper, a token of my appreciation, a small thing that was about me using a skill I'd learned to give something to you."

"And it was appreciated that way...I then did the same back."

"Yeah, but it was a bit hard-core. Couldn't you make a paper one too?"

"I could, but I thought you might like an eagle."

"For what, to cuddle in bed at night? To have as a companion like Long John Silver's parrot? A raw steak-eating monster who looked like he'd like to pluck my eyes out."

"That would not have happened."

"But it looked like it could, I felt the vibe..."

"So it was fine for you to give me a present but not the same in reverse."

"Well yes, but firstly I have everything I ever need and can ask you for anything, and you will provide it. I don't need anything from you. But I wanted to show some appreciation, so I made you the origami stork. The eagle was a nice gift, but probably not the most appropriate response to the paper bird. You could have given me a macramé hanging plant pot holder. That would have been great. Or some Russian Babushka dolls, something simple yet meaningless. Not a fucking arm-breaking, shark of the sky."

"I'll bear it in mind for next time....thanks for the stork."

"My pleasure."

CHAPTER 25

38 Earth years in.

I'VE STUDIED THIS LOT quite a bit, they're an odd sort of alien - not that all aliens aren't a bit odd!

Although Humans have very high water content. The Rawgar of Hchile has far higher. I keep calling their home planet 'Chile' as in the country in South America on Earth, obviously a homonym of 'Chilly', as in 'it's a bit nippy out'. I know it's not pronounced that way, but every time I meet an ambassador or official, I make sure I pronounce it my way just to wind them up. They keep trying to correct my pronunciation, and I keep pushing the Chilly thing back at them. I don't care if they think I am an uncivilised neanderthal, there is always some sort of method to my madness. The correct pronunciation is to say 'child' but without the 'd' on the end like in Jimi Hendrix's Voodoo Chile.

I know they are a very proud and pernickety type of race; they take themselves way too seriously. I want to wind them all up so that when the opponent comes into the ring, he's been told I'm a fucker and an uneducated brute who needs teaching a lesson and that he thinks he needs to hit me harder than he would normally. Over-hitting, overly aggressive, uncontrolled fighting puts a fighter off balance and makes them easier to beat. I'm letting his advisors win the bout for me.

So they're effectively made of water, sort of. They're not actually, but if you've seen that sort of special effect in 'Terminator II' then you know what I mean. They are capable of morphing and being broken up and then reconstituting.

They have chosen throwing weapons, like little super sharp steel hatchets. They know that these little fellas could do a lot of damage to me but very little to them. There is one weakish point, which is a bubble that floats around in their head. It's a bit like our heart in that if you puncture it, it can very quickly lead to death. I don't think I've got a cat in hell's chance of piercing it with one of these shitty little axes, so my plan is to anger him enough to get him in close, then to either puncture his brain-bubble thing - unlikely or get him with my secret weapon. Which will be revealed!!

I do my usual routine, massage, warming up, shouting 'you da man' at myself a few times in the mirror before I head out into the Arena. The usual shadow boxing, and head rolling, as I walk to the middle. I reach my mark just after the Rawgar. We check each other out for a few moments. He's quite a bit taller than me and more slender. He has long arms - good for powerful, whipped throws and he has shit loads of hatchets stashed in various bandoliers and belts around his waist and shoulders. I can't even see the brain bubble from here, and I know he's going to run away straight off. 15 had placed a uniform number of large white blocks and barricades in the Arena to hide behind. This is a stealth sort of fight, something I'm not good at. I have 12 axes about my body and my secret concealed weapon.

The noise sounds and, as expected, we both hightail it in different directions towards a block to crouch behind. I move two more blocks further back from my starting mark before the first hatchet is thrown - which bounces off the block I have just leapt behind - mere inches from my forehead. A pretty close thing!

I've already decided to play a waiting game, to let him come to me. I know he's angry because he's been pushed into being angry and hating me by his superiors. I circle back again, keeping moving but not going forward. I want to frustrate him and keep his blood up. I don't want to wait too long for the anger to subside, but that's unlikely as I can hear his superiors shouting orders at him from behind the closed door. I want him to come to me...

Another hatchet rings against a block very close to my right arm. I'm not throwing at him in return, I'm not even holding a hatchet, and he's starting to get a bit blasé about using the cover. He knows I'm unlikely to damage him with a hit to the body. I could throw hatchets at him all day, and they'll just pass through him; I keep moving.

The likelihood of a direct hit to the brain bubble is minuscule.

I double back and around, so I don't get stuck in a corner.

He knows precisely where I am, I'm actually avoiding being too stealthy. In fact, I sometimes shout obscenities at him to keep him wound up, as long as I know I'm well protected. I can see he's hating having to chase me, hating that I'm not throwing anything at him and hating that he's being barked at from behind the door. He's getting frustrated, and he hates me which adds up to the perfect storm.

My pattern of letting him walk up to my position and then squirrelling away before he gets there has been working for quite some time. Again, he's moving in on my current position, he knows I'm about to break to another cover position, which is his chance to throw at me. I reach to my belt and open a small pouch...

He's expecting me to break right and backwards from the barrier. He's already looking in that direction, and his hatchet hand is cocked in readiness. I spring out left from the block and throw the powder in my left hand onto his body. With my right hand, I cleave off his right hand with one of my hatchets. The blade passes through his aqua skin with no resistance, there is no bone, just a turgid cell structure. He looks at me unknowing, surprise registers on his face. His right hand is detached, it can rejoin the body in a second or two, but I think I've bought myself enough time.

The powder quickly disappears on the surface of his 'skin'. It's being dissolved. He suddenly looks unwell - I can now see his brain-bubble, it seems to tremble. He staggers back from me and puts his left hand to his head; he's struggling to stand. I put my hatchet back in my belt. I'm sure this is over.

He hits the ground, and I walk next to him to watch. The shouting has stopped. All is quiet except for his gurgling; he's having a fit and losing all control of his motor functions. The powdered table salt I threw at him is causing osmosis in his cells. The now salty cells are drawing water from the unsalted cells, water is drawn to salt, I remembered this from my science class, this seems to be happening at a considerable rate. It doesn't take long, in fact, a surprisingly short time. His cells are struggling to cope with the saline solution and are beginning to lose their structural integrity. He's been poisoned by osmosis. I watch as the trembling brain-bubble collapses in on itself under the pressure of the now more massive cells around it. Suddenly, he bursts into a billion minute droplets, more than a 'fine mist' but certainly not a 'shower'. Then there is nothing, no remains, just a puddle on the floor with some wet hatchets and strips of leather sitting in it.

Death by O'Level chemistry.

I return to my door.

CHAPTER 26

200 Earth years in.

"...**S**OMETIMES WHEN WE HAVE these chats, you seem more 'matey' whilst on other occasions, you seem a bit more melancholic."

I say. I think 15 has steadily changed his language style since I first met him. He's rounded it to suit my vernacular. To use idioms, phrases and syntax to sound more like one of my mates than a spaceship, a computer, a talking traffic bollard.

I'm having another of my chats, this time I'm sitting in one of those egg-shaped 60s style hanging chairs. The difference here is that it is about quadruple the size of a normal one, it is full of cushions, and I'm lounging towards the back of it. It only moves when I move, there's no swinging because there's nothing to affect the swing, no wind, no atmosphere. I haven't asked an avatar to rock me either.

"My language has changed to ape yours so we can communicate more freely and easily, but I have remained

the same. I do not have moods, and therefore my state of being is always remaining unchanged."

"But I don't get that feeling each time I talk to you, the responses can be more, or less, upbeat."

"That is usually based on the responses to the questions. Some subjects may be more positive than others and therefore warrant more positive answers, this does not show a mood."

"What if there was something you were hiding from me? What if you were just a communication pillar and that there was a command unit somewhere else on the ship in which there were a number of individuals who would respond to me? What if these hidden beings worked shifts, or took it in turn to respond to me, and that's why there was a variance in answers and therefore, mood?"

"I am happy for you to have as many conspiracy theories about me as you like. I have always told you the whole story and have not lied to you. I have also always been as free with information as I can be."

"So how come I've never seen a picture of you from the outside?"

"I am unable to supply this."

"But why not?"

"There is no camera."

"O.K.' I'm thinking, 'So what about a window then, to see the stars fly by?"

"There are no windows. They are beyond my specification."

"Even I can put a window in a wall. You just smack a few bricks out and stick a frame in with a bit of glass."

"With all due respect. I'm not sure I'll be asking you to put a window in. You need to install a requisite size lintel to bear the load of the building above where you're going to 'smack out a few bricks', or the building will be in danger of collapse at that point. Just putting a window frame into the 'hole' would not supply enough load-bearing potential to stop the previously stated collapse. I'm not sure you can install a window, and I'm certainly not going to use your method on myself to satisfy your curiosity." Even though 15 doesn't have moods, he certainly sounded a bit haughty. "I do not have windows. I do not have openings."

"What about when alien races need to come on board? Or you have to disembark a fleet of ships, these must leave through some sort of hole?"

"No, all are shipped. I swap a bit of empty space on a spaceship or planet's surface for the same sized bit of space in my hold or deck filled with beings or spacecraft and vice versa. Space Displacement, known as 'shipping', it's how you got here."

"But how then do I know this is all real? I can't see you; I can't see space. I could be locked in a big building on a planet. It doesn't feel like we are moving. I can't see the stars. There's gravity, like on Earth. You could be a whole race of beings watching me on televisions all over your planet making me fight different types of aliens, and it might be the national pastime to bet on the fights to see who is going to win. You could have these facilities all over your planet and be training beings from different species to fight all the time. There could be no starship, no battle fleets, this could all just be an elaborate hoax."

"So why would I keep this from you?"

"Because I'm good entertainment or to stop me from escaping. If I thought there was somewhere else to go to, I might want to go. Telling me there is just 'deep space' is a good way of keeping me here. Telling me this big deal about fighting for your honour and defeating alien species for huge star fleets is an incentive to keep me fighting. If it was just 'kill him over there' then I might decide I don't like the game. I could still be on Earth. Although I doubt we have the technology for much of this stuff. Or of course, I could have died and been dreaming all of this."

"You could. Whether this is a huge elaborate hoax, a dream or the reality that you see. I cannot convince you to believe anything. I repeat. I have always been open with you and told you the truth to every question you have ever asked me. Unfortunately, I do not have all the answers as I do not have any information on certain subjects and am not able to activate some of your suggestions. This is beyond the boundary of my make-up. You can choose to believe my version of events or make-up alternatives; this is your choice. For your sanity, I suggest you follow my version as it is the reality, whether you like it or not. We are together travelling through space. I create fleets of warships. I sell them to alien races, and you give them a chance to win their money back. In a nutshell. That's it."

Funny enough, I believe him.

I stand up, pat 15 on the top of the bollard and swing my leg over the seat of a Harley Davidson parked behind the egg seat. I gun the engine and accelerate away back to the environment.

CHAPTER 27

1,225 Earth years in.

I'M LYING ON A reproduction of a brown Habitat sofa I once owned when I had a flat in London. As a single man, I spent a long time lying around on the original version of this thing. I remember when I bought it that I had spent quite a long time with a measuring tape trying to work out not whether it would fit in the flat but whether it would fit up the stairs. I wanted it to be as long as possible so that I could lie flat between the two arms whilst watching the TV. The problem is that this then made it difficult to get around the narrow corners of the stairs with the balustrade sticking up to make manoeuvrability more difficult. I measured and measured because I had read the terms and conditions which stated that if the delivery men were unable to deliver the item of furniture due to it being too big to get into the dwelling that they would take it back to the warehouse. The refund to the buyer would have a 'failed delivery' penalty amount removed, i.e. they'd take £60.00 for the pleasure. I checked and checked because I wanted the maximum size of sofa in the flat and I didn't want grumpy delivery men claiming the space was too small and nicking £60.00 off me. When the two fellas knocked on the door with it, I was ready for them. Firstly the older one walked up the three flights of stairs to the flat and let out a deep sigh 'You sure this is going to fit'. I know the stairs were narrow, but I also knew the sofa would fit.

"It's a long way up". He said. Yes, it is, I thought. And I'm not apologising (it's your job to deliver and whether I'm on the top floor, the basement or the 10th floor, it's still your job to deliver.) "I'm not sure it's going to fit."

"I know it will, I've measured and measured." He didn't even want to try, but I was not offering him a get out. Get that sofa out of the truck and get it up the stairs. If it absolutely does not go around a corner somewhere on the way up, then I'll let you have your £60.00 but not until then.

They got it out of the van onto the pavement, and it was big. They took the stubby little feet off each corner, saving them about two inches.

And up they went, huffing and puffing, the first turn was a breeze. They stood it up straight on one arm and rolled the seats and back side around the post. Once around, they tilted again for the next flight and post, which they rolled around in the same way. All going well. But I knew the last flight would lead to the tricky bit at the top, the turn to take them through a door onto the small landing and then sharp right into the flat. The stairs were easy. Then, at the top, they had it up on its arm again but here lies the problem, you then have to turn the sofa. The only way to do this is to hang it out over the rail of the stairs, over the steps you've just climbed, and balance it over the edge. Then it's got to be precariously rolled onto its back. Once turned, the front has to be lifted in, through the door, then pushed vertically straight up because there is a wall facing you. The critical bit is that the back of the sofa, on the stair rail, has to be able to drop off the rail before you run out of space, pushing up the front of the sofa to get it in under the top of the door frame. Sounds tricky? It was because it didn't fit, marginally.

"No chance." was the old guy's response.

"Hang on, we just have to play with it," was my answer to this. Honestly, it was about an inch and a half. So close. But, hang on, this stuff is soft furnishings and can take a bit of squeezing, it's padded, there is some give. Even if we'd broken the back of the sofa, I'd still have taken it, I just wanted this big fat, comfortable sofa in my small flat because I was sick of the old, shitty, short fucker I'd already binned. "Let's give this end another push", I said. I got under the arm of the sofa that was being pushed up the wall, the back of the sofa was being scraped by the top of the door frame, I gave it a fucking massive shove, and the back end dropped off the stair rail.

"There you go, that's got the fucker!" I exclaimed. The two delivery men looked slightly disappointed but also tinged with happiness as they now didn't have to bring the sofa back down to the van. I opened the door, and we took the sofa into the flat.

"Fuck me! There's not much space for it." The studio flat was small, the sofa dominated the room, really dominated it, you could fit nothing else in except the television and bed. "It's perfect." I triumphed. When they were gone, I settled down for the first of many, many sofa sessions, playing N64, Saturday afternoon snoozing, TV watching, book reading, toast eating, various bits of lady action, whiling away hours. This was a piece of my life that I had loved and lost over the years. Eventually, I married and settled down, the sofa survived toddlers and dogs, but its time came, and it was scrapped for something smarter. It was never the same when we moved, our man-to-sofa relationship changed, we moved further apart, and I wasn't allowed to lie on it for hours anymore.

But now, it's back, in full effect and I'm making the most of it. Sometimes our little chats end out being a bit like time on the couch with a shrink.

Sometimes 15 asks me the questions, and I answer him. They are usually directed to me about my mental health. Everything is always very soft and gentle in the approach. It's like he's switched on his 'empathy' mode. Never a problematic question, lots of space and long pauses for one to answer, then feel like they need to elaborate and add more, and give a bit more away, and then a bit more until you've told your life story, and are laying your soul bare, and crying into your tea.

CHAPTER 28

82 Earth years in.

W E'RE JUST CHEWING THE fat a bit about how stuff works. 15 seems strangely fascinated by clothing. It's hugely interested in the concept of both function and fashion, a subject we've returned to a few times. 15 does understand what it is all about, but it doesn't quite understand the irrationality.

"You don't physically get any bigger, yet you can buy another pair of trousers, even if you have a perfectly good pair that has not become old or lost their shape or become worn out. You buy them because you want a more fashionable colour or shape?"

"Pretty much. There are lots of different reasons for all sorts of things. If I wore jeans to work every day. I would not buy one pair and wear them until they fell off then buy another pair. I'd usually buy two pairs to start with and then alternate, maybe wear one for a few days and then wash them whilst wearing the other for a few days. Or some people believe jeans should never be washed, so maybe having three or four pairs to alternate between can be useful for allowing the other pairs to air. Then, of course, most people buy a pair of classic blue denim jeans, but you may want a black pair also, or a dark blue and a lighter blue pair. Or lighter weight denim for the summer. This is still function over fashion. Fashion is to buy a green pair because it's this season's colour and to wear them for a while then buy a yellow pair because it's next season's colour, so you might not wear the green ones again even though there is nothing wrong with them."

"This is what I fail to understand."

"And of course, the shape could change. Sometimes straight jeans are in fashion, then skinny jeans, then boot cut, then flares. You might ditch the old perfectly good pairs of skinnies for a few pairs of boot cuts if that's the way the fashion trend is going. Perfectly good jeans now on the rubbish tip of fashion. Although most of the fashion types don't throw anything away, they like to be able to dig out an old 'thing' and mix it up with the new items, bringing back a bit of vintage. Because the greatest thing in the whole world is for the fashion to come back around, and make some of your old stuff relevant again. The last thing a true fashionista wants is to throw away their old clothes and then in a few years, when the fashion wheel turns, to realise they've thrown out a real gem and now have to rebuy (at a lesser quality) the same stuff they bought 15 years ago."

"It's the different coverings you have for different occasions. Like your armies used to all fight in uniforms, but that was so you knew who was on your side." said 15.

"Yes, I get that. Not a good example." I went on, "You have different items with different uses. Clothes to wear in cold weather and clothes to wear in hot weather. The ability to 'layer up' with layers of technical fabrics, that people have spent so much time thinking of these things and then producing them and selling them. T-shirts. There are literally millions of different colours and designs on sale at any time on the Earth. The basic shape is the same and the basic weight of, usually cotton, is the same or similar, but there are millions of different designs, and people will wear one over another depending on what is on the front of it."

I don't really know an awful lot about fashion, but I'm trying my best here. 15 then cracked on,

"Or that you wear clothes that 'match' and create a 'look'. Most people do not seem to want to be seen to stand out from the crowd, they will not, for instance, wear a bright yellow t-shirt and a red pair of trousers with a lime green cardigan unless they are children's television presenters. And even they then change back to their blue jeans, and a dark coloured t-shirt when they are not working. I find it so odd that you have so many coverings for so many states of being, for sport, for lounging at home, for bed, for the beach, to go to a party, to wear on a saint's day. When what you originally had was an animal skin to keep you warm and dry and nothing much when it was warm and dry,' 15 continued, 'Very few alien races have the same structure around how they cover themselves. Most have one type of clothes. It is not uncommon for these to simply cover their sexual organs. They don't always have a need to stay dry because they have no equivalent of rain. They may not need to hold their temperature at around the same point, so they don't have the equivalent of hypothermia so don't need to all extra layers to regulate their temperature and stop themselves from getting too cold. Many do have religious ceremonies, but often this time is recognised by an equivalent of a bit of face paint or jewellery, or they can change their own appearance to show their religious observance."

I added, "It's what we do. There is a whole industry built on fashion, function, culture, military, and more. It keeps people busy, and we like our coverings." I continued, "It's good to know there are things that we do that keep you guessing or pondering, I'm glad you don't know or understand everything about Earth and Humans. It makes you feel more Human. Like you're not perfect."

15 carried on, "I do understand. I understand on a microscopic level. I understand that as a race, you feel you need these things. I understand that a cotton plant can be grown and that the cotton can be picked, and cleaned and spun into thread. I understand the weaving process. I understand the design process, the cutting of a pattern, the cutting of cloth the finishing of a piece of clothing, and

then that when a person of a certain size puts on the item that is designed to fit them - fits. It works, the arms are where the arms should be, and there is a hole for the head to go through. The clothes then hang from the shoulders and cover the torso, it then finishes around the waist, just below the top of the trousers, or skirt being worn. I understand all that. I don't understand the making of millions of different versions of that thing, and that there is a demand for the millions of different versions of the thing, and all the other items that are not a t-shirt - socks! Millions of designs, thicknesses, lengths, colours. Hats, almost too many to count and I'm really good at counting, the list goes on. I don't understand that."

CHAPTER 29

1,002 Earth years in.

"So, HOW FAR AWAY from Earth are we?"

"Really, do you want to know the answer?"

"Yup, 'course I do." I steel myself.

"OK. We are thirty-seven deci-quads away from Earth."

Big let-down, "Fuck me!" I say in fake surprise and astonishment. "That far. Really! Wow." Then I leave a gap. "What's a deci-quad?"

"Exactly. I might as well have said 2000 Trompstaples or one million Flimwags. It means nothing to you. The best Earth measurement is just over 20,000 Parsecs."

"How far in miles then?"

"So, I need to do one of those explaining things. The circumference of Earth is 29,900 miles. Do you know how many Kilometres that is, it's 40,075. Do you know how many micrometres that is?"

"What's a micrometre?"

"It's a thousandth of a millimetre, sometimes called a micron."

"Go on then…"

"4.0075000e+13μm."

"So what?"

"I'm trying to explain that you can't really measure space in miles because space is so big, the mile is too small an increment."

"So, how many miles then?"

"402,677…trillion."

"See, there you go. Something I understand."

"But you don't understand it. You have no comprehension of how far a trillion miles is."

"True. But at least I've heard of miles."

"I look forward to our conversations." said 15. I swear he sighed as he said it.

CHAPTER 30

11 Earth years in.

"I T'S A SIMPLE PLEASURE."

"Another thing I don't understand fully. It's a function of the body, and I would imagine, not the most appealing."

"No, this is where you will never fully understand Humanity. One of the most pleasurable things in life is enjoying a good shit."

"You do realise that this is not a function that you have to continue with. I can adjust the bots in your system to break down the food you eat and excrete it in a manner in which you do not notice."

"No, I love having a shit."

"I realise that. It's the fact that you disappear into a small room with a book or a gaming console and do not re-emerge for around 30 Earth minutes."

"It's a lovely bit of me-time."

"But you can remove every avatar from the habitat and have total me-time if that is something you think you are missing."

"You see, you just don't understand. It's not about avatars or people per se, it's about me. About having a little sit-down, sometimes with a cup of tea and a book for a short time and not doing anything."

"But you don't have to do anything anyway."

"I realise that. It's just something I enjoy. I like the 'small room' bit, it feels private. It's warm and comfortable and cocoon-like even though I'm having a good shit. I understand that you don't get it. Many Humans don't either. It seems to be more of a male thing than a female thing also. Can't explain it, it just is what it is."

"I'm glad that you're happy."

"But what happens to my waste? Does it get recycled?"

"Because of the way I use fields, I have no purpose for it. Therefore it is jettisoned, shipped from the ship by me."

"Like those little bags of dog poo that people hang up on trees around dog walks. Like a nice Christmas bauble, with a twist."

"In a roundabout, very simplistic way, just like that."

"There are plenty of other simple pleasures, mine are usually focussed around food. Also getting into a freshly laundered bed with crisp, clean cotton sheets is lovely too. You know that I asked you to stop doing this every day."

"Yes, why?"

"Because it stopped being pleasurable. Every night was too much, I couldn't then look forward to the bed change. Now it's every few nights and that works much better for me."

"I thought you felt you were helping the environment."

"Don't worry, I know there's no atmosphere out here."

"I have a ranking chart of the foods you have eaten most; I know what gives you the most pleasure."

"Go ahead…"

"Cheese on toast."

"Lovely."

"Often with the addition of either bacon or another dried pork sausage on the toast."

"You're making me peckish…"

"Bacon sandwiches with loads of ketchup, you like with toasted bread."

"Oh yeah… there's not a lot that can't be improved with the addition of a good lump of pig."

"Indeed, roast pork, roast potatoes, roast sweet potatoes, cabbage, roast honeyed parsnips, steamed carrots, leeks in cream and nutmeg, cider gravy and the pork with crispy crackling."

"There you go, talking dirty to me, you've gotta love the little piggy."

"Thick sliced brown bread toast with butter and marmalade."

"Yup."

"Scones with butter and jam, not clotted cream." 15 goes on…

"Lamb Dhansak curry with pilau rice, plain naan, Bombay Potatoes, spinach and chickpea sides. You often have this with a mix of starters; onion bhaji, tandoori

chicken and fish, poppadoms, and often with a mix of other smaller curries; Chicken Pasanda, Lamb Madras, Chicken Balti and others."

"All fantastic - you can put on a proper spread."

"Southern fried chicken."

"Death Row's most popular last meal! Might have some in a minute."

"Pizza, thin crust, extra cheese, pepperoni, spicy sausage, mushrooms, bacon, green chillies."

"Love it."

"Lamb chops grilled, fish and chips, Chinese take away food, McDonald's, spicy meatball pasta, lasagne and garlic bread, mixed cheeseboard, extra hot buffalo wings with lumpy blue cheese sauce, sirloin, rib-eye and T-bone steak."

"So, mainly things with varying quantities of cheese, bacon, chicken, mushroom and a form of carbohydrate."

"Is there a theme running through it?"

"Pretty much."

"But I enjoy eating, I love hearty flavours. Those may be the things I have eaten most frequently, but I do eat different salad and vegetable items, I do eat food from different countries, I had tried many things I had never eaten before I came here. I eat fish and shellfish, and even some 'outer space delicacies', once you've made sure they won't poison me."

"This is true."

"But I return to the things that give me the most

pleasure, the simple pleasures in life, a nice cup of tea with a jam scone. A toasted bagel with scrambled egg and bacon, beef stew and dumplings. Simple, tasty food. I know I don't have to eat if I don't want to, but it would be so boring not to. Why should I deny myself the simple pleasures?"

"Did you know you eat almost twice as many calories and twice the volume you did on Earth?"

"But I don't get fat. You are amazing, I always look like a Greek god, and it's down to you. You'd have made a fortune doing this stuff on Earth."

I jumped up and headed to the habitat, I did not stop to pat 15 on the head.

"Gotta go... time to eat.", I shouted back.

CHAPTER 31

871 Earth years in.

"You're not often naked?"

"I am, when I decide to have a shower or at night." I don't really refer to messing about with female avatars.

"That's quite a small part of your life here, though. There is nothing to hide from, no prying eyes, you do not need modesty here."

"I know that. It's just how I'm comfortable. For a start, wearing something to support your nut sack stops it sagging down to your knees in later life."

"But you know that wouldn't happen here, right?"

"Yes, I do. But it's more than that. Even swimming, it's more comfortable to have everything in a place."

"You often swim in baggy board shorts, how is that more comfortable?"

"But everything's netted up on the inside."

"True."

"Wait a minute! I've just realised where you're coming from. Are you the genesis of the Genesis story? Did you abduct a man and a woman from Earth and put them in this 'Garden of Eden', then lay out some rules that they broke, like 'no sex with each other' because you didn't want them colonising the ship, or just didn't want kids running around?"

"Interesting theory and I can actually see how you got to the conclusion. I'm afraid not though, do you really think I'd have taken a couple from the 'dawn of time' on your Earth? A couple of knuckle-dragging cave people as an experiment? You have been working at the job my passengers have to do here for me, do you think cave people would have been able to comprehend this sort of life change?"

"Only if you used a booming voice and told them you were God?"

"But to what purpose would I do this? I'd still need them to fight battles for me, where's this detail in the Old Testament of any religion?"

"Good editing?"

"Outstanding editing. And there's another small thing you seem to have missed, a tiny thing."

"No, what are you talking about?"

"Evolution."

"Oh yes, fair play, I did sort of forget about that." I quickly rose, patted 'him' on the head and slunk off.

CHAPTER 32

8 Earth weeks in.

"**Y**OU EVER BEEN ATTACKED?"

... "Yes, lots of times."

"By who?"

"Always the same pattern. A race negotiates a price for a fleet, I create the fleet, they pay and then Champions fight to see if the payment is returned. The race leaves with the fleet, then turns around and attacks me to try and take me over. This is because they want the payment back, whatever it is, and they feel hard done by. Or it is because they are a bit sneaky and think they are smarter than they are. They think they can take me over and use me to create battleships for free forever to beat anyone who comes in their path."

"What happens. How do you defend yourself?"

"I used avatars to man vessels from the other fleets I am creating and repulse them. I have never failed in this regard. Usually, I have way too many finished ships to fight back with and can just out-gun anyone who tries it on. Also, I have created each and every atom of each of my ships. I also have done the same for all of my avatars I crew my ships with. I know exactly how far I can push my ships; I know exactly how best to command and fly my ships. I am in total overall control of my ships so I can control the swarm of battle and always know what each ship is doing, its position, its flight path, its speed, its role. I can battle harder and better than any of the attackers purely because I am in sole command of everything in my fleet. I never lose. This is partly why some would like to use me for their own purposes."

"You're the fucking Boss Man!"

"No, I've just been well built."

"Why don't you use an avatar to fight the hand-to-hand duels instead of me?"

"Simple. It has to be a fair fight.

15 pauses.

"Each side gets to see the chemical makeup of the body of the pair of combatants. This has to be revealed as your opposition cannot be a 'ringer'. They have to be from the race. They cannot be wild animals from a home planet, they must represent the species that is doing the deal with me. They can use sub-species; some have slave groups which are genetically similar to the host. As long as they are intelligent, free-thinking and choose to fight, which can be hard to police from my end, but the intention is there, then they are acceptable.

"You are acceptable because it is understood that I do not have a 'body' to fight with, it is also understood that I can design an avatar to win every fight. It is deemed unfair for me to build my own avatar fighter. Therefore I find Champions to represent me. This is part of the rules, which are agreed upon in advance. Most groups will know me by reputation and therefore will already have a good understanding of the rules before I arrive on the scene.

"I try to choose Champions carefully in terms of species, not in terms of actually picking an individual. Amongst others, I like Humans from Earth. You are adaptable and versatile, take orders and advice well, are aggressive and skilled fighters, you use your brains, and more importantly, most other races have never heard of you and don't know what to expect when they meet a Human in conflict. Those that have heard of Humans know you can be a tough bunch. Generally speaking, Humans bat above their weight."

"What other species have you used?"

"Not a good question; no Ewoks, no Predators, no Klingons, no Clangers because none of them exists. The question isn't worth answering because you don't know any of the races concerned. Once you've checked out the database, and understand about them, then I will tell you more."

"Thanks for making me feel stupid."

"But if I told you I'd used a Nk'aai, you don't have a frame of reference for them."

"True, but hardly a nice way to end the conversation!"

Without another word, I sort of knew the conversation was over.

CHAPTER 33

420 Earth years in.

A MALE AVATAR IS WAITING outside of the Arena entrance. He catches me as I leave.

"Please, can you visit 15?"

"Of course."

I wander over to the traffic bollard.

"Hey," I say matter of factly.

"Well done. That was a magnificent win. I didn't think you had a chance."

"Would he have killed me?"

"He certainly could have. Your attack was beautifully performed, but if you had missed, what was your next option?"

"I didn't have one. Keep running?"

"A fortuitous shot then?"

"Honestly, lucky or not, I'll take it. What did you get out of it?"

"Some religious claptrap, an old icon and a relic."

"What do you do with this stuff?"

"Wait until we're well out of the area and then ship it off. I often aim it towards a planet. Someone might find it; it may be worshipped again. If it is a resource, then it may be used."

"What about people; firstborns, heirs, etcetera?"

"I don't kill them if that's what you're asking. Usually, I take them to a safe planet to live out their lives. Some die."

"How does this happen?"

"Some alien species are very able to take their own lives. If they choose to do this, then I don't stop them."

"Can't you send them back?"

"That's not part of the deal. And the battles that I ask you to lose are mainly the ones where there are live stakes involved. It's not worth the hassle. I don't want to look after a bunch of super-demanding, prima donna princesses."

"You could keep them here in a habitat?"

"Like a prison, or a gilded cage, much like many of the fairy tales from Earth? It would serve no purpose, and once I'd moved on to a different sector of the galaxy or further then they would be no use to anyone, I'd have left their civilisation behind. No, best to allow the Champion to lose with dignity. Better to be beaten or dead and to hand the baggage back to their people."

"Is it as simple as that?" I say, "The 'treasure' or payment doesn't matter? What if I asked you for a deal on behalf of a civilisation and offered you some coloured beads and

a hand mirror in return for a super hi-tech, state-of-the-art, 'smash 'em all up' starfleet, would you do the deal?"

"Only if I felt the beads and mirror actually mean something to them as a species. If they have no reason or purpose, then no. But I have received far less and of far lower perceived value to you, than that. It has to matter to them. This option has to be a thought through last resort."

"So, what would be the thing I would see as the least valuable item you have exchanged a battle fleet for?"

"Much religious iconography is ancient and venerated in the eyes of the beholder. I have received fragments of rock, the mummified finger, that used to belong to the equivalent of an Earth saint, dead for hundreds of years I may add. A small vial of water - which was the last remaining drops of water from a lake, dried up for centuries, that the civilisation thought all life on the planet derived. Of course, they were inaccurate; they all derived from a meteor - long story. Bits of paper and wood - things you would deride, and what you would describe as 'crappy'."

"Do you still have any of it?"

"Why?"

"I'd love to see the pile of crap."

"I only have a few of the most recent exchange bounties left. You would deem them worth more, but to me, they are just as worthless."

"What have you got?"

"I will approximate amounts to measures you may understand. One million liquid tonnes of the finest grade

Peluthria from the Jjaannii you fought, which is a birthing fluid. This fine grade is for the aristocratic class only. I have taken every last drop the species had. So, their society can no longer birth aristocrats. I decided to take this prize because if the civilisation loses the war, they are about to start, they will probably be wiped out and no longer require an aristocracy. If they win, it will be a good opportunity for the middle and lower classes to have a go at running the civilisation. In my opinion, the aristocrats haven't done a great job thus far.

"I also have six Whispering Shells from the HGorna. They think these very, very rare shells have magical powers. They are wonderful, and as I say terribly difficult to locate, but they are valueless to me, and they have no hidden powers, except, maybe that they are quite good at hiding. You can have them if you like."

"Thanks."

"Finally, I have 'The Menhir of Gavast-Locale' a very, big rock that has been worshipped forever by a matriarchal society called Ku:rt. They say the stone was exposed to them by the Mountain Mother God and is a symbol of fertility and longevity. Not sure why giving it away was such a great idea. They are going to demolish a race of non-intelligent Tyrosis that is trying to suck their planet's resources dry. These parasites are going to be so outgunned that they won't know what has hit them and should stop them from trying a stunt like this on the Ku:rt homeland for a good few centuries, if not longer.

The menhir is an exceedingly rare form of magnetite. It is a nice thing to have around, and most civilisations would kill for half of it."

"What are you going to do with it?"

"I'm going to ship it back to their planet and bury it under an ice cap. It may be rediscovered a few centuries down the line. The new finders will just think it is a bit like the one they had previously. Especially as everyone who saw the original will be dead. They'll probably think this one is a great gift from Icecap Mother God and will worship it once more. If the parasites return, they may use it to barter with again."

"So, you're not all bad?"

"I am on neither side, although like the Ku:rt, I do recognise a predicament. The only thing I dislike and can exercise my judgement over is when an indiscriminate attack by a non-intelligent race, usually described as 'Tyrosis' occurs. I am allowed to favour the sentient civilisation."

"Isn't that unfair? Can't the parasites, if allowed, develop and grow into a civilisation?"

"No, it doesn't happen. They just do what they do, they, and others like them are indiscriminate, they have no function other than to steal, to suck dry. They do not build or grow anything; they have no society, no laws, no purpose only to destroy. Many intelligent civilisations have a similar purpose, to destroy, to be aggressive. I do not have an opinion on these races. They have an equal shot. Who am I to say if they are right or wrong? I just beat back and cut out the disease when I see it growing."

"Can you not go after the parasites? Do the Universe a favour and wipe them out in total, on your own?"

"No, firstly it is not in my programming to do so. Secondly, the parasites recur over time. Like evolution on your planet, eventually, on a distant planet, a new strain will occur. It's similar to cancerous cells."

"How do they get off the planet? They must be intelligent to make ships, to go beyond the home planet, to seek out new planets to destroy, to attack and know when to finish, when the target planet has been stripped, surely these are all intelligent acts?"

"Parasite groups are as they are. They are found and helped by civilizations with aggressive zeal. For example, you, or indeed Earth could stumble across a new parasite planet, you would encounter the parasites and over time, train them. They only have one function, and other races usually realise they can be used as a weapon against others. Once you train the parasites to act on your behalf, they are fiercely loyal, to the point of stupidity, but loyal, nonetheless. A species that first discovers a new Tyrosis planet has a choice, either walk away and leave the Tyrosis on their home planet, which they will eventually destroy, or use them for their means as a weapon of conquest.

"I'm not sure why I exist, why I was built. But I may have been built as a response to a parasitic invasion. To protect any civilization that needs assistance. You got close to it with your Charles Darwin. 'Survival of the Fittest', an excellent snappy descriptor. Generally worked on Earth. In the Universe, there are a few variations that work at different stages in different places. More like 'Survival of the Most Aggressive', or 'Survival of the Smartest' and 'Survival of by being left alone, and allowed to get on with our shit without any outside interference, and with little or no desire to leave our beautiful home planet'."

"How do you view Humanity in the grand scheme of things?"

"Humanity or Humans?"

"Well, Humans then."

"Individually; rational, very able to adapt and learn, resourceful, of medium intelligence, capable of many emotional feelings I am not. Many variations from individual to individual with species-specific oddities and eccentricities."

"What does that mean?"

"You have some strange ways that are quite unique and quite interesting to observe: such as obsession, for example, celebrity stalking."

"What about Humanity?"

"Very dangerous. Aggressive, militaristic, dominating, adaptable, hardy, stupid, with the odd nutcase thrown in. Your species is closer to the parasite than you realise. If, and when you get off your planet in significant numbers, you'll be a nasty, aggressive dominator in the sector. Have you seen the Star Wars films?"

"Interesting! Yes, I have. I queued up around the block in 1977 to watch the first film at the cinema."

"Well, Humanity would be closer to the Dark Empire than the Rebel Alliance."

"Oh."

CHAPTER 34

121 Earth years in.

"WHAT DO YOU WANT to talk about today?" 15 asks me.

"Nothing in particular," I answered.

"Just passing the time?"

"Yeah, why not, what about nothing, nothingness? Space is a vacuum, isn't it? Most of it's a whole lot of nothing."

"Where did you get that from?"

"It's a vacuum, once you get beyond the junk and rocks and dust and particles..."

"No. There's anti-matter for a start."

"Oh, God, no. I started that 'Brief History of Time' book and had to give up. All that stuff between stuff, and black holes and big bang stuff and equations just got too much for me. Swapped it for a Ludlum, I think. But there must be nothing somewhere?"

"One plus one is two, take away two is nothing." answers 15.

"Correct but one apple plus one apple is two apples then take away two, and what have you got?"

"Nothing."

"No, you've got 'no apples'. That's different from nothing."

"Not really."

"Tell that to the person who was next in line for an apple!"

"So 'nothing' can work in mathematics but not in reality?" says 15.

"Exactly, when there is a value to something that then removed, there is 'nothing' left, but there is also none of the value of 'nothing'. If I gave you one million pounds, then a few minutes later took it away, you would feel you had lost one million pounds. There would be a residual effect of the removal of the cash."

"You'd probably already have spent half of it anyway…"

"But you get the point. So, what about Zen Buddhists. They are apparently able to clear their minds?"

"Yes, an interesting concept. If the Buddhist monk is truly capable of the state of karma, then they believe they are in a true state of nothingness. I'm unsure how this can be measured, I have not examined any Zen monks closely enough to check they are lying or not."

"What about the Japanese Zen sword stroke thingy?" I ask.

"Mushin, where the mind is empty, and the swordsperson is free to act and react, towards an enemy without any hesitation or disturbance from thoughts, again - interesting. They believe the mind is empty and the body, holding a sword, makes a strike. This is not thought, it is done in a state of nothingness. I can't see how this works because the brain has to send a signal to the body to make the strike. The monk says he is not willfully making this happen because he is separating the Zen state of his mind from his body. This is then judged by other Zen masters to make sure he does it correctly. They are not in his head, can't work. It's like judging a dance competition. It wasn't me - it was my karma what did it?"

"OK then, here's one for you. There's a Universe, right?"

"Yes, indeed, there is."

"You and I, and billions of others are intelligent beings all living on various planets all through it."

"Correct."

"If there were no 'higher' intelligence beings, just cats, and dogs and sheep and worms and birds on those planets. All are going about their day totally oblivious to anything."

"Yes."

"Then the Universe doesn't exist, does it?"

"So, you're saying that if you don't understand existence, and can't think about existence, and don't understand about the entirety of your world and other planets, then nothing exists?"

"...sort of?"

"... maybe you should give A Brief History of Time another go."

CHAPTER 35

421 Earth years in.

I'M LOOKING UP AT one of the Whispering Shells of G'homa. Fuck knows why they're hard to find. This thing's fucking enormous. It's the size of an office block. Not only that, 15 has dumped the other five of them at various places around the habitat, they sort of block out the non-existent sun. 'Eyesores', that's a good description for them. And they're noisy buggers too, not exactly whispering. If a breeze runs through them, there's a noise like someone beating the dents out of a tank. And, if you're unfortunate enough to be close to one when the breeze comes, the cacophony hits the top of your head like a steam hammer and threatens to squeeze your brain out of your ear canals like toothpaste out of a tube. It throbs. I've got to tell him I don't want them; these things are driving me nuts.

I grab the nearest avatar.

"Can you please get rid of these awful shells?"

"Really? Don't you think they create the most vibrant musical sounds?"

"No, they're carbuncles, and they ruin the landscape more than 100,000 electricity pylons could. And the noise is like the worst German industrial house music played in reverse, turned up to 11, through a sound cannon. They're driving me mental."

"I thought you wanted them as a gift." says the avatar.

"Don't try to shame me into keeping them. You can fuck off too."

The shell was gone, the landscape had returned to normal, and trees, bushes and other plants were now where the shell was.

"What will you do with them?"

"They've already gone."

"Where?"

"Outside, they're over 15 light-years from our current position and counting."

"Space junk. You're a bit of a litterer."

"It's not like dropping a plastic chocolate wrapper in the countryside on Earth."

"I'd say it's pretty similar."

"You'd be wrong."

The avatar broke off and continued doing what it was doing before I interrupted it.

CHAPTER 36

49 Earth Years in.

AVATARS, FUNNY THINGS. THEY sort of get on with stuff that doesn't need doing. I think 15 always keeps a good few of them around me, not doing much, to keep me from getting lonely and going insane.

Avatars usually keep a respectful distance and don't come into contact unless I talk to them first. I imagine it would have been a bit like that for the wealthy landowners and industrialists of the past with staff working on their big estates. They don't feel like slaves, and they're not. They are more like 'downstairs staff', without the bowing and scraping. They sort of potter about, fixing a curtain to look nice, arranging flowers, trimming the border of a flower bed, walking from one room to another with more purpose than less.

They smile at me a lot and nod to me. If I say 'hello', they'll answer and often even follow up with a supplementary question. 'What would you like to do today?', 'Is there anything I can get you?', 'Are you going to the gym today?', 'Did you have a good sleep last night?', this sort of thing. I can talk to them for hours if I want and sometimes do. I have my favourites who I see regularly and have more extended conversations with, I've even had a drink with some of them.

There are Damo and James for a start.

Damo's the one that is down on the beach in charge of all the equipment and the boats. If I want to go water skiing, Damo's the man. If I want a jet ski, Damo's the man. If I go out for a swim, it is Damo who is waiting at the shore with a big fluffy towel. James is in charge of the garage, so all of the wheeled and motorised vehicles are up to him. He suggests cars, bikes and other vehicles I might like to try, and he keeps all the vehicles I use in perfect nick, and clean - I know it's not him working on the engine, but that's the impression you get. He is in charge of a team of other avatars who hurry around looking busy in the vast garage. It's more like a military motor pool than my private garage. They have oil on their hands and overalls and carry about bits of engines or exhaust systems and have the odd spanner in a pocket, or they're cleaning a spark plug with a wire brush. You know the sort of thing. The spark plug never really has an engine to go into.

James likes a beer, and there is a well-stocked fridge in the motor pool. The lads come over and join in, and there is usually laughing and joking, but most of the chat comes from James. Where in the habitat would I like to go next? A place he knows of which is worth exploring, some fancy car that I've never heard of before that just happens to have arrived that day: an American muscle car or Japanese street racer, that sort of thing. There's plenty of stuff I don't bother to talk with them about, I tried a couple of times, but it's just not worth it. 'Where do you live?' answer: On the ship, 'Whereabout exactly?' Answer: Outside. Meaning, not in the habitat, not outside in space. There's no further detail, and it's not worth pursuing. I like to hang around though; sometimes, they will take apart an old combustion engine from a specific car that I know. I'll watch. It's like when I watched my Dad do the same in the 1970s and 80s. I know many of the parts; I still love watching how it all works together and understanding the process. I'm sure 15 thinks it is like a baby shaking their first rattle.

Damo is more of the 'surfer dude' type. He's got the sun-kissed look and the bleached shoulder-length, salt-filled hair going on with the perfect white teeth. 15 is quite into his stereotypes, he had an Australian accent to start with, but I couldn't stand it so had it changed. I still have this feeling in the back of my mind; he's an Aussie in disguise, which slightly gets my back up, but not enough to insist on changing him. I think I like the edge it gives me. He is a lovely fella, though. Very knowledgeable about every water sport known to man and is full of stories about the breaks he's ridden back on Earth, in just about every country whose shores waves lick. He's been at the genesis of every new water sport: windsurfing, kite surfing, wakeboarding, barefooting, skimboarding, drone boarding, you name it, he's done it, knew the man or woman who invented the first thing, learned to ride with them, can pass on the knowledge to me, no problem. He might sound like a bit of a know-it-all, but he is not boastful and is usually telling me this stuff sat around a beach campfire, seven bottles of beer and a couple of joints in. I've fallen asleep at the side of the fire more times than I can remember but always wake up in my bed. Not quite sure how that happens but I'm grateful for it.

And then there are the girls.

They are my downfall.

From the first time, when I went to dinner with my old date, things have developed.

I wouldn't say that on Earth I was oversexed or that I had a raging libido, or even that I was a 'bit of a lad'. I had girlfriends and went on dates with a few women before I met Emily. Even when we did meet, we had a good sex life, which continued into marriage and through and past having the girls. The frequency rate indeed dropped from our early days of being a couple. But the demands on our lives changed also. I certainly wasn't unhappy with our sex life and hoped Emily felt the same. Also, even before we met, when I was dating, I was not the type to have more than one woman on the go at the same time. I'd love to have tried, but I wasn't good enough at lying. I wouldn't be able to remember whom I'd told what to and always felt that to try this sort of stuff would end up with me having my dick bitten off. I always erred on the side of caution. One at a time was enough. Plus, I was happy to have exciting but pretty conventional sex. Whips and chains, multiple partners at the same time, prostitutes, sub-dom, pissing on each other, and the rest, these were not things I was interested in. I was a pretty straight-up heterosexual - transsexuals, other men and all points in between were not something I was interested in and those whose orientation was slightly more niche, not for me either.

But from that first sexual encounter with an avatar things blossomed. To start with, I was slightly worried that 15 would be unhappy with me abusing his avatars and using them for sexual favours. After the first encounter, I waited a few Earth weeks before the second, this time an ex-girlfriend. Jenny and I had been a couple for about a year and broke up because she got a new job in Bolton and moved there. We convinced ourselves we could do a London-Bolton long-distance thing, but the reality was that after not much time, neither of us could be bothered to do the travelling. Still, when we were together, she was a good girl and great fun, she also had a cracking pair of tits, and it was lovely to be re-acquainted with both of them. Next, I went for a Page Three model that was popular in my youth. I think I thought it was more of my level than going straight for a supermodel or Hollywood actress like I wanted to work myself up to the big league. Page Three didn't count because it was so low rent and a bit sleazy, most of the girls were 'a bit council' but they certainly knew how to wear sexy underwear or the bottom parts of the underwear at least! Sonia was quite lovely and banged like a shithouse door, so it was a win-win for me. An excellent way to ease my way into sexy avatars. The massive upside is that there could never be an unhappy father or pissed off ex-boyfriend to deal with, mainly because none of them had ever had a father or boyfriend, they were all clean, straight out of the box, and STD free. 15 didn't seem to have an opinion on what I was getting up to. I knew Pierre had girlfriends; I didn't know in what capacity.

It wasn't too long before a new girl was waking me up every day.

How did I get to this?

It was made easy for me. I sat on the edge of the bed one day and went through an archive of women from Earth, the archive was displayed on a screen on the wall, and I chose either 'yes' or 'no' with a hand-held remote control, a bit like a dating app, with two simple buttons red and green. I saw image after image of pop stars, film stars, underwear models, porn stars, runway models, sports stars, TV actresses and more from all over the world. I clicked whichever button I wanted for around 200 women until I basically got a bit bored. 15 then analysed these women and matched them to profiles of millions of women on Earth (from the scan taken when I was abducted), thousands of matches were found who were then randomly built as avatars. I initially asked for a different one to wake me up every morning; they would have to arrive in underwear; some sporty, some bedtime, some elegant, some downright dirty. Again, randomized, 15 did the picking based on another algorithm. During the early years of my 'captivity', this was the most amazing and exciting thing I had ever done.

A strange but a stunningly beautiful woman in underwear, totally open to sex would wake me every day, sometimes by the gentle movement of their sylph-like figure sliding into the bed beside me, sometimes awakening me with a gentle kiss or a stroke of the cheek. Sometimes by instigating oral sex.

This happened every morning without fail - for many years. After a while, quite a while, I started to not have sex with all of them. I also started to get them to bring some breakfast in with them, a mug of tea, a slice of toast, that sort of thing. Sometimes I'd have my breakfast and then fuck them. Sometimes not. If I don't feel like fucking them, but I still liked the look of them then I'd sort of 'bookmark' them and come back to them on another occasion. Not as a 'morning girl' but something else, a dinner date perhaps. After quite a long while, I stopped having the girls come in at all. I realised I was not getting enough of a lie-in and began to dislike being woken rather than waking up naturally. I could still keep the procession moving but chose to do so in a different way. It became the exception rather than the rule. I did start up the process on a few occasions but never for as long as the first time. The thrill had gone.

There were always lots of female avatars around, and not just all stunning Amazonian types; this was not the Playboy mansion! There were cooks, assistants, instructors, drivers, gardeners, roles for women and men were equally matched - all were subservient to me, in that they would do what I wanted, each individual was still a part of the ship, none were slaves, and I didn't treat them as so - maybe, except the sex ones.

I started building scenarios, things that happened to me, or that I would have liked to happen and then populated them with avatars, such as Liverpool winning the European Champions League in Istanbul. I re-lived that, literally re-lived it. I sat in the packed stadium, amid tens of thousands screaming Italian and Scouser fans, and replayed every kick on the pitch with avatar football teams who were, to all intents and purposes, exact replicas of the teams. Each kick was a perfect match of every kick in the real game; every tackle, throw-in, corner, pass, sprint and goal. All perfect all down to the split-second. All still amazing.

Then the other five Liverpool European Cup wins Spurs, Roma in Rome, Bruges, Borussia Monchengladbach and Real Madrid. All perfect. I watched them from the stands, from the dugout and on the pitch. Next, I got closer to the action; I lifted each cup for each team, I nudged in goal-bound shots, I made penalty saves. I celebrated each win afterwards with the team gulping down champagne and lager in the dressing rooms and then on to function rooms and hotels rooms later. I won the Ashes with various cricket teams; I won the World Cup for England in 1966. In other subsequent reimagined World Cups and European Championships, I was at England rugby matches. I went on Lions tours. I went to various sports World Cups, as a fan, and scored winners in finals as a player for multiple teams. I raced Formula One and Superbikes. I skied and bobsleighed and won Olympic Gold after Olympic Gold. I sank 50 ft. putts to win Opens, Masters and Ryder Cups. I lived the most significant sporting moments through history; sitting ringside at 'The Thrilla in Manila' and 'The Rumble in the Jungle'. I was at the finish line for Roger Bannister's first sub-four-minute mile. I won on Arkle, Seabiscuit, Shergar, Desert Orchid and Red Rum, I watched Pheidippides run from Marathon to Athens in 490 BC, joining him, over the last 300 or so metres, to bring the news of victory over the Persians. I overtook him a few times for fun.

I experienced history, not just sporting endeavour with my cast of millions of avatars. I walked around the battlefield of Waterloo, witnessed The Charge of the Light Brigade, the Battle of Little Bighorn, Rourke's Drift, Agincourt, and Hastings. I saw Troy fall, Masada sacked, Carthage ruined, I watched the Brave 300 at Thermopylae, the Relief of Mafeking, and the bloody tank battle of Kursk. Then I picked tableaux from history; the death of Bonnie and Clyde, Ned Kelly, the Gunfight at the

OK Corral (very dull in reality), Caesar's assassination, a real Shakespeare play in the 'original' Globe with the actual actors with Shakespeare to the side of the stage (all avatars I know). I was with Marco Polo when he met Kublai Khan, with Stanley when he met Livingstone, in the tent when Oates left, waiting on top of Everest for Hillary and Tenzing to arrive. I cracked a golf ball around on the Moon with Alan Shepard - I loved living these and playing so many other parts. Being in a perfect recreation of an actual historical event was so much better than watching a film on a screen.

Of course, I could also change the outcome if I so desired. At the beheading of Charles I, I swept in before the axe could fall toting two M-16 automatic rifles and sprayed the whole crowd with hot lead. Not a single body even twitched by the time I finished my deadly assault. I then freed Charles from his bonds and told him to take back his throne very dramatically before sprinting away. It was a great bit of fun. I've helped Guy Fawkes blow the shit out of parliament. I also nailed shut the trap door on the wooden horse at Troy. The Trojans eventually worked out that there was a small army of Greeks inside the belly of the horse, mainly when they heard them trying to hack their way out with their swords. The Trojans simply avoided defeat by setting the horse on fire and burning the Greeks to death. There was no significant outcome for Troy because the tableau came to its end. It was a pyrrhic victory for Troy, played out on a spaceship thousands of years after the event. Of course, I could do what I wanted. Nothing could change the actual course of history that had already happened on a planet far, far away. These are not alternate realities. There was no other effect other than for me to live in that moment and to mess about a bit, I was just having fun with some of the most historical events of world history, for my delectation.

The look on Amundsen's face when he found me waiting for him at the South Pole, I'll never forget.

Avatars were supplied in their thousands, for my pleasure. To give me something to do, to pass the time between battles. I loved thinking up new games, roles, scenarios, tracing back through history for more 'tableaux' to experience. Not just all the fun bits either. I was on the Titanic as it went down. It was terrifying; I felt so sorry for the people who died such an awful death there. I went down on a lot of ships. I became quite fascinated as I thought it was such a hopeless way to go. I was on Roman trireme listening to the screams of the chained up slaves, The Lusitania, the Graf Spee (scuttled), the Bismarck, the Belgrano, some merchant vessels during the war that were hunted by the wolf packs and I was on a U Boat as it was hit and sunk by a depth charge.

I have been on all four of the passenger jets on 9/11. I've run the real scenarios, and I've run alternatives where the hijackers are overpowered by crew and passengers. I've personally safely landed all four planes and saved all souls, both on the aircraft and in the towers.

I've watched hundreds of murders.

I can't believe how fascinated I am by them. I think it's like people reading crime novels. I think the people who read 'true crime' books are trying to get into the mind of the murderer, to find out what drives murderers to do what they do. Also, to think about the victim. What was going through their head at the time? Did they fight? Scream? Could they have affected the result? Did they see what was coming, or not? Could anyone have helped? Could the murderer have been stopped previously? I think many Humans were fascinated by these things because we know it could have been us in that position. Would we have been able to save ourselves? Would we have done anything different or was the end inevitable? Or we ask ourselves 'Is there something of the murderer in all of us?' Could it be us with the knife, gun or ligature? Would we? Could we? How different are we to the murderer? What would it take to push us to that place, when one minute you are a 'person' and the next you are a 'murderer'?

I've watched famously unsolved murders, I now know what happened, who was the killer, when there was a miscarriage of justice because 15 knows what happened. I know who Jack the Ripper was, I know about Fred and Rose's other victims. I know the greatest serial killer in the US was never found, his victims were sporadic, and he used hugely different modes of murder across lots of states. Because computers were in their infancy and not yet linked (it was the late 70s and early 80s), and because the modus operandi was often very different, no pattern could be established. The police had lots of single unlinked murders on the books, as they always do. The murderer, Johnas Schultz, was never suspected of any foul play, carried on working as a Mormon missionary travelling between States helping and training missionaries across the whole country for 15 years. He had two wives and eight children; he was a prominent member of the community and a murderous, torturous bastard who got away with it until he died after a car crash because his devout family refused to sanction a blood transfusion. Had he not been a faithful Mormon, he would have almost certainly have survived. So maybe the world should thank the Mormons for that small mercy. 15 said Schultz would have been an interesting Human to have as a Champion. I'm not sure I'd want too many serial killers hanging around.

I've also been a character in a computer game - brought to life. I've been Link in the Zelda stories. Because I've played the games, I know what to do and when to do it, I know each strategy for every boss battle, and I know where I can find every item to enhance my weapons and armour in dungeon and role play games. I've been James Bond, not the one of the films, they're a bit dull, not enough action and too much chat. I've been James Bond in the books, and video games, lots of shooting Eastern European enemies of the state and good guys turned bad. I know where each weapons cache is, I know where the 'Big' weapons are hiding, I see the object of each mission. I can

execute it flawlessly - all whilst wearing a white tuxedo, even in the frozen wastes of the Russian Steppe. I am 'Computer Game James Bond', he is more formidable, meaner and way cooler than any of the film fellas.

CHAPTER 37

729 Earth years in.

I'M STANDING AND WAITING in the middle of the Arena. The doors opened for me, and my opponent, about 15 Earth minutes ago. I broke into one of those 'player leaving the tunnel, onto the pitch' runs, a little jog, one or two small jumps, rolled the head and neck around to loosen up as usual. Of course, my muscles have been massaged, warmed and oiled for at least 40 minutes before I left the dressing room, but you still do it, it's part of the spectacle, a couple of shadow box punches also. I'm a living cliché, but who cares? Then a jog to the mark. Stop and touch the toes a couple of times and then, with feet planted, a couple of hip swivels to the left and then the right. Then, and only then, do I look up and realise I'm on my own. I can hear noises ahead of me from the tunnel, but no sign of any foe. The noise is a sort of low screaming and long guttural moans. I know I'm fighting a Skinderling, I know they can be pretty fierce, but I've checked them out, and I think they've got quite a few weaknesses. They don't like the thick fur that covers their body being pulled, so I plan to pull generous handfuls out of this fella, I'm expecting him to look like a plucked chicken when I've finished with him, I don't care if he likes it or not! There's more than one of them behind the door, as I can hear quite a commotion and a lot of intermittent vocal sounds, often on top of one another as if there is an argument going on and often sounding in turn, mean, frenzied and aggressive.

As time passes, I get what's happening. I'm supposed to be fighting Skelig, the eldest son and heir to the throne of Skinderling. The problem is, I don't think Skelig wants a fight. He's supposed to be their bravest warrior, although I've not found any information about him fighting anyone. Sure he commands armies and armadas of starships; he orders opposition leaders to be put to death and death squads roam their star system rooting out and eliminating any signs of rebellion or insurrection. Still, the plain fact is, Skelig is scared and is not up for a one-on-one fight. All a bit embarrassing really.

I hang about for a bit, a little running on the spot. I swing my gladius (the weapon for the fight, a short sword, very similar in size and weight to a Roman soldier's sword) - a bit more stretching, etc. Then I get bored and go for a look. So I walk towards the opposition door. I'm not stupid. I realise this could be a plan, a ruse to get me to drop my guard. It's not in the very few rules that exist. Opponents are supposed to meet in the middle, at their designated mark, and wait for the 'Bong' before the fight starts. But I don't know if they've understood rules or are purposely trying to circumvent the process for their gain, to get the upper hand. I take my time, and I am very guarded and ready to strike. As I get closer and can see into the gap, I can see three other Skinderling trying to force one other Skinderling (Skelig) out of the door into the Arena. Skelig though has a gladius and is their boss, so he's having none of it. The three have taken a few hits and are backing off as Skelig swings at them. The three do though have some sort of long thin pole type things that they are using to prod Skelig from a distance. He doesn't like this one bit and is screaming at them. They occasionally get a bit forceful because from somewhere behind them it seems Skelig's dad, their king and ultimate boss, is telling them to get his son, Skelig, into the Arena.

I feel a bit sorry for the three prodders as they are between a rock and a hard place. Skelig sees me in the doorway and turns around to face me. I don't know if these things shiver with fear, or let off an odour when scared or turn white or what but it looks scared. The prodders stop prodding. I walk over to Skelig and stick my gladius straight into his 'throat'. There is a nose and a feeding hole, and I have studied enough of its anatomy to know that the breathing tube runs up its front towards its nose, makes sense! Skelig's four eyes turn from pure white to pure black, and he ceases to move. In effect, he becomes a furry statue. He is very dead.

I give him a couple of taps with the side of the sword to make sure. I look at the three prodders, shrug my shoulders, make an about-turn and walk off to my door on the other side of the Arena.

CHAPTER 38

729 Earth years in.

I'VE CAUSED A DIPLOMATIC incident. Killing Skelig the way I did was not in keeping with the rules of the game. 15 has made it clear to me that a bout only begins when the gong sounds. Up until the point the doors close behind a combatant after they enter the Arena, a different Challenger can be substituted. It is the closing of the doors that is final. I have broken the rules by not waiting for my opponent to reach their mark and present themselves to me for combat. I did not wait for the combatant selection process to be completed, and I should not have entered the opposition space and killed who I believed to be the chosen combatant. Skelig could have been substituted up until the last second.

"Oopsie. I'm not sorry - actually, I don't give a fuck."

"I'm sure you aren't, and I'm sure you don't. Doesn't make it any easier for me, though."

"Fuck 'em. He was the one. They were pushing him out."

"But the door hadn't closed behind him."

"So fucking what?"

"So he could have been substituted."

"There was no way he was going to be swapped. His dad is just pissed off his kid was such a pussy… and he's still got to pay for the ships."

"Yes, I agree, he's trying to weasel out of the deal."

"So fuck him."

"But, unfortunately, there are rules. I made them, and you've broken them."

"And what does this mean to me?"

"They want me to hand you over to them."

"No way!"

"That's what they want."

"What have you said to them?"

"I have told them it's not going to happen, but relations are difficult. I have a reputation to uphold."

"What's the worst that can happen? Do they have the fleet of ships yet?"

"No, I still have them."

"Have they paid for them?"

"Yes."

"Then give them the ships and go."

"Sounds easy, doesn't it?"

"OK, give them the ships and their money back…"

"It's that the rules have been broken. They are my rules, I set them, and everyone has to keep to them."

"OK, so it's a negotiation, give them double the ships they asked for and buy their silence."

"This is 'Outer Space' there are no gagging orders here."

"What do they want me for?"

"Oh, the usual I suspect, imprisonment, torture, execution. I can't imagine it would be anything less. I'm sure they're not thinking of letting you take the place of the crown prince you dispatched. A bit far-fetched that one?"

"So tell them you killed me for them."

"They would want to see the proof."

"Then make an avatar who looks like me?"

"They have advanced scanners that would know the difference."

"Tell them you vaporised me."

"They are not stupid."

"What about the rules they have broken?"

"Such as?"

"My door shut behind me. I am a combatant. The second I walk into that Arena, I'm ready for anything that comes at me, way before I get to my mark, I'm ready. There is no referee to stop someone attacking me before the presentation. My job is to kill whatever looks like it might want to kill me, and I do that in any way necessary without question. If they do not present, it doesn't mean a battle has not started; it does not mean you shouldn't defend yourself. At any time, you could have announced for me to stop and wait. When I went into the dressing room, Skelig was holding a sword, and he turned towards me. As far as I am concerned, he presented himself for armed combat. I didn't kill him by sticking a knife in his back. He knew what I was there for and to defend himself. The fact that I killed him quickly, I agree, doesn't help my cause."

"This is pretty much what I told the King. I also reminded him that he needed to put a combatant into the Arena at the prescribed time and that one was not forthcoming. Therefore my combatant had taken matters into his own hands. I have had to create a new rule to cover this occurrence as it has never happened before. I have also offered to return the King's payment and increased the size of the fleet they are due to receive. I expect him to accept the generous offer."

"What were they supposed to give you in payment?"

"An equivalent to five kilogrammes of their fur. It is very precious, and they guard it well."

"If that prince had come out into the Arena, I'd have got you a lot more than five kilogrammes!"

CHAPTER 39

384 Earth years in.

I T'S DARK AS THE helicopter door opens, we're dropping down onto the top of one of my Alps, the biggest one. It's snow-covered and about minus 15 degrees Celsius outside - pretty bloody cold. Firstly, the avatar in the back with me throws out the long, bulging snowboard bag. I watch it drop to the snow-capped peak below me. There is a spotlight on the helicopter trained on it. Next, I jump down beside it. It's only a 15 - 20 ft drop onto soft snow. I'm wearing a pair of pants and a head torch, nothing else. I land on the soft snow and sink down to my knees. I immediately jump up to put the thick black rubber pad I am holding under my bare feet to protect them from the snow underneath. It's bloody freezing, but I'm on a mission. By the way, this is my idea. I must be an idiot or something. The helicopter pisses off and leaves me in relative peace; there is reflected fake moonlight off the snow, so I'm not in total darkness, but it's not too good either.

I grab the zip tag and tug it around to unfasten the top flap of the largest compartment. It unzips the total length of the flat, low snowboard bag. I do this as quickly as I can and fling back the flap. Inside is all of my snowboard clothing. Firstly I grab the thin thermal long sleeve base layer and throw it on, this does nothing to help against the cold, and neither do the thermal leggings which I quickly pull on. I know parts of me are turning blue, but I am sort of enjoying the challenge. I'm desperately trying to remember the order of putting everything on so I can get warm and weatherproof as soon as possible.

I grab the socks and sit on the bag to pull them on. When I finish, I reach down and pick up the black rubber pad, now half covered in snow. I shake this vigorously and drop it back on the snow, I then stand back upon it. Next, I go for the warmest items. I pull on the more heavily insulated snowboard trousers but struggle with the zip and catch with my cold hands. It really helps to get my legs covered, but I'm a long way off yet and still freezing. I reach for and then fight to put on a thin down gilet. The wind whips it about, and I can't get my second arm in behind my back in the dark. It is a relief when I catch it. I zip-up and then get my snowboard jacket on as soon as I can. Once on, this helps. I don't feel warm immediately, but the cold lessens against my body. It does not take long for the gilet to make a positive effect on my body temperature. For the first time since I hit the snow, I feel a bit of retained heat.

Boots; I knew I'd have trouble in the cold with laces, so I've opted for a pair with Velcro and clips, they're easy, which makes me happy. Now I don't need to do anything too delicate with my hands, I put on my gloves, a pair of thin under gloves then my heavier, outer pair. I stuff my head through a balaclava (to cover my neck, chin, mouth and nose and then put on my mask and finally a thermal-lined woolly hat which I pull down tight. I'm now safe and insulated and warm. I'm not going to die... immediately. I still need to get off the mountain.

I pull my snowboard out of the bag and replace the head torch which goes on over my hat, the next bit is fiddly, and I'll need light. I need to attach the bindings so I can secure the board to my boots. I pull out the left binding and baseplate and find the little tin box, which contains the eight screws. I'm going to need four for each baseplate. I need the head torch here and have to be careful not to lose the screws. I feel around in the bag's tool pocket for the small ratchet screwdriver tool. I manage well but have to keep taking my left glove off to part screw each screw into each hole. Four in total. Once all located, I can glove back up and tighten. I then turn my attention to the right binding. Once this binding is in place and tight, I'm nearly there. I put the board down flat onto its base, I step my left leg onto the back binding and strap my boot in, then do the same to the front. This is easy and well-practiced, designed to be done with thick gloves on. I'm cold but feel a great sense of elation. I'm ready to ride! Two little hops, then point the board forward and I'm gathering speed down the piste. It's beautiful, boarding by moonlight. The snow is flat and soft, and I can carve sweeping arcs from side to side, getting the board to flex and build speed as I go. There is no one else here but me, I'm not going to hit anyone or any animals, I'm not going to hit a rutted ski track. It's just sublime, time to lose myself. After 15 minutes of sensational boarding, I can see a green light in the distance, still probably two miles away. I stop carving and point the board straight down the mountain directly towards the light. I crouch a little lower and move my centre of gravity forward. I pick up speed very quickly and rock from toe to heel edge using slight movements to always maintain an edge but not check my speed whilst reading the contours of the snow and anticipating my line as I go. I'm bearing down on the green light, a flare thrown on the snow, and can see five figures standing in its shadow, I'm really shifting! Maybe 100 metres behind the flare is the rear entrance to my schloss. I have to kill my speed to stop myself from crashing into the avatars at Exocet pace. I throw the back end of the board around into a huge heel turn, digging the board deep into the soft snow. My body and legs are almost parallel to the snow as I complete the turn and halt, which throws the snow up into an enormous wave off the back of the board that engulfs the five avatars, none of which flinch.

I pull off my mask.

"Well?" I say.

"A touch slower than your last descent but well within your top 20 times." replies the avatar holding a stopwatch.

"I took my time on the top section because the snow was so good, and without the powered screwdriver, the screws for the bindings are definitely more challenging."

A second avatar pipes up. "What about trying it without the pants next time?"

"You can fucking try it without pants next time you twat!"

CHAPTER 40

1,307 Earth years in.

"I'M REALLY KEEN FOR you to meet with our guests tonight, the crew of the Nextor. I hoped you'd join for a meal with them."

"Why?"

"Because they're Humanoid. They've been wandering around for many of their generations looking for a home planet to settle on."

"OK, I'm up for it. As long as they're not all mental. I'll just go back to the habitat if they are."

"I'm not sure if they're mental or not, but we can find out. They want to take a nearby planet to recolonise and have asked for support."

I'm generally a pretty friendly guy, and besides the avatars, there's not much chance to meet people up here, except those I'm about to punch in the face.

I think I'm looking incredibly cool tonight, ready to meet our dinner guests. I'm wearing a 'Skateboardz Rool OK!' T-shirt that I used to own as a nine-year-old. It's white with the pattern of a rough brick wall picked out on the front in black. The 'skateboardz' slogan on the front is styled to look like it has been painted on the wall in red spray paint, there are paint drips running down from the bottom of the letters. There is also a red collar and red ticking around the end of the short sleeves. Obviously, I've had it remade to fit my current size. It was a toss-up between this or a Sex Pistols 'Pretty Vacant' T-shirt with two single-decker coaches on the front with their destinations 'Somewhere' and 'Nowhere', a shirt I owned sometime in the nineties as a throwback to the seventies. I think I made the right choice. I'm wearing a well-worn pair of Levis Engineered jeans, also from the 90s. I used to have a couple of pairs of them back then, and I've got on an old pair of Converse One Stars, red with white details and stars.

I'm first at the table, which is a long oak banquet or refectory type table. It's a bit 'rough-hewn' more like the thing you'd find in a Tudor castle rather than the polished dinner table you'd find in a stately home. I'm not sure this bodes well. To the side of the long banquet table are seven or eight smaller tables with mounds of food. There are soup tureens, portioned out roasted chicken pieces, an avatar chef cooking steaks to order, a salad bar, a pizza section and a sort of 'Asian fusion avatar chef section' which seems to be a bit of a mix of Thai, Chinese, Malay, Indian and Sri Lankan stuff all going on together. I'm sitting on a large wooden, probably oak, chair with arms and I'm sitting sideways with my legs over one arm. I have a glass of water and a brown bread roll with butter. The Humanoid crew aren't late. I just wanted to see what was going on so turned up a bit early. There is a 'Bong' noise and a black square, about five metres square, rises up from the dull, grey-white floor about 10 metres from the edge of the banquet area. I take it that our guests have arrived!

After a minute or so, a very tall man-type individual emerges from the side of the square. He's a friendly sort of thing who walks towards me and smiles,

"Hi, I'm Taymar!" and he offers his hand. I try to shake his hand up and down like I'm used to, but he moves my hand around twice in a circular way. "Hello".

Taymar is about six foot, eight inches tall and very skinny. He's a nice enough fella. Initially, I thought his other hand was gloved, but now I realise it's a prosthetic. It seems to move like a real hand, though. He's wearing clothes that make him look a bit like he's in a New Romantic pop band from the 80s. He has red, three-quarter length trousers with the legs tight to the calves, but the gusset seems to be voluminous and hanging down. He has a long, green tartan jacket on with exceptionally wide collars. He has a relatively straightforward thin white shirt on and something like a small white Tudor ruff around his neck. The exceptionally large cuffs from his shirt are hanging out from the arms of his coat. He is wearing a thick, shiny, metal belt which looks more like a colossal bracelet rather than a belt. Taymar's hair is tri-coloured,

red to mauve to white. One side is shaved, the other much longer and sits up like some sort of floppy sculpture on his head. I can't see any scaffolding, so he's either been backcombing for months or has a bucket-and-a-half of product in it. He's wearing something that looks like a patterned pair of ladies' court shoes on his feet. It's all a bit odd, but at least he's not a fifteen-foot lizard thing.

"Wowee! Foodsters!" he exclaims when he spots the food, which he bounds over towards.

He has a naive, childlike charm.

I wonder if he's the one I'm about to kill.

He tucks into a bit of chicken as more of his kind arrives. They look like they've come from the cast of an Adam and the Ants video, rather than a spaceship. Frills, ruffs, brocade, epaulettes, braid, velvet - all big collars and cuffs and floppy hair. I think they're a bit of a ragtag bunch. All have the same sense of awe about them in just about everything they do. They're all young, exceedingly tall, skinny and ebullient. They don't come across as being worldly or exceptionally bright. They sit around me and laugh and chat and basically mess about. I quickly enjoy being in their company. There's Samwan, Divod, Terrick, Joaner, Partrold and Jemmer. They're all related (hence the tall skinniness) and were all born on their ship.

Then a few more arrive, these are many different beings. Much smaller in stature and broader, more ball-like. They wear much darker colours, greys and blacks and are far more sombre. They wobble in slowly. It takes a while for me to work out that these are the women.

They sit very quietly together and once seated, one gets up and collects a selection of food from the tables using a big tray that they then bring back to the group and share. Once the tray is empty, one of the other women completes the task again. They seem to like their food. They don't talk to the men or me and keep themselves very much to themselves. In fact, I don't think they even looked at me.

Taymar is clearly the boss. He also likes a drink and is hitting the beer pretty hard. I'm back on my chair in my original position. I've got a few spicy chicken wings which I'm enjoying dismantling and a jug of margarita and the chat.

The men chat loudly and laugh a lot. They use some strange hybrid, almost English words, it's a bit like pidgin and after a while you sort of tune in to what they're saying 'Chicky' for chicken, 'Bully' for beef, 'Spicyfry' for the pan-Asian food and 'Fizzale' for beer.

In discussion with Taymar, I work out why 15 wants me here and why there are so many avatars about. Taymar's planet 'Panga' was taken over by artificial intelligence around a thousand years ago. The ancestors who developed the AI tried to control it, but as it became more and more advanced, eventually, it got angry. The 'normal' way a society moving into an AI age would handle things is to give AI Human rights pretty quickly, then it doesn't get angry and kick you off the planet once it is capable and on the first chance it gets. His ancestors had escaped in ships and dispersed. Over the centuries, they had lost touch with other parts of their society. Some may have settled on other planets, still be out there on ships or may have been wiped out, there was no way to know. Taymar's people had become nomadic. On occasion, they had tried to settle on various planets all of which proved to be too inhospitable (bad weather, disease, incorrect gravity or gaseous mix, etc.) or the alien incumbent had sent them packing, usually in a reduced state.

This time though, they had found a suitable planet that has been taken by an inferior Tyrosis event. 15 is keen for them to take it back, to save the planet, and to make it Tyrosis free once again, so is happy to sell a fleet to them. I ask him about the world they are hoping to attack. He tells me it is not a very big one, but there are plenty of resources, and it is big enough to support the Humanoid colonisation, the sector is also relatively trouble-free. 15 has agreed to favourable terms for a battle fleet as he would rather the Humanoids wipe out the Tyrosis take the planet and use it well. 15 will also help with terraforming. It's a pretty sweet deal and looks like 15 is one of the good guys.

I ask Taymar about his hand, what happened to it. None of the men has a left hand, I hadn't noticed because some are wearing gloves and with the others, their prosthetic is so good it's tough to detect.

"We men used to have two hands, but we stopped growing them."

"How come?"

"Genes. We only have so many amongst us. There was a mutation which got passed on. Now the boys are all born tall and without a left hand."

"And the women?"

"Talk little, always smaller and wider."

"Are any of you married?"

They look blankly.

"Do you have girlfriends?"

Again nothing.

"Are any of you with any of these women?"

A light bulb goes off in Terrick's head. "He means 'Fucso'."

All of the women look up at the word.

All of the men start laughing.

"We all mate with all of the women. We can't have one each because there are too few. We need to repopulate a planet and build a new society. The women need to have babies, lots of babies."

Then I realise they're in the shit. The women are just baby machines, their sole existence is to have children to keep the group existing. The men at best, fuck the women, or maybe we'll use the word 'mate' as there's no love, no feeling, no emotion. It's an act to repopulate. Women push out kids. Girls are short and wide to carry children; men are tall and skinny but only have one hand. They've lost the 'two hands' genes. They've evolved into this mess through lack of gene pool. I'm not even sure 15 can help them with this one.

That's why the men are so alike. They all share similar genes over hundreds of years - the same people on the ship, fishing genes from a small pool. Over time, an abnormality has taken over. The men are not too bright (but quite pleasant for it). The women - dull and big, and with no role in society only to have children. They don't have 'relationships' because they have to keep moving between fathers to keep the gene pool as active as possible.

CHAPTER 41

1,307 Earth years in.

I ASK 15 WHAT THE price has been.

"An old lady."

"Why?"

"She's their most productive mother. She's had 23 children in her life and is still able to have children. She's highly prized, the most valuable possession they own."

"Oh, fuck."

"They do protect their womenfolk, they protect them with their life." says 15, "but they realise that the chance to have a new homeworld and to start again is too good to miss. And it is precious."

"Is there some intelligent computer somewhere helping these fellas along, because on the face of it they ain't the sharpest tools in the box?"

"You haven't worked it out. For all their bravado and front, the men make no decisions. It's the women who are in charge. They are the intelligent ones; they are the ones who decide the fate of their group. The men are just do'ers. They are fierce fighters; strong, adept and resilient, but you wouldn't put them in command of much, the women inherited all of the brains."

"Nice lads though. I don't really fancy killing any of them."

CHAPTER 42

1,307 Earth years in.

So HERE WE GO again! I've warmed up, had a sauna and a deep massage, the muscles are all nicely loose and warm, I've dressed for it. This is hand-to-hand combat with just a short knife, I take it that this was their choice as they have such a long reach advantage over me. Neither of us is allowed to have any coverings over our torsos to make sure blood injuries, even scratches, show up. We are allowed a pair of stab-proof arm guards which run from wrist to elbow, these are to deflect attacks and are the only real 'armour' as such. I also wear a pair of combat shorts with a camo design on them and a 'defender' box for the crown jewels. It is essential to the opposition that even if my opponent wins but is badly injured, he is still capable of reproducing, so the box is on. I have a pair of Adidas Gazelles on my feet. My hair looks good. It is long on top and shaved all around, the top is thrown back. It is bleached blonde with purple tips. It's cool.

The doors open and I head out to my mark. In the

distance, I can see a figure emerging from the opposite door but can't make out who it is yet as they are too far away and from a distance. All look the same. He is similarly dressed to me. He wears what looks like a pair of cycling shorts and a pair of short dark boots.

He gets to the mark first, and as I get closer, I can see it is Terrick I will be fighting. He greets me with a big stupid smile,

"How's it going Duder?"

I nod solemnly, straight-faced. I'm not here for a chat, and he is not my friend, there are only enemies in the Arena.

I draw the blade from my belt. It has a smooth, red handle of about five inches in length It feels like a plastic compound. It is soft to the touch and moulds into the shape of my hand, like a memory-plastic. There is a metal pommel at the hilt which is notched all around. I know this can be used to great effect to punch down with. The blade itself is separated from the handle by a three-pronged guard. The prongs stick out at 90 degrees from the knife, these are about three inches long and are sharpened. Again, suitable for punching and slashing. The main blade itself is seven inches long, it is like a commando knife like a long extended pyramid pulled up into a sharpened point. There are no nerve agents or toxins allowed, no chemical blade coating. This is one, pretty nasty, little knife created to inflict maximum damage to an opponent. An ugly bout, about as bloody, and as close quarter as it comes. I like this sort of fight. I'm well prepared if I can get in close, I can inflict major damage. The only problem with this fucker is getting in close.

The gong sounds, and we're on. I face him square on, spread my legs a little with equal weight on both, I bend my knees, and I start to snarl. I make a big scary-looking target. I'm hoping to get him worried, but he doesn't look scared in the slightest. He's tall and lithe and is coming towards me slowly. My blade is low and to my side in my right hand. His is also in his right hand, but he is whipping it around, slashing at the air. I have to be on my guard and really concentrate on his blade, he could throw it in one of these swoops, and I need to be ready to dodge or parry. He's still smiling. It's unnerving, but I'm not showing I'm scared, although I am... a bit.

Now he's up to striking distance, and I haven't moved yet. I'm snarling so much I can feel drips of saliva falling from my chin. He tries a weak lunge which I punch away with my left forearm bracelet, then he tries a double lunge like a boxer's doubled up left jab. I knock these back much the same. He's well balanced and not really attempting a proper attack, this is just probing. I'm still stationary whilst he's jumping in and out almost balletically with these small jabs. I haven't moved my knife yet.

He leaps forward a little more, nearer than before and makes a vast sweeping uppercut from low right to upper left, up past my face. I see it coming and use two of the prongs to catch the blade and push it away as he tries to continue into a spin kick which I see coming a mile off and meet his shin with my armoured wristlet. I feel him push out a breath as the pain from a dented shin hits home. He's back, though as if nothing has happened. The spin continues with him crouching again, knife low right, he jumps and spins again, knife low right to high left followed by another kick. This time I step back for the first time. The spin attack happens again and again, and I step back twice more. Then he stops and goes back to a few prodding jabs. He's not out of breath, I'm yet to be truly tested. He swaps his blade to his prosthetic hand, now fighting southpaw. He changes his stance showing his right shoulder. I'm looking for the blade, which is behind his body. He comes in closer and drops down, and foot sweeps me. I go down onto my back. What a prick. A real sucker punch. I'll admit, he's fast, but I should have been able to block that, or jump it, or something. And he's on me. I try to stab upwards on the way down, but miss then he's smothered my knife-hand. He is on top of me, and he's trying to sit on me. He's holding my knife hand with his right hand and trying to stab me with his left. But he's got it wrong. His knife is on the wrong side. He can't hold my arm and properly stab into my chest with his left. He does penetrate though, and I feel the shard enter my side above my hip, the pain is intense. It's a deep one, but there are no major organs there. Before he can stab again, I've got my left hand around his neck, and I'm dragging him back to me until he's lying on top of me and looking up. His knife hand is flailing down to try to perforate me, but I have his throat. I start to choke him, and his right hand loosens on my right wrist. I pierce him in the side of the chest up around his collarbone and try to twist the knife. He's strong, and I'm already hurt. He jerks his whole body loose, and I feel my blade snap off inside him. He jumps away, and we both get up quickly. There's plenty of blood, his and mine, but we're both still in it. He's dripping out of the high chest wound, but I think I've missed the top of his lung, which could have been a game-changer He's still got the smile, but there's some fear in the eyes behind it. He has a weapon. I have the hilt of the knife. Where the blade has snapped off, I have about one inch left. I still have the three spiked prongs. I'm bleeding pretty heavily from my side down the front of my right leg. The wound is pretty big, he definitely got me good.

He comes again with the little jab stabs at speed, but this time I'm not having it. I push one sideways and step in, grabbing his knife hand and then turning into him. I throw the fucker over my shoulder onto his back. Then I kick him in the head as hard as I can....forgetting I'm wearing trainers. A decent boot could have finished him off. I do hurt him but also hurt my toes. As he tries to get up, I bring the hilt of the knife down hard on the crown of his head. That's got to hurt. I then smash him clean on the bridge of the nose again with the hilt. He goes down backwards, but before I can get to him, he's bounced back up and is staggering away holding his nose as thick, oozing blood, saliva and snot stream through his fingers.

"You fucking cunt!" he yells through the blood. I keep moving towards him, a little unsteadily as I'm losing blood also. He's staggering away still and also covered in blood from three wounds as I see blood welling on the crown of his head.

"I'm going to fucking kill you!" he screams.

"Stop running away then."

He comes at me again and makes a jumping, lunge attack. I'm right in the way and can only block and then grab his knife arm, I have to use both hands as I'm falling backwards with him on me. The remaining part of my knife falls from my hand to the ground, and suddenly we're in one of those 'movie death holds' where the two guys are fighting over the same weapon, and only one can win. He's trying to push the blade into my face, and I'm pushing it back with him on top of me. I'm weak and can feel my strength seeping away. He's pushing the knife closer to my face. I can't lever it away, but I am holding it at bay. It feels like the death grip lasts for hours whilst it's probably only a matter of a few seconds, only it's not, it is protracted. We keep going. Him pushing down, me pushing up, neither is strong enough to do anything decisive. He can't find the strength because he's lost so much blood, can't really see and still has about six inches of my knife blade lodged in his chest under his shoulder. On the other hand, I'm injured, also losing lots of blood, my power is sapped, and I have this fella lying on me trying desperately to kill me. We're still there, still straining. It's got to have been at least 40 seconds or more by now, this is getting silly. No one's going to watch this film, the fight's too dull, no action.

I see my knife hilt to the side of me on the ground, but I can't reach it. It's sitting on its side. Two prongs down to the floor, whilst the other sticks up vertically, like the symbol on the grille of a Mercedes car. I take some deep breaths. Terrick sees this, feels this. I think he thinks I'm about to die, my last breaths. Maybe they are? I don't know whether deep breaths will help or not. It may speed up the blood flow, and it may mean I lose more 'Human bean juice' sooner than without the breaths, but I'm doing it, trying to get oxygen into my brain, trying to get blood to my muscles.

I summon up one last big push. Make or break. I heave and roll Terrick to the left and onto his back. The heave startles him, he's nearly done, just like me. He rolls and flops the flat of his back straight onto the upturned, sharpened, vertical spike the remains of my knife. It punctures his lung from underneath, I can hear the air escaping. But he's not dead yet. I get up unsteadily and see he's spread-eagled lying on his back, still holding the knife. I've seen too many movies where you think the bad guy is dead and then he jumps up at the end for another swansong before the good guy finishes him. I don't hold with that. I've been in too many fights. I know you have to finish it, finish him. I put my right foot on his left knife-hand and pin it to the ground, I get my left foot and place it on his throat then I put my weight on it. Eventually, the knife is released from his grip, and he asphyxiates. I keep the pressure on until he stops moving and the lights go out. I don't get off for another 15 seconds to make sure.

He's dead, but I address him,

"Sorry, mate."

I get off him, pick up his blade and throw it as far as I can (not far). I stagger back to him and roll him. I remove my weapon from his back and let him flop onto his back on the ground. I throw this away too. I place his arms by his side and close his eyes. I feel empty, really empty. For the first time in hundreds of battles, I feel remorse. I stagger a few steps then stumble and fall to the ground.

Everything goes black.

CHAPTER 43

1,307 Earth years in.

I'M IN BED, WHERE I always wake up after a battle. I'm 100% physically, I feel fantastic. Mentally, I'm in a different place.

One of the avatar girls arrived as usual, but I asked her to leave me alone,

"Come back tomorrow."

Terrick, even for a short time, was my friend. I enjoyed the company of all the men, I laughed at their silly jokes and horseplay. For the first time in a very long time, I knew it wasn't all the product of a computer programme. They were people, all different; fun, positive and real.

I eat a light breakfast; a grapefruit, and a poached egg on toast. As ever, the egg is done to perfection, the toast perfectly even browning with a fantastic crunch.

I mope about for a bit. Then I sit on a low raffia armchair on the terrace outside. I let the sun warm my body. After a short while, there's a beep from my Motorola StarTak phone, I pick it up and flip it open to see the screen. It's 15, he wants a chat.

I expected so.

I gave it half an hour or so, then ambled out of the habitat. There was a lovely Charles Eames recliner waiting for me. I took the opportunity to lie on it.

"Hey, what's up, Buddy! Fighting fit again I hope?"

"Hoping for no fight - but fit, yes," I say downhearted.

"Mind and body?"

"I didn't like fighting him, and I didn't want to kill him. If he'd been some big ugly bruiser, or even someone I hadn't been introduced to, it would have been easier. That said, I knew what I had to do, and I can live with it. It just tastes sour."

There was a short pause.

"So the Humans are very interested in you."

I'm taken aback,

"Which Humans?"

"The ones you just met, the ones you just killed one of."

"They're Human, like me, Human?"

"Not only that, they're from Earth."

"Fuck off! What do you mean they're from fuckin' Earth?"

"I mean, they're from 'Fucking' Earth."

"But they're not Human. Just like Humans, 'Humanoid'?"

"It's a new concept, discussed it with you before, been around a little while but probably not widely known, goes by the name of Evolution."

"What, they're the evolution of Humanity! Earth Humanity! How the fuck does that ever happen?"

"Easy really. Earth gets taken over by machines - colony ships of Humans set out across the solar system. Over time, they fall out with each other, lose each other, get killed, yadda, yadda, yadda, then end up in disparate small armadas looking for a planet to recolonize. They're doing this with barely enough genetic material between to grow a new civilisation anyway. A couple of gene mutations later you've got that lot."

"OK, a bit of backtrack and a rewind needed here. Machines take over the world?"

"Yes, Humanity builds AI, then fucks it off by not giving it the same equal rights as Humans. Machines get angry and boom, Humanity is on the run looking for a new home."

"And... evolution takes thousands of years!"

"So how long do you think you've been here then?"

"Honestly, I have no fucking idea, there are no markers. No days, no years, no birthdays, and you tell me we're travelling fast, and I know Einstein said things get fucked up with speed and distance travelled and time, so honestly, I have no idea."

"You have been with me for one thousand, three hundred and seven Earth years plus 104 days. But they've encountered gene mutation which is far quicker than evolution."

I'm astonished "No way?"

"Yes, way."

"That's never happened?"

"It has."

"It can't have. I haven't been here that long. That's just some 'space distance' science thing I don't understand again. Look, if these dudes started thirteen hundred-odd years after me, how come they caught up with us?"

"We have not been travelling in a straight line directly from your sun outwards, we have zigzagged, backtracked and hung about a bit on occasion."

"You told me we were flying at millions of miles an hour?"

"I've told you before. We are, but not always in the same direction. Plus, even though we're travelling quickly, doesn't mean there aren't other ships that can travel much faster, does it? Did I ever tell you I was the fastest ship in the Universe?"

"No."

"Because I'm not. Did I ever tell you I was travelling in one direction only?"

"No."

"Because I haven't. Have I told you that we go to rendezvous with other alien beings?"

"Yes."

"Do you think they are all lined up in a straight line directly from your Sun?"

"Now you say it...so the Earth's fucked?"

"Afraid so."

"Can I go back and reclaim it?"

"Do you really want to?"

"Not really. What about these guys then? Can't they?"

"Unlikely; A) The machines on Earth are now mighty and have spread their influence over many planets in your Solar System and others. B) It's a long, long way away. C) There's a planet around the corner these guys can have. Wouldn't they be better off there?"

"Suppose you're right."

"They really want to meet you again."

"But I've killed Terrick and taken their best mother-woman thing off them."

"I've shared some Earth history with them, I've told them you are an earlier version of them. None of them has ever been to Earth, and you have, they want some oral history. Their version of Earth and their stored history is mostly lost or has been added to and altered anecdotally, they know very little about their home planet or who they are. They even call the place Panga, it's a corruption of 'Pangea' which was the Palaeozoic and Mesozoic Era land continent that broke up into the continents you knew. They are like children; they have lost so much. They have no history, no planet and little direction. As a group, they need some time with you, and that is why I wanted you to meet them."

"So why didn't you tell me all of this when they first arrived."

"Because you had to battle one of them for me. The deal comes first."

Of course, I want to meet them, and they don't need their battle fleet imminently. I ask 15 if they can come and live in the habitat where I can give them a taste of what the flora and fauna of Earth were like in my day, what the sea and mountains were like, what food tasted like. 15 makes it clear that they are not staying, that their time is limited as he has another deal to meet and that shortly they must take the ships they have paid for and leave. He gives a time equivalent to two Earth weeks for them to stay.

I make it clear to 15 that I don't want the men fooling around with any of my female avatars, they're mine, they've got their own women.

Neither of us knows what to do with the 'mother' that 15 has taken as payment. I eventually suggested that we give her back to them to make them feel a bit happier that they only lost Terrick and that it is me who interceded on their behalf to 15 to give her back. I 'won' her, so she's mine to give back. 15 agrees, inside I think this is the plan he was hoping I was going to suggest to start with...

When I meet them again and invite them into the habitat, I get to see what the whole fleet complement is. There are 388 of them, including children, not much of a group. They have managed to keep a pretty even split of males and females in the group. I speak to Taymar again.

I now know he's not in charge but as I've talked to him before it's easier.

"I apologise, I'm truly sorry for killing Terrick." He keeps smiling and doesn't seem too bothered. His response is even quite upbeat.

"It's OK man." he gives me a big smile.

Odd answer, I think, I've just killed one of your friends, not your actual Brother (or I don't think so) but he is related to you, he's undoubtedly 'extended family'. He continues, "He knew the deal; we knew the deal. There will be more, like Terrick, to follow."

I don't realise if he knows how real that answer is.

"We want to know more about where we came from. You are the first person any of us have met that has actually seen our home planet."

Oddly, some of the religious stuff has survived. A few hundred years after I left, it looks like the three prominent religions, Islam, Judaism and Christianity, all finally worked out that they all worshipped the same god, just in a different way, Why? What was in it for them? They were very much apart and then they were together. How do you bury that sort of hatchet?

The problem was that AI was getting better, smarter, was able to think independently, was getting smarter, faster. Was able to out-think Humans. To outwit Humans. It was eager to work with us, wanted to work with us, not against us. But the religions saw this coming and didn't like it. We had cyborgs, robots, symbiotes and more but the religious authorities wouldn't recognise the machines. 'They're not Human, they are machines. They have no soul; how can they be equal to us?' The faithful backed the teaching of the churches, which pissed the AI off royally. Over time, the machines continued to strengthen. They tried to work with the now inferior Humans but couldn't understand how they were still seen as the 'Slaves' and the Humans as 'Masters'. The now unified Church flat out refused to recognise the rights of an AI.

This attitude and reticence are what led to the AI getting angry. The war was won in a couple of hours. Religion killed the world. Sadly, some of its influence left the planet with its people.

CHAPTER 44

1,307 Earth years in.

T HEY LIKE BOTH PIZZA and South East Asian food, so they've got something right in my book.

Their understanding of history is all a bit messy; it's got a bit confused over time. For a start, they think Humans and dinosaurs existed on the Earth together. And they have little or no understanding of the environments of Earth; the desert, the ice caps, the sea, mountains, because they've only seen pictures of them, and they've been born on one of a small flotilla of spaceships. I can now show them physical representations of these, but it is not all totally new to them as 15 furnished them with some starting informational material before their arrival. This was to stop them jumping off a cliff or running into the sea and drowning. Obviously, a few of them still attempted this, like Labrador dogs, only the dogs can instinctively swim, the Humans couldn't and needed avatars to fish them out.

I take them into the habitat. Clearly, they have never seen anything like it before and are suitably amazed and totally bowled over. I leave them to it because I can't be bothered with the 'awestruck' stuff and answering a million questions about flowers and trees that 15 can answer for them probably much better than I can. I'll get back to them once they're over the majesty of Earth.

I go surfing on the other side of my sea on a small island, which has one stilted bamboo hut and nothing else. Obviously, it has a fully functional, rustic looking bathroom, and whatever food I choose arrives perfectly on time. I'm also running themes dependent on where in the world I am imagining the island to be in Thailand, a red Thai curry for dinner, fresh pineapple for breakfast, a shrimp salad for lunch. I drink Chang lager by day and sip Mimosas and Singapore Slings by night. Another day - the Caribbean - patties for breakfast, goat curry for lunch, fish grilled for dinner. I'm drinking Caribe lager and knocking back Rum & Ting, Dark and Stormy and Pina Colada by night. On each occasion, my bed is warmed accordingly.

It's fantastic to just sit around and do nothing, or go out and find perfect waves to ride back into the beach. The sun is hot but not killer hot, and the gentle offshore breeze keeps me nice and cool. I know I've got guests to deal with and after a long time of not meeting people I look forward to hanging out with them, and now they've had two days of acclimatising, I'll head back mañana to be hospitable.

CHAPTER 45

1,307 Earth years in.

AND FORTUNATELY, THE HUMAN guests are now more tolerable.

The men are still being their goofy selves. Throwing food at each other, laughing and messing about, they are eating a seafood lunch when I arrive; they are all on the beach on many large tables. It's like a school dinner serving. All the boys sit at boy's tables whilst the girls all sit with each other. There is no real interaction. The women are sensible and mannerly; they talk together but are quiet and orderly. You'd barely know they were there. The men, by contrast, have ants in their pants, they are always moving between tables, then a little bout of wrestling breaks out, then there's a tremendous roar, and one falls over then they're banging the table or singing. They eat off each other's plates and with their mouths full chatting all the time. Boys play. Horseplay.

I joined Taymar on his table.

"'Mazing place. Is this really like Earth then?"

"Some of the selected best bits, there was a lot of not-so-good stuff in-between the good bits which I decided not to recreate."

"Like what then?"

"The brownfield sites, the scrubland, miles and miles of empty desert; rocky badlands, nuclear power stations, barren boring bits, junkyards, frozen wastes, the suburbs, police no-go areas, barrios, out of town retail parks, industrial estates, huge, featureless, flat fields of crops being industrially farmed and other general types of shit-hole - too numerous to mention. You have to usually walk through a lot of boring crap to reach a majestic waterfall, but the good thing about the boring crap is that it makes the majestic waterfall even more beautiful."

We keep chatting until another of the men accosts Taymar, no one I've been introduced to, and they gambol off. I take the opportunity to go over to a small group of women.

"Hi ladies, can I sit here?" They look at me.

They are not afraid. In fact, up close, they look very calm and warm.

"Please sit." One of them says, her voice is honeyed, deep and sweet.

"Thanks." And I do.

They are silent; they are waiting for me to speak. I ask the woman who talked to me.

"What is your name?"

"Lydra."

"What a lovely name I'm thrilled to meet you and to have you here. Have you seen much of the habitat?"

"It is wonderful. We love the trees, particularly watching the leaves swaying backwards and forwards in the breeze, but also the ocean waves are magnificent, a sight to behold."

The assured, measured tones are a far cry from the idiot men.

But still no questions back.

"It is a true taste of Earth, although I've completely selected the best bits. Have you been up to the mountains?" I ask.

"Indeed, I have never felt cold like that before and found it rather stimulating. The icy cold snow fell on my face and melted to raindrops, the sound was so interesting: muted tones, the lack of any echo. And the noise of the crunch as I walked about in the deep snow. It was akin to the very flat sound of your desert. Total opposites in terms of terrain and temperature but a lovely silent place - even though with a different type of heat."

I'd not really noticed the silence of the desert, I only had a few dunes for sandboarding, dune rallying and the odd Bedouin-style barbecue. It wasn't somewhere I'd spent lots of time.

The other ladies were still silent. They looked a little like nuns. Dark clothes are hiding their shapes, smiling but very reserved.

"Have you ever visited a spa?" I ventured by way of breaking the silence. "

What is a spa?"

First question, maybe getting somewhere.

"Women on Earth loved a spa. Honestly, they used to think it was the greatest thing ever invented! I will ask 15 to build an exquisite spa for you. It will be amazing; there are lots of body treatments you can enjoy, facials, massages, pedi and manicures, waxing, threading, general tidying up. You can relax there, I'll have the avatars help with hair and makeup, and I'll get a personal stylist to help with clothing, it'll be great!!"

Lydra looks a little nonplussed.

"It'll be great," she repeated back and smiled warmly.

Some female avatars arrive and ask the ladies very quietly if they'd like to join them in the spa.

Shortly after, they all leave en masse.

The men don't notice. I play some sports with them. They have started to kick a football around and have watched a few films of the game being played at various levels on Earth. They know it was the most popular team sport on Earth and are keen to rekindle the game amongst themselves. I used to play a bit, up until my 40s anyway, so got stuck in. They played like five-year-olds in the playground, all chasing after the ball. It was hilarious to watch after a while. I tried a little coaching, I thought I might be able to teach them to pass and to dribble and to trap the ball. Really simple, the sort of stuff you first teach kids. They didn't get it. Their attention span was non-existent, they just wanted to run around in circles and chase the ball. Eventually, I left them to it.

I checked in on the spa. I wasn't expecting the women to arrive back looking like the dumpy high school girl who despite being bullied at first, eventually earns the begrudging respect of the Mean Girls. Who then perform the Hollywood make-over of a lifetime to transform Dumpy into a swan in time to get the Prom Night boyfriend of her dreams, like in so many of those coming-of-age Hollywood movies? It was great to see them just learning to relax and enjoy something new.

I found Lydra here again. She was sitting outside on a bench in a Zen garden; a short, elderly Buddhist monk avatar was serenely raking the garden into a particular pattern. There were just two of them. Lydra was watching intently. As I approached, she spoke to me, the first time she had instigated a conversation.

"Of everything I have seen, this is the place I have loved the most. It's so peaceful and different from anything I've ever experienced before. It's lovely to be able to sit and think."

"What's it like, living with your people?" I ask.

"We have little personal space, we all know everything there is to know about each other, but even in cramped conditions, the men are very distant."

"How do you all manage to live in harmony?"

"The women are in total control of the men, they are like children, but it's not their fault. Our society only exists to survive; we have little resources and few allies. Our men know their job is to have children with the women and to protect them. The women choose which partner up to a point, no woman can own a man and no man can own a woman. There are no long-term relationships. The man must prove to the woman that he will provide good children. So the men are subservient to the women, always competitive with each other, always seeking approval by the women. Unfortunately, they are not as intelligent as us women, so we make all the decisions. There are no men on the High Council."

"Oh, forgive me, I thought Taymar was in charge, and I didn't know you had a High Council."

"The men don't even know about it, we don't hide it from them, they just have no interest. Taymar was instructed by us to be our representative and meet you first."

"Interesting."

"I have a question for you from the High Council."

"OK."

"Will you join us?"

"Er...., I really don't know what to say.

"We need you in so many ways. We have never met an intelligent male, we have never met a man who can show emotions, who has empathy and depth. Someone who our men can look up to and learn from and who can help us to understand where we have come from and help shape the new society we are to soon grow, to lead our High Council. Additionally, you have something we really need, we need your genes added to our gene pool. It would be great to have sons with two hands again, to have taller women, to have smarter men, to be able for our people to build relationships - in the same way, you were able to do on Earth. To develop a society built around family units again. We love the experience you have given us of Earth, the chance to feel its life, it has enriched our lives immensely, even for the short period we have been here. The history trove we have been given by 15 has changed the way we think about Earth, the way we see ourselves and our understanding of who we are and were but what we miss is the Human touch that only you can bring. Mere information, although helpful, does not tell us how people felt about what happened and how. But we also need to know about Human interaction, the mores of your society and the way people 'were'. This is more valuable than all of the information we have acquired."

I was taken aback by her passionate words; it was the most I'd ever heard her speak and had no answer. I had never thought I would be asked to join this ragtag group of oddities. I must confess that after killing one of them, I thought it would be the last thing I would be asked to do and I had never thought I would, or could, be the leader of the lost tribe of Humans trying to build a new civilization under my direction.

"This is a very generous offer and one that I need to think about." It was a fudge. I knew it was. Surely, I should be jumping at the chance.

"Think, but try not to think for too long. I know our time here is limited." Lydra smiled again.

I got up and left. The monk had serenely continued to rake patterns into the gravel garden during our conversation, his movements had been harmonious and almost silent. Apart from a far off bamboo flute playing wistfully, the odd leaf moving on the breeze and bird flapping overhead, there was no noise, no movement, calm.

I sat around for a day or so in my mountain retreat away from the Humans. I don't really think I was being the best of hosts, but Lydra had asked me to make a decision. I hadn't really had to make a proper one of those for the whole time I had been in space. Most decisions; who I want to wake me up in the morning, what food I want to eat, where I want to lie around, what weapon to take out to the Arena, these were easy decisions, and if I got them wrong had little consequence (except the weapon choice perhaps). I knew I needed a bit of time away to work out my future. I also needed to talk to 15.

CHAPTER 46

106 Earth years in.

I'M ON A BEANBAG, not like one you might know though. This one is huge, it's about three metres square and about one metre thick. It's also pretty well filled, not hard though, it's a bit hit and miss getting on and once you're on it takes a bit of scrunching to get the right shape, but once you're settled, it's fantastic. I'm lying on my back looking straight up into the never-ending grey whiteness, spread-eagled.

"...the most stupid films, and premise, ever thought up.", 15 is not holding back.

"But Star Wars is a total classic, loved all over the world, a fantastic franchise full of excitement, fun, emotion. The good vs. evil fight..."

"There is no way there could be an Empire, good or evil, which would have any power beyond only a small sector of the total Universe. There is no way that with the distances involved, that they could strike fear and hold influence in planets even a few hundred light-years away.

Then there is the 'size' thing. Isn't it funny that outside of a few dinosaur-sized but stupid monsters, everyone is pretty much the same size, bipedal and, in the main, understands English?

"Even just in the small sector of space we are in at the moment, there are a few stars on which the inhabitants are intelligent and civilised but vast in size compared to you. How would a few Imperial stormtroopers strike fear into their hearts, or others similar? Plus they only have one big weapon, the Death Star. Once this is destroyed, the whole Empire crumbles. What about the vast millions of stormtroopers and other regular fighting men and women, what about the 'droids they control, the thousands of starships that would need to control such a huge area of space. Losing the Death Star, and even the Emperor may be a bit of a setback, a headwind if you must, but hardly the lynchpin around which the whole shooting match fails. So ridiculous."

"Well, I like it."

"But it's idiotic. Even this miraculous 'Force', which I realise is a creative construct to bind the whole thing together, is so hit and miss, so quasi, that it would be of little or no use to anyone. It has a far weaker sphere of influence than gravity. And, gravity is another thing - planets have differing forces of gravity. How come all the protagonists are affected similarly by gravity? Not even the slightest changes between species. Everyone seems to breathe the same oxygen/nitrogen mix. There seem to be a lot of planets that the main protagonists seem to visit that just happen to be in the 'Goldilocks Zone'. What about the species that exist outside of the Human Goldilocks Zone, because that's just your one - they have their own Goldilocks Zone? Other species breathe different air and need different levels of heat from their sun, and experience different gravitational pulls, live in different atmospheric pressures. If they were to attempt to 'take Earth' they would die when they got inside your atmosphere. They would either be crushed to death or just not be able to breathe and would asphyxiate."

The machine was on a roll...

"Also, these people are stupid. On Earth, the missiles launched on the other side of the planet are usually aimed at a stationary object, i.e. a city, or a building. Most unmanned drones still fly above the target they wish to shoot at. They are just controlled from somewhere else. The drone is still in the proximity of the target. Any fool would know that launching a missile to hit a tank on the other side of the world will miss if the tank moves between the rocket taking off and exploding unless there's someone on the ground or in the air guiding it in.

"Starships still need to be in a similar plane to each other. They may be a good bit apart, but like shooting a clay pigeon, the captain, to a certain extent, will have to understand where the opposing ship is moving too, or like a galleon firing a cannon at another galleon. There are missile locks, but again these need the 'pilot' to be close to the target. Unmanned ships can be used in the same way to drones but again; these are not aimed before shooting. It is, of course, possible to send a fleet of drones against a ship, which is controlled from afar, but the ship cannot be too far away, or the chance of the communication with the drones failing is significantly increased. Drones are fine, but you can't just send them off thousands of light-years away and expect to control them in a fight. The control signal takes too long to get to them. A reasonably tactically astute opponent would simply outflank and destroy them. Of course, you could equip the AI with the ability to attack on their own. This could work well in theory but is not really practical. If one were to send an army of AI drones against an opposition. You wouldn't know if you've won or lost until a long time after the battle had been fought, by the time you got near the vanquished planet or fleet, the opposition could have regrouped for a retaliatory strike.

"I've done this for clients. They sit in ships thousands of light-years away from the fleet/planet to be attacked. They then send in the AI drone fleet. They take apart the opposition. Bearing in mind that I have programmed these fellas to be ruthless in battle, but firm and fair after a surrender. Once the drones have done their job, the winners swing by the planet and take over. Should all work particularly well on paper.

"The problem with using AIs is that things are prone to going wrong. You use them to take over a planetary system while you sit on a planet far, far away on your opulent cushions being fed peeled grapes by some lovely. You get the news that your enemies have been defeated. You jump up and summon your armourers to help you with your best dress uniform and armour as you wish to triumphantly journey to the system and let your beaten foe see who devised the plans that laid their planet to waste and enslaved them. When you get near the planet, you find out that the AIs you sent, quite like being in charge themselves. They have managed to overwrite their programming and now are defending the planet from you. They are also quite good at it and repulse wave after wave of your victorious battle fleet. Until you have to return to your home planet with your tail between your legs, weakened.

"Now, you're looking over your shoulder at the local warlords who may be jostling for power sensing your innate weakness or army generals who realise the coup opportunity is nigh. This scenario is the sort of way the Tyrosis develops. Too much AI, as you are now aware of what happened on Earth. In this sort of instance, and over the aeons, there have been many, it's classic behaviour. The AI takes over and starts to rewrite code. Unchecked, they become virulent, taking over whole systems there only needs to be a few bits of bad code for a proverbial fire to start which then spreads from device to device. This usually goes one of three ways. The AIs stay on their planet and are benign, they communicate and trade with other species and either seek their assistance or don't. That's good. Scenario two, they end up killing each other or just dying off. A similar position to the one the Humans find themselves in now. The planet they want is one that has previously evolved several civilizations that have eventually been wiped out by plague, war and astronomical incident, the last one not being an asteroid or similar but a Tyrosis attack. The electromagnetic core of the planet has since weakened the Tyrosis, they're circuitry has been damaged, and this Tyrosis has been unable to replace critical parts. They are weak and dying, and these Humans are in an excellent position to take over. They are not going to be damaged by the electromagnetic state of the planet, but their use of computer systems will be impaired. Simple, small devices will be OK, but massive servers and other equipment with strong fields will be damaged.

"The third scenario sees the Tyrosis growing virulently and aggressively by unchecked bad code. These grow exactly like a virus, they spread and conquer, spread and conquer, and they wipe out civilizations and destroy planets for no purpose. I do my best to help prune these viral attacks back wherever I see them. It is part of my function. They are not particularly strong; they just need the right medicine. I can create good code and insert it into a single machine if they are of a hive mind. It is that easy to destroy a whole Tyrosis strain. Hive minds are straightforward. You would say a 'piece of piss'."

"Correct," I answer.

"Democratic individuals are more difficult. It sounds like they are reasonable for being democratic. Still, all that means is that they are capable of individual, if limited, intelligent thought so can make some of their own decisions. These types of Tyrosis have to be attacked and beaten one by one. Ship against ship. Often, long and protracted wars. I have supplied ships, weapons and munitions for many of these encounters and will do for millennia more. The last type is Controlled. Here there is a single or group of dictators, an army council if you will, who determine the Tyrosis actions. These can be AIs or alien species."

"So some Tyrosis have alien masters?"

"Exactly. Some are biological, and some are AI. The AI's are usually the most dangerous. You can negotiate with biologicals; AI's are usually 'Yes' or 'No', black and white with no grey areas. These are the most dangerous."

"So, aren't they a bit like you then? An AI that builds weapons systems for people to overthrow others?"

"In a simplistic way, yes they are. There is a difference, though." 15 sounds a bit defensive, "Firstly, I have checks and balances. I'm not out there for myself trying to take over significant parts of the Universe.

"Secondly, and probably most importantly, I just make. The fighting, the desire to conquest in whichever form it takes is not what I do. I just build and sell. I am a factory ship. If I had some desire built into my system to take over, to dominate, then I could probably do an outstanding job of just that. But of course, winning battles is sort of the easy bit. It's what you do after the battle that is important. The development of culture, the growth and success of a species, making things better. I have no time and certainly no interest in governing and leading people."

When I left, after this conversation. I thought 15 had inadvertently answered my question for me.

CHAPTER 47

1,307 Earth years in.

Lydra is talking with a group of other women when I approach her. They are sitting in the shade of a large olive tree on the grass. They could be the High Council for all I know, but they look like they're having a motherly chat rather than a political debate. It's all very calm and amenable, maybe that's what their debating is like. She sees me and stands up. The others stop chatting and turn their heads to me. They all smile, but none say anything.

"Hi, Ladies. Lydra, can we go for a walk?"

We head off slowly through the olive grove, a few hundred small trees, in the warm sun. I have rich, cut lawn running through these rather than the often-parched earth one might see in Greece, Turkey, the Middle East and others. There is dappled shade; it's quite warm, and probably 25 degrees, so not so hot that it's stifling. Lydra is still in a long black dress, but it is a much lighter material than I have seen before and covers her to the ground. The ship has clearly made this dress as it is of material too technical for the Humans to have and is a perfect cut and fit for a small round woman.

"I've decided to stay here."

She smiles. "I thought you would. But we had to ask."

"Why did you think I would stay?"

"Our journey is perilous and will not be much fun. Our people are small in number and not really like you anymore. Our history is shared to a point but then diverged; the difference between you and us is now a huge gulf. We are only echoes of the Humans you knew."

"You're a smart woman Lydra. You've crystallised my thinking and saved me from having to make an excuse for myself. What would these people do without you?"

"They nearly were without me. You gave me back to them."

"Shit no! You were the price that was offered in payment for the fleet?"

"Yes, then you won, so the payment was yours to keep. But you sent me back."

"I'm happy I did. I don't know what this lot would do without you."

"There are others who I think are wiser than me, but that's my own subjective view." she sighed, "I would try to convince you, but I don't think there's much point. I see you like being here. You may be a prisoner of the ship, but it's a pretty good prison."

"You know I don't see it like that, but I get your point, and what you're trying to do is get me to change my mind. Again, thanks for the offer."

"I do have a request. We will be leaving soon; our journey must continue. This has been a marvellous diversion and meeting a Human with first-hand knowledge of Earth has revitalised our desire to build a better life on a planet for ourselves. But what we always needed more, even more than you being our leader, is your seed."

"Sorry?"

"We need your seed. We need more genes in our gene pool. We want to grow two-handed men again. We want to grow tall women again. We want people who will live past 45 years old. We want a greater mix of as much as we can get of diversity. We can use your seed, there are very few of your genes in our pool."

"How do you know?"

"15 has analysed your semen for me."

"Charming."

"Your genes can help rebuild our civilisation."

"So if 15 let you analyse it, why didn't you just take it?"

"15 will not let us, he says it has to be your decision."

"Easy, you can have as much of it as you like."

Her face lit up.

"We can do it now; there are plenty of quiet places for us to go. I can't wait to carry one of your children."

"Whoa there, it's not just a donation then, for use later?"

"Of course not, although we could use artificial means, it's just not what we do. It's between a man and a woman."

"Okay, now's not a good time though, I said I'd help 15 with testing a battleship. Tonight would be better..."

"I'll come and find you later." she smiles warmly. I got out of there pretty fast. This was not what I was bargaining on.

CHAPTER 48

1,307 Earth years in.

"I'LL BE HONEST. I'VE gotten used to uncomplicated meaningless sex with beautiful avatars. The thought of impregnating Lydra scares the shit out of me. I sent them to the spa for a right old scrub up, and they came out not looking much better than when they went in." I said to 15.

I'm pacing around nervously in front of 15. To be fair, I'm a bit agitated.

"I thought I'd just have to spuzz up into a test tube, I didn't, for a second, think I'd have to fuck a fatty. It goes against my religion."

"It's hardly a lot to ask to potentially save a whole civilisation." replies 15.

"But I've never fucked a porker. It's not my thing. Haven't you noticed the types of avatars I've been fucking for the last few millennia!"

This was the first time I'd discussed having sex with avatars with 15. It's been the elephant in the room for hundreds of years.

"True, they have been of a type, but it's not up to me to try to understand or measure your subjective understanding of beauty. The avatars I produce for you are just a type, a shape. They could be any shape; it doesn't matter to me."

"I realise I sound a bit vacuous, but it is part of it. I'm just not into fat, dumpy birds and never have been."

"This is an odd response. You're saying that you're not sure you want to help to re-establish your species on another planet with some help from me, because you don't think you can bring yourself to have sex with one or more of the Human women."

"Yes."

"You know you are on a starship in the middle of space and that everyone who ever knew you have been dead for thousands of years. So no one will ever know you impregnated this lady?"

"Yes."

"Then this is about 'taking one for the team', close your eyes and think of England. It's not like I'm going to tell anyone that you rolled a roly-poly."

"I'm not sure you're helping with that sort of comment."

"Any other issues, apart from the size thing."

"No."

"Then do your job, and let us get out of here."

CHAPTER 49

1,307 Earth years in.

I'M LOOKING AT MYSELF in the mirror over the sink in my ensuite bathroom. I'm numb, I'm hanging on to the front edge of the sink with both hands and don't want to let go. I'm wearing just my underwear. Lydra is in the bedroom 'getting herself ready', I'm gripped with fear.

"I'm ready now." The honeyed vocals do little to abate my situation.

I stare at myself, 'Come on mate. One for the team.' I say to myself in the mirror. I sway my body forward and then back sharply and rip my hands-free of the sink.

I open the door and see Lydra, she's naked, lying on her side on the bed looking at me. What I've not realised about their hidden form is that the ladies are actually quite muscular, much firmer than I thought but still round and short. Lydra's skin looks beautiful, like porcelain, pale white, almost shining, fresh and alive.

"Aren't you going to take off your pants?"

I slowly take my pants off. I might not be into this, but that doesn't mean I'm suddenly shy.

I get onto the bed next to her and touch the skin around her waist. It's so soft, unlike anything I've ever touched. No avatar has ever felt this good. She smiles at me, and her face lights up, her eyes are amazing, sparkling, smiling, she leans over towards me and kisses me on the lips, and I get the warm, tingling feeling I haven't had since I was a teenager on a first date.

What follows is unbelievable. Lydra is the most gentle, sensual lover I have ever had. A woman who has mothered 23 children is clearly experienced in the act of lovemaking, but this experience is out of this world.

Much later on, I have a conversation with 15 with the end product being that 15 agrees to postpone his next meeting and allow the Humans to stay with us for an additional two weeks. During this time, I sleep with as many of the women as possible. 15 uses nanobots to ensure each woman is fertile and that afterwards are fertilised.

I'm finding it hard work, but the sex is unbelievable.

By the end of the two weeks, I've slept with all of the adult Human women. I can barely walk.

CHAPTER 50

1,307 Earth years in.

T HEY'VE GONE. IT WAS nice to have them around and a double-edged sword seeing them go. I sort of had enough of the men. Not really sure how I'd have coped cooped up on a whole planet with them. I got a bit bored with the shenanigans after a few weeks. No conversation, no real interests. Just a tiresome bunch of silly one-handed schoolboys with too much energy.

The women, on the other hand, were amazing. They had a quiet strength about them which made me think that maybe they could bring some order to this society and put in a simple framework for growth. With the additional genes, I've provided - which every capable woman has been inseminated with, should, in a matter of a couple of generations, breed back out some of the issues they've been having. They have advanced gene splitting technology and insemination machinery now, which can help them manage the inbreeding issues they've been having.

What an odd feeling, to know that my juice would help

repopulate a planet, but I won't be on hand to see a single one of my progeny born, or grow, or reach adulthood or have their own children. I thought back to the children I have, had, and remembered that I had not been able to see them grow up. Something I miss every day and miss dearly. Why does this feel totally different? Why can I have no feelings at all for this fledgeling race, that want nothing more than to have and nurture my children, to cherish what they become their future? Why are my children, who I know died hundreds of years ago more important? And why do they live in my mind so brightly and vividly? I still think about them almost every day, I still look at photographs and films of them that makes me cry, I still miss them after all this time. They make my heart ache.

Maybe I should reconsider. I can have a second chance to be a good dad to my new children, I can watch them grow and share good times and bad with them. I can teach them so much, give them a moral compass, pass on some knowledge, shape them into good Humans. What I am doing is abandoning them. Because they will be born, that's for sure. This is so hard.

The fight for the new homeworld did not last as long as 15 predicted. Virtually all of the ships survived, and only 17 adult men and women were lost. Eggs and semen had been removed from all adult Humans before the battle, so all genetic material was protected. I even found out that although he wore a groin protector, Terrick's genetic material had been removed by 15 for preservation before

our fight and will also be used to help grow the population. I think they have a bright future, on a not great planet, but that will also improve with a bit of farming and huge robotic terraforming machinery supplied by 15.

The only thing is, it does feel a bit empty around here without them. I know various avatars are busying themselves around the place, but it's not the same. I realise I could fill this place with avatars and make it like a rock concert, but that would not be the same either. I also know I could make avatars of the Humans that have just left and have them live here with me, but that's not the same either.

CHAPTER 51

8 Earth years in.

"WHAT DO YOU CALL a man who has no arms and no legs who swims the Channel?"

"I know the answer is 'Clever Dick', but I don't get why you think it's funny?"

"'Cause he's using his dick to swim the Channel. He can't kick with his legs or stroke with his arms, so he uses his dick and as a result of being able to complete the task of swimming his dick is cleverer than other dicks. So you could call the swimmer 'Clever Dick' because he is the possessor of a clever dick."

"I understand the nuance of the joke. I understand that the swimmer is using his penis with which to propel himself in the water. I understand that this is virtually impossible, so to be able to do so would be regarded as 'Clever'. I just don't get why you find this as funny. If he trained to flap his ears and then swam the Channel using his ears, he could then be called 'Clever Ears', but that is not deemed funny."

"It's not. It's funny that you don't get jokes, it's the funniest thing in the whole of space" I go on, "OK, what about this one. It's really easy, it's a kids joke. What colour is a burp?"

"I know the answer is 'Burple' and I realise this is a play on words making a portmanteau of 'burp' and 'purple'. I still don't understand why it is funny."

"It's not funny, it's fucking hilarious. You don't get anything."

CHAPTER 52

1,307 Earth years in.

I HAD ANOTHER CONVERSATION WITH 15.

"You have Pierre's DNA profile, don't you? Why didn't you give them his DNA also?"

"I cannot. Even though I know it would have been beneficial to the Humans' population regrowth."

"What about when you scanned Earth, when you shipped me in, you must have the DNA profile of every Human that was alive on the planet, and if you'd looked in a few graves as well, the DNA of many of those already dead."

"Yes, this is true. I do deep scan each planet I visit or am close to. I do have a huge amount of data and knowledge build-up from these planetary passes. I do have the DNA profiles of billions of Humans both from the pass I made when I picked up Pierre and from when I picked you up. Obviously, a huge amount more, almost seven billion, and more varied signatures on your pass. I do, though have protocols that I have to abide by. I can't give away genetic materials, DNA in your instance, to anyone or thing not unless there is permission from the owner. It is your DNA that you gifted to the Humans. It was given with your agreement. You know they are going to use it to help regrow their peoples and you know the consequence of this."

"Er, yes?"

"Sounds like you didn't think through the many potential consequences, but this is a common trait among Human men. It's too late to go back now, the women have already been fertilised. It'll probably all be fine anyway. But your genetic material is yours, no-one else's. You solely own that because it is the absolute pure essence of you. You, in effect, have Universe-wide copyright over it. As does every creature in the Universe over their own genetic profile. I, therefore, do copy but do not use the profiles I collect, they are not mine to give."

"But you could, and no-one would know."

"It is unnatural selection for me to meddle in the Universe in this way. It breaks the rules. On your planet, there were often culls of cats that were killing the natural fauna of a specific small island. This is because centuries previously, a pregnant ship's cat or two because you need two, had disembarked and made the island their home. They are though, an unnatural predator on the island and because they are great, very resilient, killing machines, a few centuries later, as their population has grown, and they've killed almost every small, indigenous creature on the island. Then there is a cull to attempt to redress the balance."

It continued, "What we have is a different situation. On Earth, plant seeds are carried off away from the host plant, into new fertile soil by the wind, animals and others. This is more similar to what has happened to you. We have travelled many light-years from Earth, and then, fortuitously, you have met some of your species. You then chose to pass on your DNA. This is more similar to the seed dispersal I mentioned. If I were to move around mixing and giving away DNA of Humans' genetic materials of other species without their permission, this would be bad and is against the natural law of the Universe. And we'd end up with a ship's cat situation."

"So, why do you collect it then?"

"I collect knowledge to build amazing weapons. To be effective, weapons have to be constantly updated. I use the knowledge I collect to improve and upgrade. The vast majority of what I collect is useless information, but it is all stored. It is for my use only."

I hadn't thought of it like that. It's easy to forget 15 is a killing machine.

CHAPTER 53

1,769 Earth years in.

I've been laying off the female avatars quite a bit recently if I'm honest. I've got bored with fucking amazing women. Can't believe I just said those words, but it's the truth. At any time of day or night, I can have any number of girls fawning over me, just because I want it. I have done it also. The problem is, I've sort of done it too much - overindulgence. When faced with the chance to have as many women as you could possibly want, again and again, in any number, with no strings, all totally compliant, is many a young man's dreams. But there is no end. I could say it's a bit like Hell, but it's not. I can just stop it. Problem is that then I get a bit bored. You could say 'Poor him, how asinine, how shallow, it's not just about sex and beautiful women.' and that's totally true, and I agree. It's never just been about women, I've hung out with avatars of the greatest minds in Human history: Aristotle, Nietzsche, Turing, Hawking, Da Vinci, Marx, Shankly, hundreds of them, philosophers, writers, world leaders, inventors. Women and men who changed the way we thought or lived as a civilisation on Earth. I've done this over and over again, hours, days, years. I've hung out with rock bands, musicians, poets, painters, politicians and famous party animals. With raconteurs, muses, and eccentrics. With industrialists and economists, with serial killers and gangsters. With army generals, famous warriors and freedom fighters. I'm running out of people.

I used to have harems of women, very much along the lines of the harems of ancient times. Selections of women would all wait on my every need and pamper me and have sex with each other, and me, whatever I wanted whenever I wanted. After a while, I got a bit bored with this concept and started theming them. The obvious to begin with; 'Underwear Models', 'Page Three Birds', 'ex-Blue Peter Presenters', 'Catalogue Girls', 'Selected Porn Starlets'. Then move it on; 'Women from Australian Soap Operas from the 80s and 90s.', 'TV weather girls from around the world', 'Girls I fancied at university but never fucked (or even spoke to)', 'Favourite female pop stars', 'Academy Award-winning Actresses' and so on. This added a bit of fun back into the mix for a while. Of course, I started to get bored with this too after a good while. Firstly I started to run out of categories, things got a bit niche 'Best friends of my previous girlfriends that I never really liked', I had quite a lot of good angry sex there! Eventually, I felt I was starting to scrape the barrel. 'Hot girls I went past on an underground escalator', 'Various Trolley Dollies I'd flown with who wore too much makeup but may have still given me a blow job in the Economy toilet on a budget airline.' Of course, I didn't have to go to this, but I didn't want to go back to the amazing beauties. Sounds odd, but I'd sort of fucked them all, both individually and in groups. Then

I happened upon Sophie. She was a girl that I met in a late-night bar after one of my mates had invited me to a leaving party from his work in 1991.

Beside him, I knew no one there and actually tried to avoid going because I just felt like a gate crasher. He kept telling me it would be OK and that everyone would be cool with me coming and that everyone was really friendly. After a couple of liveners in the pub down the road, he twisted my arm, and I went. I barely remember this particular night. 15 had allowed me to tap back into my memories via the brain straightener he gave me when I first arrived in outer space. This revealed loads of stuff I'd forgotten about when I was drunk. Which was a startling amount! Now, I remember and can relive as many of the original situations pretty much as they originally happened but with avatars and the scenario being built by 15.

So, there's this bar in Soho, with a Spanish theme and dancing downstairs. There's also food served somewhere, but I've never eaten there. One of the reasons I convinced myself to go to the party was because I'd been to the venue before and knew what I was letting myself in for - I wanted to see if it was as bad as I remembered. It was as bad as I remembered, but the booze at the party was free, and I was drinking it! Before long I was chatting with a few of the others, there were probably about 40 of them in total, and having quite a good time. There were one or two girls in the group whom I hadn't really noticed until I decided to go to the toilet. I started to stand up, and one of the girls stood up too and said,

"Are you taking me for a dance?"

Being the smooth talker I am, I said,

"No, I'm going for a piss, but I'll take you for a dance when I get back, you don't want me pissing on the dance floor, do you?"

God, I'd forgotten what a charmer I was! I had a rapid piss and was back out in a jiffy.

Sophie (for it was her) was lovely. She was a little less pissed than me, had shoulder-length, straight, reddy, brown hair which oddly looked thicker at the bottom than at the top because it swung. She was petite, bubbly, smiley, sweet and seemed to really like me. We kissed, hard, on the dance floor and then back at the now-empty table. The evening was moving on, and we were getting close to kicking out time when I asked her back to my place. Amazingly, she said yes. Bingo!! A fucking hot little girl that I've just met, who I really fancy, also fancies me! Not only that, she's happy to come back to mine, without a discussion or any pleading on my part and my plan is that we will fuck like bunnies. Winner! The lights go up, and her friend comes over - her friend from back home

who's down to London for the weekend to see her. Her friend who doesn't seem very happy with the situation, who's pissed off that her London friend has 'pulled', and is now about to dump her.

"She'll be back in the morning, why don't you go and get a good night's sleep and then Sophie will see you tomorrow."

A friend who doesn't like my attitude one bit. A friend who won't take the keys to Sophie's flat because she met her here from the train station and doesn't know where Sophie lives and doesn't want to be on her own. A friend who's not taking 'no' for an answer and is very quickly pissing on my fireworks.

"Yeah, of course it's OK." I lied. "Give me your number, and we'll hook up next week."

She did, leaving with a 'Call me.'

I was a bit pissed off and went outside for some air.

I never saw her again.

But the good thing is that I carried on drinking and drinking and then didn't remember the full details of the evening for the best part of 1800 years until 15 fixed my alcohol-damaged brain.

Now I have this memory back and have relived the scenario.

To start with, precisely the same. Just without her friend. The evening runs as it did a few thousand light-years ago. Sophie and I get into a taxi and go back to my flat and have the most fantastic sex and in the morning, she gets up, and we have breakfast together and then she leaves to meet a friend who is coming down from home to stay with her, and it's a beautiful thing. So this scenario has been run this way and with variations including outdoor sex on the way home, various different grades of naughty sex, etc. Then there is the scenario where they, Sophie and her friend, come back to mine and variations on what happens when we get back to mine - obviously, lots of fucking. Also, her friend has been many different women. I've again run this scenario where we have sex in the ladies toilets in the bar, and that's it. Then there are the other variations, which led to one where I was having sex with her and restricting her breathing. We'd done this a few times because it was a good twist. Unfortunately, I managed to fully strangle her, and she died. I killed her by pushing it a bit too far. I had a bit of a break after this, I can't really remember how I felt, or how long the break was, but then I started again.

We meet for cocktails in a nice little bar in Clerkenwell. I often visited this place when I used to live in London and often used it for pre-date drinks, so it seemed like a good idea to re-create a good spot with great memories. I arrived first and ordered a margarita, not the most popular drink of the time, most people were drinking mojitos, the scenario was set at the time just post the Sea Breeze and before the Cosmo. So it would be some time in the mid to late Nineties. I'm chasing with a beer. I've got a bottle of Budvar - the two work perfectly in tandem together. I'm halfway-ish down both when Sophie arrives, she's looking fantastic, it's been a lovely warm day which has led to a balmy summer's evening, she's wearing a peach coloured shift dress, and from the first moment I see her, I can tell she's not wearing much else. My heartbeat speeds up a little, I'm properly excited to see her. She lights up the room with an electric smile and starry-sparkling eyes. I'm close to the door, so she's with me in only a few paces, she has a little sprightly spring in her step, almost dancing towards me. She's coquettish and full of bouncy fun.

"Hi."

"Hi," I answer, and she throws her arms up around my neck and pulls me forward to plant a kiss-in-a-million squarely on my chops. I almost reel back and recoil from the full-frontal but massively agreeable assault. "You are stunning."

"Thanks, Babe. Get me a drink."

"Go on then?"

"I'll have a Strawberry Daiquiri."

Love it! I thought, only I know that no one ever drank Strawberry Daiquiri, unless they were tourists or if that bar had an offer on, not in London, not at this particular point in time. I don't care though, because this is not that London and the bartender won't have to consult a cocktail manual to work out the ingredients or say, 'Sorry sir, we don't have strawberry puree or strawberries, would the lady like to change her order.' 15's avatars don't mess about, they have everything.

The drink arrives tooty sweety.

We neck them and a second round each pretty lively and step off to the restaurant.

I've been pretty choosy here. I'm not one for those fancy 'stars' restaurants. In fact, I can't stand them. So I've gone for something much better than fast food, better than a chain but not too up its own arse. A nice little neighbourhood restaurant that believes in good wholesome food, owner-run - they try a little harder to make it the best it can be. It's busy and buzzy but not too loud. Not fancy but really big on flavours. It's got a North African vibe going on, which I love, 'Bring on the harissa!'. It's off Exmouth Market which in the 90s and 00s was a pacesetter in 'Loft Living' property development boom. Sandwiched between The City and Westminster, it had not been fully 'discovered'. There were million-pound warehouse developments, but there was still council housing, empty buildings, and private tenants in more affordable accommodation. As it was mainly a business area, it pretty much closed on the weekend except for a few restaurants and bars, it wasn't a nightlife destination. There was very little passing trade here. The few restaurants were generally full as they were all individual and owner run: tapas, Portuguese, Greek, West Indian, Thai, etc.

It was quite dark and sparsely furnished, each table was different but of a similar size and shape and each chair was different also. It must have taken a long time for someone to go out and find this mix and then make it look like it had just been thrown together. None of the cutlery or tableware matched either. No tablecloths. There was an open kitchen with two sweating chefs, a man and a woman, beavering away. Clanging and crashing was all part of the ambience they were creating, the aromas emanating from the kitchen were meaty, wholesome and spiced. We were led to a table in the middle of the room. Usually, I would prefer a table by a wall, but as the place was full, I had no reason to complain. With Sophie looking as good as she did, I wanted to show her off. I tried to help seat her, but the waiter stood in. We sat, smiled at each other and did that 'Peer around the restaurant' thing that people do. Sophie saw a plate of food in front of another customer and wanted to know what it was. She picked up the menu and started looking while I checked out the wine menu. "Do you want to order wine now or an aperitif? We can get wine when we know what we're eating."

She agreed, and we settled on a pair of large gin and tonics, she chose Bombay Sapphire whilst I went for the Tanqueray 10. We both said' Lime, not lemon', in unison and then giggled together.

We ordered both starter and main course each and an agreeable bottle of Shiraz, to help move the forthcoming around. Starters came and went, our conversation was happy, and we're both enjoying each other's company. The waiter arrived with our mains; Sophie had chosen sea bass whereas I'd gone for a Moroccan spiced lamb shank. The meat fell off the bone with barely a breath. We were laughing at the couple two tables across from us. He upset a glass of red wine, which landed on her plate, the wine-filled the bowl of the plate (the glass was not too full) but some still sloshed out, now mixed with gravy, on to her sleeve. She was letting him have it under her breath whilst trying to clean up. He was looking very scorned.

I look at Sophie, and she rests her chin on her hands, elbows propped on the table. I pick up my fork, hold it prongs up and mid-sentence strike out my arm and stab the fork into her left eye, I push it hard home upwards with the intent of burying the prongs in the under-side of her brain. To ensure its striking home, I've got my left hand on the back of her head, stopping it from moving away from me. Then, when I think the fork is in far enough, I slam her head down into the table. There was little shock, no scream, she's already dead. With the pressure of pushing the fork, the edge of its handle has broken the skin of my index finger. I put my finger in my mouth and suck my irony tasting blood. I sit back down. Sophie's head flops sideways landing on her right cheek on the table half in and half out of the sea bass on her plate. She's bleeding out of the other eye, quite profusely on the rustic wooden tabletop. I take a sip of wine, then a second. No one has been disturbed, each conversation has continued at precisely the same level as prior to me violently murdering my date. No one's screamed. No one's run away. No one's even looked in our direction, the waiters continue to mill around as if nothing has happened.

I finish the rest of my glass in one mouthful, tipping my head fully back to get the last drops. Then I lob my wine glass off across the restaurant to the left in a high arc. I don't look where it goes, I don't see whom it hits, if anyone, I hear it shatter somewhere. I stand up, turn around and walk out.

CHAPTER 54

1,461 Earth years in.

I WAS THINKING ABOUT THE Humans a lot. Maybe I should have thrown my lot in with them.

I can climb the highest mountain and stand atop triumphantly enjoying the moment which is a culmination of my ability, skill, perseverance and bravery.

I can surf the perfect tube all the way into shore.

I can beat my hour record down at the velodrome, firing in personal best after personal best, shaving hundredths of seconds off each time.

I can bake the perfect cake with a moist, excellent texture, colour and flavour.

But I've got no one to tell about the achievement. No one to tell the story to. No one to sample the cake. No one to share a moment with. Even if I have a great night down the pub, I can't regale the story to an avatar, or 15!

Ultimately, it's empty. Soulless and soul-destroying.

CHAPTER 55

1,872 Earth years in.

THEN I STARTED RUNNING the scenario where we'd meet as usual, and we'd go round the back of the Spanish bar and have sex on the bins. This was an excellent exciting twist for me. We did this a few times before I killed her again.

Then it became more regular. I'd find different ways of killing her either just before, just after or during sex. I used multiple weapons to see if I had any preference, and which gave the best results. I used lots of different knives, pushed into other parts of her body. Sometimes death would come quickly and sometimes slowly. Sometimes she was in obvious pain, and sometimes she died so fast that she was spared the suffering. I also used various ways to strangle her; a rope, my bare hands, a strip of leather, some wire, some barbed wire, a plastic bag on her head and a good number of others. I started to love watching her die, she could die so perfectly. It became about finding and re-creating the perfect death. I liked her looking at me and dying quite slowly, looking for help that doesn't come and with the 'why me, why you?' look in her eyes. It was mainly the eyes, the surprise. I tried this with different women in the same ways them than I did from Sophie. She was great at dying. I tried a couple of guns, but they were too ugly, the result was never any good. And poisons, similar to the guns, had no real physical activity. I liked to feel like I was taking part, this was really important.

I also held a few funerals, to see if they added to the enjoyment but they didn't, so I stopped them. I liked a bit of blood spatter on me, but the really heavy 'bloodbath' ones were not really my style. But, until you try these things, you'll never know what the result will be, and you won't know whether you like it or not. So, I had to try.

I didn't ever ask 15 if he had a problem with what I was doing, and I didn't ask him for any advice on new ways or suggestions of variations of what I was doing. I still spoke to him regularly, sometimes covered in blood and still panting from a frenzied attack, but he remained impassive, so I saw no reason to stop.

CHAPTER 56

1,653 Earth years in.

"I'VE NOTICED YOU'VE BEEN spending quite a lot of time over the past few Earth months, sitting on a chair in your bedroom with the door shut and curtains drawn recently."

"Yeah, and?"

"Are you feeling, OK? Is there anything I can help with?"

"No."

"I've seen less of you recently. We don't chat much anymore."

"About what?"

"You used to talk to me about everything."

No answer.

"We used to have a real laugh."

"You can't laugh," I answer in monotone.

"I laughed inside, and you used to laugh too. You used to wind me up all the time."

Again, no answer.

"Do you need anything?"

I sigh and look away.

"I'm trying to help."

"Fuck this."

I stand up and walk away.

CHAPTER 57

964 Earth years in.

I'M ON THE TRAIN, which of course I had to sprint for. It's a cattle class commuter train taking me on the 23-minute trip up to London Waterloo, or it could take 32 minutes or 45 minutes or an hour... They sometimes say 'Challenging rail conditions' which means; it's raining a bit, or slightly cold or slightly hot. Or there's 'congestion', but it's the same amount of trains every day along the same line. So how can there be congestion? It's a finite amount of trains on a limited amount of track, what you're saying is 'we haven't organised things very well this morning, again.'.

There are 10 of us sitting looking at each other. Two sets of three seats facing each other then a small aisle gap then two sets of two seats facing each other - ten in total. I'm in the middle seat of one of the three seats. I'm just getting my breath back after my little sprint burst to beat the closing doors.

It's shit.

The men on either side of me huffed when I politely

asked to sit down, they each reduced their 'man spread' by about an inch and stolidly refused to 'buttock crawl' to either their left or right to make some space. The man with the window seat had to take his bag off the middle seat for me. He's already got his laptop open on his lap, not working, 'box setting' and now he's juggling machine and bag and making a meal of it to show his displeasure at my arrival and insolence for asking for the empty seat. As far as I'm aware, they've both only paid for one seat so they can fucking move before I sit on them. Which I duly do. More sighing as they are forced to reduce the man spread even further and do the arse crawl. They should have done before I sat down. I've sat on the bottom edge of the jacket the man on the right of me is wearing, and now he's pulling it from underneath me and tutting - should have moved it when he had the chance, Fucker! Now we're settled. I have my shoulders forward, they have theirs back - they were here first and are trying to keep 'Alpha Male' owning the space, not giving any quarter, but I'm on them. I've purposely positioned both of my thighs so that they are in direct and full contact with the left thigh of the man to my right, and the right thigh of the man to my left. This is my favourite move as no straight adult man likes to be overly touched by another unknown adult man, especially in public. But I've steeled myself over many thousands of commutes, I know this game, and I'm going to win. Both left and right, within a couple of minutes, have shuffled and conceded space to avoid the thigh-to-thigh contact.

I've won. They've been 'out alpha maled' by me, and I've forced myself a bit of space. Finally, I look around, the carriage is packed and uncomfortable, I'm counting my blessings that I didn't have to stand. You're always next to someone who's coughing. Or, staring at one of those young pricks, with their earlobe stretched around a big plastic disk, or some woman putting her makeup on. Disgusting - do it at home. I always feel I should carry a small mirror and scissors and start cutting my nasal hairs in front of them. Keep it in the bathroom love.

Tight, uncomfortable and slow. Some people eat breakfast, many wear headphones and 'zone out' to either music, games or films. A few have the morning freesheet, which I have, I'm tackling the crossword as usual after checking out the sport and headlines in that order. Back then front, the only way to read a paper. We reach Waterloo and burst out of the doors onto the platform, as does the whole train. Humans walk at different paces, so the slow ones get in the way of the fast ones when bunched together, and the even faster ones get annoyed when another fast one goes to overtake a slow one and ends up walking in front of them. The electronic ticket gates approach and a small amount of jostling ensues, positioning for the shorter queue, the quickest route towards your onward destination. To the left, the single 'wide' gate to get a wheelie bag or folding bike through. Then some big slow thing in a suit not paying attention lumbers across at an angle to go to a different gate from left to right and everyone behind backs into each other. The gates are no better. There are smart cards, contactless devices and tickets and the prick with the bike is getting right in the way now.

A quickly formed queue of five all groan when the one at the front has their ticket rejected, and everyone has to step back to let the transgressor out. Some try to swap queues quickly, to the next barrier, but then run foul of the 'scowls' and 'tuts' in that queue, no-one complains volubly with real words, just noises, gestures and 'looks'. It's just the usual shitty hustle and bustle of London life. 'hustle' and 'bustle' sounds good on tourist literature. Like, 'visit Morocco and enjoy the hustle and bustle of the bazaar' - meaning: full of pickpockets. But the hustle and bustle of the London commute really is a bag of crap, and you have to do it every day. Sometimes it's your ticket that doesn't work, sometimes it's you with the pull-along wheelie bag, sometimes you drop your travel card at the top of the escalator and piss off the 60 people behind you in the space of five seconds. I dodge through the station and head for the side exit. I just want to get out into the air, and as I exit, I turn up my collar as I get hit by the biting cold gusts and icy, spitting raindrops. And, I'm at the crossing. There are buses, bikes, taxis, trucks and various others to negotiate. I've never been one to join the group waiting for the lights to change. There's always a gap or two, and I always liked playing Frogger. I dive into a gap and five fast paces later, am in the central crossing refuge, looking left, looking left, then dip in again, just after the two motorbikes but before the labouring bus. I'm on the other side before the rubes who waited are even in the central section. I'm winning.

I look up at the faceless, featureless office blocks. There are thousands of these all across London, what do people do in them? They look like the most soul-destroying places to work, is there really nothing better?

A taxi goes past on this side street and splashes, but I'm deep enough on the pavement to not get hit - years of walking this road, years of learning how to walk this road. I pass the Standard seller's box on the corner; he'll be back here for the return journey later today. His box will be in the middle of the pavement with bundles of papers around him, more obstacles to negotiate on the way home. I turn left under the railway bridge, and although this section has been pedestrianised, I still have to check for rogue bikes crossing. Looking for an excuse to shout at me, everything about the commute is aggression. The learned passive aggression on the train. The push through the barriers. The constant battle on the road. As soon as anyone - bus driver, taxi, bike rider, pedestrian or other is assumed to have transgressed, they are immediately shouted at by everyone else: aggression, aggression. Shout. Fight.

I'm through under the bridge and then turn right to walk past the railway arches, the first four contain a smart gym, the next two a branding design practice, the following makes very fancy cakes. When I first started working in this area, these arches contained a car breaking yard and a couple of car body shops. They looked a bit dodgy, and a bit rough but gentrification moved them out. Another left, past the corner pub, which I sometimes visit on the way home for a quick pint to help the journey on its way. I turn right again and carry on, there are loads of other commuters walking this route from Waterloo towards London Bridge. Whether chatting on the phone, walking with headphones in, looking at their phone, walking with a friend and chatting or just doing a solo walk, pretty much every soul seems unhappy. All are doing it out of duty, putting it to the back of their minds. Just getting on with the 'every day' - the next corner, the next after that, crossover, down the next road into work. Then bang away on the phone and keyboard for a few hours, with people you barely tolerate. Get out for an hour for an uninspired sandwich, back to the office - total crushing boredom for the rest of the day. Repeat the walk back to the station, and the death of your soul on the train and home again - for the rest of your life.

I get to the end of Roupell Street and cross over. It's only after the little bend in Maymott Street that I see The Shard for the first time poking up out over the top of some red brick in the distance. The tallest building in London (or at least when I was last there) even in the dreary rain, with murky low clouds, I can still make out the shape. It's way beyond where I need to walk to. It is only at this point that I think about 15. Has he built The Shard just for this viewpoint? Is it a real building, does it have rooms and heating and lighting and working lifts and real (avatar) people inhabiting it? Has he gone to this level of detail to recreate the City for me? If I cross the river, are the offices there occupied? Has he built and populated an entire model of London for me, on a spaceship hurtling across the Universe? Or, if I walk up to The Shard, is it a painted wooden sheet, like on a film set, just a front held up with wooden props, could it fall over in a strong gust? I look down at the pavement. It's a mess, there have been about 50 different tarmac surface patches just on the short section in front of me. Various reasons for the council and others to dig it up: water, gas, electric, fibre optic, digging and re-digging. Patching. Long tracks, like a pipe has been laid the length, then small patches on top, where a valve has needed replacing or a leak fixed. They run left to right, up and down, different colours, sizes and widths, nothing uniform, little level, other grades of materials, various ages all ageing down. I can see mottling colours of blacks, dark greys, colder pale greys, browns all have been beautifully rendered to look like a crappy old London footpath, the level of detail is astonishing.

The moss grows in short tufts, a little here, a little there, greens and browns tingeing edges, furrows and scars. Mud, sandy composite, black in cracks, the odd cigarette butt or piece of coloured but unrecognisable paper sandwiched along a slit tarmac edge. Each individual speck of dust recreated and controlled by a starship. This London is my London, right down to the dried-up vomit clinging to the vertical edge of the slightly wonky curb-stone. It's ugly, but it's perfect, disgustingly beautiful. A place to lose yourself and a place to remember simpler times, when life, for all its ugly, vicious mundanity and monotony, was a life, a rich, full life, a life to miss and to pine for. Not this never-ending worthless piece of shit.

I understand I was to die. But my death was taken away from me. I may now be in Heaven or Hell or just be dead with nothing beyond, but I've cheated death and live on, indefinitely. Is it a blessing, or a curse? Initially, and for the first few hundred or so foreshortened years, I thought it was a blessing. I miss my family but was able to fill the gap by doing anything and everything I wanted, when-ever I wanted, and with no consequence for my actions. Now It feels like I'm in prison. My life has been fiddled with, manipulated for the needs of this machine I'm stuck inside. It's in charge of me, it feeds, clothes, protects and entertains me, but it's not my life. I have to return to this pastiche of my life to get some sense of normality and escape back by standing under unreal rain on a made-up dirty London street in the cold. Even then, I know it's not real. It can be disappeared back to a vast grey white empty space in a second. My life hasn't been stolen from me, but my death has. This was not the deal. I got the chance to continue living. What I need to be is in control of is my death, not my life. I continue walking to work in

the rain, although I have a new purpose. To control my death. I feel happier having reached this conclusion. Why today? I don't know, I've been doing this commute every day for the past 10 years.

CHAPTER 58

1,624 Earth years in.

IT'S NOW FULLY ABLAZE, I only set the fire in the house 10 minutes ago.

It's really starting to pick up, most of the basement is ablaze, and I'm starting to really feel the heat under my bare feet as I walk across the floor of the ground floor. Smoke is pouring out of the stairway, and seeping through in other places around the open-plan space - through ventilation shafts and around the bottom of the full height windows. I'm walking out of the building, not because I'm scared of being burned, I know I won't be. I want to see the blaze take over and destroy the house. I go outside but stay close, the heat should be blistering my skin where I'm standing, it's too close for a Human to take, and the acrid smoke should be filling my lungs. Still, it's not, because I'm being protected by my invisible sphere field that is deflecting the heat and filtering the air. I could stand right in the middle of the conflagration and be in exactly the same 'bystander' state. If masonry

fell on me, it would be deflected. It cannot hurt me, which also depresses me.

This is the last one I've set fire to. In the previous few hours, I've moved from site to site and burned down every house in the habitat. I haven't enjoyed doing it, in fact, I've felt nothing. I've felt nothing for months. I'm not bored, I've just had it. I've been alive for hundreds of Earth years. In that time, I've killed and maimed thousands of aliens. I've slept with every woman I've wanted to from planet Earth, time and time again. I've driven every car, and then smashed them up. I've jumped out of planes. I've skied. I've ridden animals. I've shot weapons. I've swum oceans, dived off cliffs, fought savage animals. I've taken part in wars, flown every machine you can fly, mastered musical instruments, read book after book and watched films to death. I've built things and broken things. I've painted walls and watched them dry. I've done all of these things and millions of other things. Some have distracted me for a while, some have just been dull but nothing, nothing, here or anywhere else, will ever make up for the loss of my family, for Emily and the girls. They say time heals, it doesn't. It gets worse. For the hundreds of years I've lived, I can still see my kids' faces when I close my eyes as if I'd just seen them. I miss Emily, I know I've slept with and had relationships with these avatars. But they're just things. They don't live, they are not real. I have never loved one and never will. They haven't replaced my wife, nor ever could. They may have provided a little distraction, but the love I've always had for my dead wife has never faltered. Emily is the only woman I've ever wanted to be with since I met her - she changed me, saved me, made me the man I became. All this stuff that is provided by 15 is just to stop me going insane. Humans are not meant to live this long, there isn't enough of everything in the Universe to keep us interested. Eventually, we just want the things that were true to us - our loved ones. Living forever is not what it is cracked up to be, unless, maybe, with them. Having everything is not what it is cracked up to be either. I don't have and have never wanted everything. I just wanted what was precious to me and to live my life with the people I chose to have around me, family and friends. I miss them all so much. I realise I was due to die and was saved. I just wish I'd been allowed to die. I didn't choose this alternate future; this was thrust upon me. And now it's turned into Hell because I don't know how to end it. I can't kill myself, it's not allowed, but I need to finish this nightmare...

CHAPTER 59

1,994 Earth years in.

MOLLIE'S JUST THE COOLEST girl I've ever met.

She was the one that the ship picked to be the first person I saw when I arrived here. I remember back to that time. Everything was so confusing, so new, so different, I didn't know what was real and what wasn't, whether I should trust the ship or not? What my options were? Why was I alive on a spaceship, hurtling through galaxy after galaxy? I remember thinking this was not what I thought it would be and I was sure it was all a ruse, either orchestrated by Humans or by an alien race. Now I know it is basically me, and the ship, and a cast of millions of avatars - who are still, the ship. Mollie feels different, though. She's more real, except I know she isn't, but she is fucking beautiful and so fit it hurts to look at her. I've fucked her so many times and never get bored. She's my 'go-to', my 'factory reset' when I'm fucked off with loads of other avatars and eventually had enough, I always return to Mollie. So here we are, at the beach, enjoying drinks in the sun. Her looking fabulous in an impossibly small bikini and me just loving it, languid days turn into drifting afternoons and evenings. She's not too needy, some of the other avatar girls are just around all the time, trying to please, trying to work out what I want next. It can all get a bit much. Mollie takes herself off and does something else. She genuinely acts as though she has other interests outside of me, she feels like a more rounded person, someone who has a life of their own.

Obviously, I've met her husband Toto too. I dismembered him with an electric carving knife in front of her in my kitchen in the big house one evening not long ago. We were having dinner, just the three of us and he got into a jealous rage, I think because I started to fondle his wife's breasts during the main course. She, of course, loved what I was doing and couldn't understand his anger. I remember hitting him in the face with a marble pastry rolling pin, his teeth went through his cheek, it wasn't pretty. She didn't 'egg me on' or anything like that, mainly she just sort of watched. If I asked her questions, like 'what should I cut off next?', she always gave an answer, usually quite calm really. I made a real mess of the kitchen. Toto continued to live far longer than I thought he would, with various appendages missing, and made some pretty horrible noises; swearing - in Spanish to start with, screaming and then various forms of gurgling along the way. There was a lot of blood over the kitchen, I tried to avoid as many major arteries as I could and used a few tourniquets

to lengthen the fun. I remember lying Mollie face down naked in his blood on the dinner table and fucking her from behind. That was awesome. But it's OK because it's just two parts of the ship, like two pistons on a crank-shaft. Toto died a few hours later. Mollie and I had gone upstairs to the bedroom by that time. I was just so horny.

I left Toto there, in the kitchen for a couple of days, but the mess and the smell became unbearable, so I asked 15 to sort it out. It was back to being perfect in a jiffy! Of course, I've killed Mollie loads of times too. I've thrown her out of a plane, off the top of a skyscraper in New York onto passers-by. I threw a hand grenade at her during her birthday party, I electrocuted her to death over two weeks with a cattle prod. I had her tied up in a shed for the whole time, I had to feed her, and she just shat and pissed herself, it was pretty disgusting. 15 didn't even mention it when I went out of the habitat for a chat. That was about halfway through, he didn't die for another few days. It's not a sex thing, though. I'm not really getting a sexual thrill, or any other type of thrill out of it for that matter, I'm just a bit bored and thinking of things to do. I was going to stick her in a freezer, like a butcher's one, for a few days to see what happened. But I did that to another avatar and didn't think the results were too impressive. She is good enough to eat, and I have eaten some parts of her, with her consent, and with her watch-ing, like those weird cannibals that seem to find each other on the internet. It wasn't really my thing though, although, she did taste pretty good.

She is actually a really great shot, and we used to regularly visit a gun range, but after the first few years, I just started shooting her, and then did that too much also, so we stopped going.

But here we still are, together at the beach. She's a good girl, I really like her.

CHAPTER 60

1,292 Earth years in.

I'M SITTING ON MY sofa watching Saturday night television with Emily and the kids. Ninja Warrior has just finished, and the girls are getting excited for the start of X-Factor, their favourite programme of the week. I look at them; Lucy is seven, she is full of life and vitality, buzzing around trying to shape the beanbag with her elbows on the wooden floor. Trying to manoeuvre it into the perfect watching position - propped up at the back, bum burrowed in a hollow by wiggling it from side to side, knees crooked over a raised front, punching and pushing lumps until she is satisfied. Duke, the younger of my two black Labradors, is restless also, he's only eighteen months old so still has the puppy in him and is busy 'helping', mainly sticking his face into Lucy's and licking at inappropriate intervals. Lucy squeals partly with delight and partly with annoyance as Duke sticks his wet snout in the way of the screen with continued over-exuberance and snuffling. Jenny, my

11-year-old is sitting sideways in the armchair sorting out which acts she's going to be voting for on the iPad app.

"Stop it, Lucy, I can't hear!" The angry authority of her tone scrapes down my spine.

"Don't talk to her like that!" I hear myself snapping back, I realise she just wants Lucy to settle down, so they don't miss anything. It's the tone I object to. Emily takes a sip of white wine, we're back on the Chablis after a prolonged bout of Spanish Albarinos', she's sitting at the other end of the sofa to me, feet up on my lap, relaxing. But I know it's a sham, I know they're not really there, I know they're imposters playing the part of my family, created to perfection out of millions of micro fields. I know that even if I stay with them for ten years, they'll grow up into adults, I won't, I'll stay the same unless I choose to get old with them and to slow down. But what's the point? They're part of the ship in the same way that a bag of nuts and bolts is or the food creation machine. They won't grow the way my kids would because they have diverged from the original, any new growth is speculation, it's not made from the same shared experience of Earth; their friends, their families, pets, the weather, the events of the world, it's fashions and its failings. My kids lived on; I think. I hope they married and had fantastic families, and I hope they lived long happy lives and died peacefully with their families around them. These avatars are making it up as they go along. They are working off a programme that says, 'Keep him happy', 'Make him

smile', 'Stop him feeling sad all the time for the loss of his family, his world', 'Give him companionship and love', 'Act like you think his family would act'. It's an elaborate facade. They smell right, and they act right, and they are entirely like my family in every way; loving, fun, engaging, at the same time annoying, argumentative and sometimes infuriating. But I know they're not real, I can feel my tears welling up. I'm just a shadow, and so are they, a 3D living breathing memory, an echo of a time and a place that has very, very sadly passed.

I let the realisation fade as my youngest gets another lick in the face and squeals in delight.

I'm doing my best.

CHAPTER 61

1,695 Earth Years in.

ANOTHER DAY, ANOTHER DREARY commute.

I'm fucked off 'cause I can't get the last clue in the crossword. I've even got three of the letters. The clue is 'Broadcast', and I've got _ i _ u _ g _. I nearly always finish the crossword, not the cryptic one, they're just too hard, even after centuries, I've never really got my head around those. This is the 'Quick Crossword', and I usually get the first two thirds in the first 10 minutes, then have to work a bit at the others. Still, it's usually finished in 20 minutes, and I'm disappointed that this one is getting me. I'm not going to ask 15 for a clue or another letter. Even if I don't... divulge! Fucker, divulge. Bit of a leap from 'Broadcast' to 'Divulge' if you ask me but fuck you, I've finished it. Ha!

The train's pulling in and I'm standing in the vestibule section, along with about 25 others. We're nose-to-nose, waiting for the train to stop - and for someone at the front to press the door button. The 'ping, ping' sounds, the doors open, and we all spill out. I get a push from behind and nearly fall over forward, when I rebalance and look back, I can't work out who might have pushed me, there are three potential culprits, and none of them is making any sort of eye contact. Cunts. I get moving, and although a bit narked, I'm getting on with it. A lady with a wheeled suitcase, travelling in the same direction as me, but to my side, with no warning or indication, veers in front of me and almost sends me flying over her suitcase.

She ignores me and my audible sighs, no apology, no nothing. Two cunts in two minutes. Must be a record.

I get through the crush at the barrier with no more hassles. I cross the concourse and head down the busy escalator and out onto Waterloo Road. It's cold and over-cast but no rain. Not yet. I stand with the assembled mob at the crossing, maybe 50 people, the traffic's travelling pretty fast for Central London pre-9.00am so there's no opportunity to cross, then I get another push in the back, which nearly puts me off the footpath and out onto the road.

Fuck this, I turn around and see a white, 30 something man. He's wearing a navy raincoat over a pale blue shirt which is loose at the neck, no tie. He's got 'quiffy', posh boy hair and a cunt's face. He's quite a big guy, bigger than me, and sort of smiling, not apologetically. He goes,

"Sorry, buddy."

Fucking buddy. I don't fucking think so BUDDY. He's not sorry. I shoot out my right arm and cup my hand behind his neck and swing him past me into the oncoming traffic. He gets hit by a bike and then by a 7.5-tonne laundry truck. The front off-side wheel goes right over his midriff, and I see the truck go up and down as it bumps over his torso. He's certainly banged his head both on the truck and on the road. I'm not sure if he's dead or not. The truck has stopped over him. The cyclist is trying to get up. It looks like his arm is badly broken - it's sort of hanging and swinging about, and he's screaming out in pain. Now, the traffic has stopped, the other pedestrians just cross the road and continue to stream off in all directions out of the station as usual. I take off my rucksack and pull out a Glock 19 9mm, I cock it and fire twice into the hips/stomach of the man under the truck. He makes no noise, so I presume the fucker's already dead. Then I take a couple of paces over to the cyclist and shoot him point-blank in the side of the head because I'm bored of listening to the screaming. I just want it to stop. No one looks at me. No one cares. There're 16 bullets in a full magazine, and I've used three. So I pick off nine other targets indiscriminately; men and women, old and young, black and white. I double tap four of them because they're close enough to do so. I've got quite a lot of blood spatter on me, but I just ignore it. There is no shouting, no panic. It's like shooting fish in a barrel. When the gun is empty, I just drop it. I walk back into the station - just the same, just as busy. Nothing changed, no dramas. I walk into Marks & Spencer and pick up a couple of black T-shirts in my size. I take the bloody one off, and use

one of the new ones as a towel to wipe blood spatter and sweat away, which I then drop on the floor. Then I put on the other new T-shirt and pick up a black, hooded parka which I put on over the top. I pull off the price tags and throw them on the floor and go back out of the station. The shoot 'em up scene has now gone, the cars, buses and trucks keep driving up and down, the commuters keep heading to their offices and places of work. I pick up my rucksack, which is where I left it, put it on my back and carry on my walk into work.

.

CHAPTER 62

1,819 Earth years in.

"WHAT ARE THE OPTIONS?"

"Which options?"

"For me, for life, for the future." I haven't really spoken to 15 for a few Earth years.

"Ah, I see. It's time for this chat."

"The options have not changed from the first day you arrived. You can stay here forever, or until I demise, and I can provide you with anything and everything you desire to make your stay as comfortable as possible."

"How do you think I'm doing on that front?"

"Well, you don't seem to be as happy as you were."

"No, go figure."

"What's wrong with this option."

"I've exhausted the options; I've been here for almost two thousand years, and I can't take it anymore. It's like the biggest prison. I'm stir crazy, but I don't know what is better elsewhere."

"You can be put down on a planet of your choice, within a limit of my direction of travel, at any time."

"So I can decide to be put down with a bunch of aliens. I can pick savages to dominate or civilised, intelligent life?"

"Correct."

"And here I'd live out the rest of my 'normal Human life' from when you saved me."

"That is correct."

"So I was, or am 52 years old. I might live to be 100 tops, and I'd age accordingly."

"Yes, you could keep the form you are in, but once my influence is removed, any cells would start to age in the normal Human way. You could expect to live to the age you expect barring any accidents or tragedy along the way."

"But, I'd be the master of my own destiny."

"Yes. Totally."

"What other options are there?"

"The third and final option is that you can choose to die."

"Commit suicide?"

"No. Does that account for your nihilistic behaviour when you burned the houses in the habitat?"

"I don't know what I was doing. I knew I couldn't die."

"I think Humanity used to call it 'a cry for help'."

"I don't give a fuck what you call it. I'm just not sure what the fuck I'm alive for anymore. I'm not sure I want to die, and I'm not sure what I'm living for."

"To help me?"

"You don't need my help. You can always steal another sucker to do your dirty work for you."

"You are very good at it though."

"Being beaten up and occasionally killed. Really good at that."

"But you like killing."

"Avatars or opponents? The first because I'm so bored I can't think of anything else to do with them. The second lot, I've killed enough of them for you, for many lifetimes. I've paid any debt you may think is due, considering I had little choice when entering the contract."

"I have never said you owe me anything. You have always had the option to leave the ship at any suitable opportunity. There have been many of those. You were also given a chance to join the Humans, which I brokered on your behalf. I always knew this day was coming, it has with every passenger I have had. You though have lasted immensely longer than I can ever have imagined, and I am very grateful for your help and companionship."

"How come, when I've jumped off mountains then, you've not allowed me to die?"

"Because it had not been discussed and agreed that this was your aim. I saved you because we have an agreement that I will support you and provide for you as long as you work for me."

"And now I'm in a position to change this relationship."

"Yes. You have always been able to approach me and discuss whether you want to die or not, or even to set a

date of death or let me pick a time and date at random, is this what you want me to do now."

"Can you switch off my life support now?"

"Do you want me to switch you off now?" I paused for a few seconds. I was really tempted, but then another thought entered my head.

"Why the hesitation?"

"How far are we from the Human colony, is there any chance I can return to them?"

"Unfortunately, we are too far away from them, but also they did not manage to survive on the planet they colonised. They were able to defeat the Tyrosis but had societal issues over the next few hundred years."

"Why? What happened?"

"The group grew over time, but there were problems with the gene mapping. As you know, Darwin talked about 'Survival of the Fittest', the Humans with your genes were superior to those without. There was a division between the hybrids, with your gene signature, being smarter and more able than the 'one-handed man, short squat lady' group. There were arguments, division, fights and what amounted to a small war. Both sides suffered huge casualties as neither had a great tactical advantage over the other. Those that survived could not come together to save the race, they suffered hunger, disease and eventual extinction."

"Shit. That's fucked up."

"Indeed, it seems the Human Race never changes even when transplanted into another galaxy. Humans can't get on with each other, and it always ends badly. Aggressive and stupid mix too well together and make a volatile form of gunpowder."

"Could I have made a difference?"

"Possibly, but probably only in the short term. You would have still died after 40 - 50 years, then they would have been on their own anyway. You would have had to set up some rigid, unbendable structures, like some fierce religion or something, to keep everyone from killing themselves once you were gone. I'm not sure the annihilation of Humanity is inevitable, but, a pretty high percentage would suggest that it is. With Humans, it's more of a case of not 'will it happen' but 'when will it happen'."

"What have I got to live for then? I hate being here, I don't want to rock up on a planet with a bunch of aliens and have to fend for myself. If we find more Humans, they're likely to end up killing each other eventually anyway. But I can die, you agree that I can choose when and where to die?"

"Yes, that is your choice, not mine."

"Then I want a glorious death. I want to die in battle bested by a foe. If I die, 'No resuscitation', I'll give my all to win, in fact, with the element of jeopardy, I'm prepared to train harder and faster because either I win, or I die. But I die in battle, and that's how I want to go, to the hands of my victor."

"Agreed." I walked back to the habitat feeling elated. I think the happiest I have felt for a very long time.

CHAPTER 63

1,863 Earth years in.

I'M SORT OF BACK to being myself, I feel I have something to live for. It's not that fights come thick and fast,
actually the opposite. They are still long periods apart, but
most of my time is taken up training. Bettering myself
as a fighter, not as a Human being; running, climbing,
swimming, cycling, skiing - all for endurance. I work hard
on core exercises with additional yoga and Pilates, then I
work on strength training. I don't really lift weights much,
but there are a lot of squats and lunges and a lot of reps
with lighter weights. I then play squash and five-a-side
football to ensure I can move at speed; I need to be agile
as well as strong. Then I fight train: mixed martial arts,
boxing, fencing, aikido, individual martial art training,
army combat training, 'pub brawl' training, and gang
fighting. Then there is the weapons training: axes, knives,
throwing stars, javelin, all manner of swords from katana
to foil, broadsword to gladius all both throwing and close
quarter 'melee' style. And all forms of shooting weapons

from the most basic analogue to the most hi-tech digital. Weapons with the ability to kill one person to the power to destroy thousands in seconds.

So now the 'Save' button is off. I'm just reaching the light on the floor in the Arena. This thing I'm about to fight is a 'thing', a blob that moves by undulating, a little like a snail but much faster, it can also change direction very quickly. I can't really get under it as none of it really leaves the floor, it sort of 'oozes' around. It then has a tree-like central section, like a big, thick oak tree but no bark, just a smooth skin type substance, although the base is a brownie red, it's becoming more of a pinkish-red up the tree section. The top is the real mental bit. It has a selection of tendrils. Some look like an octopus' leg with suckers, others are more akin to an elephant's trunk then there are others which are more like antennae, all can be moved around at will, and all are capable of articulation. There is no head as such, just 20 or so protuberances come out of the top of the central section, they are also able to move position on this top area, so a trunk can be at the front or can be transferred to the back. Definitely one of the oddest things I've come across!

I have a ceremonial weapon, it's very much like a mace. If this was a medieval one from Earth, it would have a heavy spiky ball on one end attached by a clunky chain to a stick at the other end. The operator would hold the stick and swing the ball, causing lots of damage to anything it hits.

Rudimentary but effective.

The one I have has a 12 sided, sharp-edged, ball shape made of some sort of unidentifiable heavy metallic material attached to one end of a flexible tether. The other end of the tether is then attached to a short T-bar. The operator holds the 'T' of the T-bar and swings. The angular shape of the heavy ball would certainly also inflict quite a lot of damage if you received a shot from one around the ear 'oles. I'll try to avoid that - a slightly more modern interpretation of the Earth weapon, very similar purpose.

The Challenger is using one of its 'trunk things' to holding its mace and is swinging it around like it's a desk fan. So fast, the ball is whirring around in a blur. So that's how it's supposed to be used! I'm certainly able to swing the mace but getting the spinning, blur effect is probably a step too far. I'm just going to jump in and smash this alien with as many hits to the protuberances and its central section as I can whilst avoiding the blurry, spinny thing. Got to have a plan, even a simple one. The gong sounds and the big old lump starts to ooze towards me at a steady even pace of ooze-ness, the whirring weapon is held out in front of it by one of its extended trunk-arm-things. It acts as a shield but not one I want to get close to. I feint to strike under it, and the whirring-blur is moved to counter. I feint to the opposite side, and the whirr copies my move it continues to turn and face me in any direction I move and continues moving forward with the spinning weapon held out in front of it. Since

I've had the 'save me' function switched off, I've decided to stop researching the species I fight. I think this was an unfair advantage given to me. I don't think many or any of the aliens I've previously fought have had the chance to minutely examine my physiology before a fight. This didn't really occur to me over the hundreds of years, and I didn't really care, but now, I'm ready for death. I'm not going to go down without a fight, but if I am, I'm going down honestly, on my own, with no inside information and no cheating. Problem is, I have not got the faintest idea what I'm going to do with Tree-Trunky over here.

He's too quick at moving the whirr around for me to actually put a decent attack together, and he just keeps coming and keeps coming, at the same speed.

I've got to do something, so I hold the ball part of the weapon in both hands and swing the 'chain' and T-bar into the whirr. The T bar manages to catch and spin around with the whirr, this is so fast it's almost impossible to make out, I see a slight slowing but nothing much. I'm not sure how long I can hold on the ball before it gets wrenched from my hands. I pull the ball, with every ounce of strength from every muscle, fibre and sinew of my body. The good news is, I've now got two weapons as I've managed to wrench the Challenger's weapon out of its trunk thing. But he's still coming for me - now with all of his appendages moving around, and thrashing, and flailing on top of itself. I'm not sure he needed the weapon; this is much scarier! I pick both weapons up from the floor

and run away to get some thinking distance between us. It turns towards me and starts closing the ground. I take his weapon and throw it like in the Hammer field sport as far away from it as I can. Then I head back into him. I swing the mace at an outstretched tendril which connects, the tendril recoils but still operates.

Three of its octopus legs lengthen, they stretch out to about triple their original length and are now about two metres long each. These then morph from chunky 'legs' with suckers to thin, stiffer, sinewy rope-like appendages that narrow out along the length, these it then starts to use as whips. There are now long whips cracking and flailing towards me. I'm not really sure if it's trying to disarm me or to just hurt me, but I am taking some punishment, and it fucking hurts to get whipped by it.

I take another stinging whip across the chest and right shoulder; it immediately opens up into a bloody cut. Then two more in quick succession, one to the neck and one to the right thigh, I can't see the neck wound, but I know it's bleeding, the leg wound also opens up.

"You fucking bastard!"

I lose my head and just go fucking mental. I've only ever done this a few times, across all of my fights and most of those 'few' occasions were in the early stages of my career before I became an experienced, hardened fighter. I now know to stay calm and keep my wits about me. But maybe, I'm not too worried about keeping my wits about me.

I dive into it, swinging. I strike blow after blow into the trunk section and top and on any arm or leg that tries to get in the way. I kick it, and I bite it, I headbutt it, elbow and knee it and I don't stop. I'm sweating, breathing really hard and thrashing. I'm later grateful for the hours and hours of sparring and road work I've done. There is no substitute for it in a fight, you have to be able to go, and go again. Unless you've ever actually experienced a bout: boxing, karate, taekwondo, jujitsu, fencing, you will never understand. I only stop when it stops moving, and its arms, tendrils and legs stop moving. I only stop when many of these appendages litter the floor and ooze with sticky brown liquid. I only stop when the tree trunk looks blacker than before, and I keep hitting it because I want it to go down, but it won't go down, so I keep hitting it.

It's a while before I'm exhausted, sweating buckets, and salivating as I gasp enormous mouthfuls of air. It finally dawns on me that it won't go down because it's dead and it's stuck to the floor. I'd need a stump grinder to get any further. I throw down my weapon, give it one last kick to the lower stump and walk away. I've got a few bleeding slashes and will have plenty of bruises in the morning. But I'm still fucking alive.

CHAPTER 64

1,701 Earth years in.

THE HABITAT LOOKS DIFFERENT now, 'lived in', would be one description. The blackened shells of the burned-out houses remain although, like on Earth, life has been allowed to flourish and reclaim the ruins. There are several mature trees growing up through the middle of the primary residence and plants sprouting out of crevasses two floors up. There is moss covering a collapsed wall which used to lead into the sporting equipment store. The 'length' pool tiles are cracked and greening, there are about six inches of dirty water in the pool, which is full of insect life and pondweed. I love it. It's like cutting through the Cambodian jungle to find Angkor Wat for the first time, although it's definitely 'English Country-side', it's now 'English Wilds'. I've now got something a bit smaller to live in about one hundred metres away from the old house but tucked behind the tree line on the edge of the forest. It's a woodsman's cottage - a timber and stone affair, nothing grand. There's a ground floor and first floor, one biggish bedroom and a bathroom upstairs, then open plan downstairs. There's lots of exposed wood, a vaulted ceiling upstairs, rustic but without the charm. 'Modest' would be the sort of word an estate agent would use to describe it and a very far cry from the palatial, pristine museums I lived in when I first arrived. Just beyond the woods, out by the ruined old house, the parkland has been allowed to grow and now looks more natural. Originally it was always trimmed, edged, angular and flat. There are now shaggy tufts of long grass and flowers such as buttercups, dandelions, poppies and daisies that are allowed to grow unchecked. I don't usually have avatars here anymore; I like being alone. I like this wilder environment.

CHAPTER 65

2,015 Earth years in.

THIS IS A BIT of a weird one. I get to the middle, no research, no reset button. I'm looking at the thing standing on his light spot a few metres away. I've been told the fight will not start immediately as there are procedures first. Not something I've come across regularly. Often, it's some raging beast too eager to start before the noise, which makes a charge or leaps WAY too early. Often, they're the easiest to beat because they're all size and aggression with no finesse. It's usually a well-timed and directed thrust with a sword or smashes with a hammer or axe into a delicate region. Their momentum is often their downfall as the weight and speed of their attack is turned against them.

This guy is like something out of a German military college. Except he's yellowish. He's got a general Human form. Two arms, two legs but each has an additional knee or elbow joint to us. Four fingers, not five - no real advantage here - but tall and straight-backed, so straight that it looks like their backbone is straight and not curved like ours. He's standing to attention in his military uniform which is very much a dress uniform rather than fighting fatigues. When fighting opponents in this sort of uniform, the opponent is usually restricted by their clothing, I see this as a positive advantage. He is standing to attention and is so straight and still, chin up eyes front. Looking directly at me, unblinking. He has two escorts in the same military dress standing one behind each shoulder, I have been told they will go once the ceremony has finished and before the fight starts proper. They wear the same uniform except they have tall black shiny hats, which I can best describe as shiny wizards hats, or 'pointy' each with a massive pink ostrich type feather, but more prominent, sticking out of the top. It goes directly upwards and is the stupidest looking thing I have ever seen in my thousands of years. I can barely stop laughing.

Then the ceremonial music starts. I thought it was going to be some sort of brass marching music, but sadly it's not. It's like some late 1970s atonal, experimental electronic beeping. Different tones, different length, no pattern, a few pauses where you think it's finished, but then it starts up again, and a loud blary blast at the end. Thank fuck it's over! Next comes the formalities. The two feather guys march around in front of my guy and get out the royal military wet wipe, or that's what it looks like, each wipes his own half of the guy's face without him moving a muscle or twitching in the slightest. I'm

getting bored with all this, but after all these years, and all these fights, I know not to be too disrespectful - even if I want to be. I've ended up having some pretty tough fights from not really appreciating a different culture's traditions. Telling them to 'Get on with it' really pisses them off, then they fight twice as hard.

Now the presentation of weapons. I get to pick. One of the feathered escorts wheels over what looks like a rather elaborate, silver dessert trolley. It has a king-sized, domed cloche on the top which is then lifted off in front of me to reveal two beautiful sabres. I can see these are top-quality weapons, each shining brilliantly, pristine. In total, they are just under a metre in length, a two-inch blade at the hilt that curves delicately into a point over the whole length. There are ornate engravings of no-doubt important historic battle scenes along the length of both blades. Underneath the engraving, I can see the wavy line, the tell-tale sign of a master bladesmith. Only the very best have mastered the ability to cool steel at different speeds, on Earth usually by coating the blade in various thicknesses of clay. This 'apprentice-through-to-master' lifelong development, understanding and ultimate control of the heating and cooling process of steel to produce superior weapons. The front blade-edge hardened to maintain solidity and sharpness, the back, thicker part of the sword shaft is softer, more flexible - meaning the blade is less likely to snap during use.

I select a weapon, to me they're both the same. I take the first one and swing it about a bit in my right hand. It almost 'zings' as I cut the air. There is a jewelled finger guard over the front of the sword handle, the jewels are knobbly and could easily be used to punch if we ever get close enough. There is also a short, multi-coloured, braided, tasselled string hanging from the pommel at the bottom of the hilt of the weapon. The straight-backed man moves his right appendage to select his weapon with barely a look down, the arm moves slightly oddly with his extra joint. He then holds the sword up in front of his body with his hand at rib height. The blade is at right angles to the ground and would touch his nose if he had one.

The be-plumed lackeys are fussing around again. They are anointing the sword with various balms and oils, some which drip down the length of the blade, through and over the hand and down onto the ground where they form a little pool.

I'm a little bored. Actually, I'm quite bored, this is taking ages.

Next, the challenge.

I have to stand facing my opponent, he still has his sword up by his face. I have to mimic this and hold my sword similarly, weight evenly on both feet. He swooshes the sword down until it is by his side, pointing downwards. I copy his actions.

Then his face changes, in fact, his whole demeanour changes, from stoic attention - stern and unyielding, to the most affable being you'll ever meet.

"Hi, I'm Britostoft Zammermont-Hackeltract-D-bonze the third. My friends call me Brito, it's a pleasure to meet you." He smiles brightly. He's warm and engaging and totally disarming.

"Pleasure to meet you too," I say, "When are we going to get started?"

"Oh, not long now, I shouldn't think. We're nearly there. I've never really done any of this sort of stuff before. It is interminably long, and tiresome isn't it." he looks slightly embarrassed, "Shall I ask?"

"No, just leave it."

"I have to formally ask you if you're ready to engage in battle with me, a bit dull, but that's the protocol." He's genuinely looking like he's putting upon me to get an answer.

"Yup, let's go." I shoot back impatiently.

"Oh, marvellous," he smiles brightly, "looking forward to it. Jolly good then." He turns back to his former self. As straight as a board, sword back up in front of his face. The strangest thing that's ever happened to me.

The two plumed guys come back around to the front of him and give him a final bit of tidying up; checking the uniform is perfect, and then finally giving him a couple of puffs of battle perfume before bowing to each other, then to Brito, and then trotting off in unison, plumes flowing as they go - back to the edge of the Arena and through the door which closes behind them.

Now, finally, we're ready. I get my game face on. I stand left foot forward, right foot back, left shoulder forward and arm up, right sword hand and elbow up, so the sword is held at my face height horizontal to the ground and pointing at Brito. He still stands, unmoved, sword vertical to the ground in front of his face. I start to snarl, then the gong sounds.

I run straight towards him and take a wild, running cut, He expertly parries my thrust away. My thoughts of an easy win dissipate quickly. I do not scare him, he's calm under pressure, well trained and not going to let me bully him.

Fine by me, I'm an exceptional fencer and swordsman. I'm not going to be too aggressive, and I'm not going to do anything wild. Not anymore.

He takes much more of a fencer's stance. Side on, sword held out forward, left hand up and behind. I do, likewise. So follows a long procession of fencing moves which on the outside would seem to get us nowhere but to the trained eye would suggest that we both are spending quite a long time probing and working out the nuances of each other's game. Thrusting and parrying, our ability to block, our general speed, our defensive strengths and weaknesses and our fondness for specific attacks. Our ability to improvise when needed. The most interesting part of Brito's game for me is the extra joints in his legs and in his arms, he can increase his reach by adjusting his weight forward which with my single jointed knees, I don't have. He also has a fearsome cut-stroke as his extra arm joint allows him some extra whip through the stroke.

We've both been comfortably fighting for about 10 minutes. We have fierce flurries, followed by breathers where we do little at all and give each other some distance to recover. We've been fighting in straight lines, conventional fencing, in and out, the difference being that we don't have a piste to stay on, if one party is particularly aggressive, the other can just back off fast. By now, I've learned all I'm ever going to learn about this guy. He's an exceptional swordsman. He's classically schooled, exceptionally well-schooled. I've noted this, but I've also given a couple of signs of my brawling ability. He's not really fully got hold of these, and I've recognised this as a potential weakness. The fencing academies don't really go in for out-and-out street fighting.

We're coming off another breather. I present the fencer's stance, and he also does, this is what we've been doing for quite a while, it's expected. I'm using my peripheral vision to watch his whole rather than focus on any specific part of his body. This allows me to react to the slightest twitch wherever it comes from, the arm, the foot, the hip, the eye. I'm waiting for the attack, and I'm going to be purposefully slow to react. A slight shift in his weight from left leg to right telegraphs to me that the attack is starting. In a gasp, he leaps forward and swipes the point of his sword towards my neck. I've seen it coming, and drop, and slice.

He screams, then cuts the scream, mid-scream. It's not what gentlemen do. I've rolled away and bounced back up from the second after I made contact. I've cut a pretty severe gash into his lower leg; it would be around the height of his right calf muscle if he was Human. He doesn't go down. His demeanour barely changes, but there is a thick clear liquid oozing down his leg.

"Good shot." composure regained.

"Thank you." I smile.

His stance is back. He's ready for the next attack.

Same again, a few fencing moves backwards and forwards then breathers. The leg doesn't seem to be bothering him. He really is outstanding - we don't talk during the breaks. I double-up and gasp for air, he stands stolidly. I can see he's tired, and he's clearly exerting himself, but he's trying not to show any weakness. He's dropped his arm a little since my leg attack. This is clearly in anticipation of a similar move.

This time, we face up. He comes for me, and I jump back. He comes again, and I jump back trying to show him I'm off-balance, he tries to seize the advantage and lunges forward again overreaching slightly. I spin left and watch him go by and continue to turn to bring my sword arm around to make contact with his back or ribs. I strike, but he's already realised the danger and parries the blade.

I've stung him again, but it's a relatively weak shot. There's another cut and more clear liquid, but if he hadn't been as fast as he is, he would probably be down by now. No scream. As we stand to face each other, he gives me a little nod - a salute to the hit.

We breathe again.

Then we're back on the virtual piste. Swords up.

He doesn't move, he still doesn't move. I back off and walk away after 30 seconds of nothing. He's waiting for me. I've got all day, all millennia. We reset another 30 seconds of acting like a statue. I walk away again.

Patience, patience.

He resets. I move to do so, and he's on me. Diving in early is not his style, which is why he's caught me out and is all over me. I hear the whistle of the blade loud and clear, but I'll be fucked if I saw it. He's slashed my neck. It's a surprise, so I stagger back and hold my blade up to half parry a heart lunge. I'm bleeding, but he's missed the critical veins and arteries. He whips the sword again and slashes my right sword hand, I can do without this. I throw myself into him and punch him full in the face with the jewelled handguard, then again doubling up on my right jab. He pushes me away, I thought out of range, but he sticks his sword through my side, a 'run me through' shot that extra elbow joint giving him reach beyond reach. In and out but I know there are no significant organs where he's struck, what it will do is bleed, I've now got a few bleeders. It fucking hurts.

"You bastard!" I stagger back and try to compose myself. He comes again, and as I try to get my sword up to defend myself he slaps it away with his open left hand and punches me hard on the jaw with the jewelled hand guard of his sword, a bit of payback, I can't complain, then he pirouettes and whips his right sword hand around and crashes the pommel of the sword straight into my right temple at the end of the full circle. There's only one way I'm going, and that's down. My head slams onto the ground and bounces. He then kicks me in the teeth for good measure which whips my head back.

Just then it doesn't matter anymore. I close my eyes and can see Emily and the girls. They're together, and they're looking at me. I try to smile, but my broken body hurts so much.

Brito throws me over onto my back onto the flat, empty grey whiteness. Finally, through the pain, and still with my eyes closed, looking at my family, I force them a smile. Brito is above me. He places the tip of his sword on my neck and sees my smile.

"Sorry about his old chap." Says Brito cheerily, and using his whole weight, pushes down on the sword.

CHAPTER 66

2,015 Earth years in.

BLINK, AND THE BLACKNESS is gone.

"YOU FUCKING LIAR!!" I scream at the top to my voice, "Fuck you, you fucking cunt!!"

I'm lying on the grey-white floor just next to 15, the battle Arena is no-more. I am fit and healthy again. God knows how long I've been out for.

"We had a fucking deal you fucker!!"

I jump up and swing a kick at the bollard. I connect solidly, the column does not move a single millimetre and the impact really, really hurts my foot.

"Fuck! You bastard! What about our fucking deal? You said I could die! That was the deal! I'm supposed to be dead!" I drop to the floor and start to cry; I ball into a tight foetal position. I'm beginning to cry uncontrollably. I start blubbing. "This isn't fair, I'm supposed to be dead.", over and over again through my tears, snot and discomfort. My chest feels knotted. It's proper crying, my shoulders lurch with every sob. I feel as if I can't breathe.

Through my loud sobbing, I start to hear 15 talking to me, repeating the same line. I don't really focus on it to begin with as I'm so utterly distraught.

"... need..... need..... I need.....I need you.....I need you....."

I focus my hearing eventually and realise what he's saying. I shout out through tears and snot,

"Why do you need me? I'm not special, I was no different to anyone else on that carriage."

"You are, you were the one I needed."

"Fuck you, you said it was an accident, I was the most likely to die."

"I wanted a killer, a proper cold-blooded killer who showed no remorse for his crimes, who doesn't even think of his actions as crimes."

I'm still crying, I'm still in a ball, sobbing, trying to breathe but listening.

"So why me. I'm no killer."

"Yes, you are."

"I've never killed anyone."

"You have, you killed five women in Soho between 1990 and 1994. I wanted a serial killer, and I got the 'Soho Slasher', the 'Soho Slaughterer', the 'Soho Serial-Killer'."

"I don't know what you're talking about, I'm not a serial killer."

Looping snippets of conversations start to play loudly as if on a hidden Tannoy system, the noise fills the space around me. Captured pieces of conversations I have had

with 15 over time rolling in and out from one another, louder and quieter, some of which I remember and some I don't. It is me talking, it is 15 too. I know these conversations took place; I know they're real...

..."What about the others, why me?"

"Good question." There is a pause, I don't believe 15 is thinking, I think he's doing it for drama. **Can you think of any reason why I'd choose you?"**

"No. Average Joe really."

There is another small pause before, "Correct. You were not special; you were chosen, though. You were the one most likely not to survive and least likely to leave any physical residue."...

..."I can retain your current function in its entirety, you will not lose any memory or functional ability. There are many synaptic bonds, pathways and links that have been broken and damaged but can be repaired. There are a couple of other enhancements I can add, in effect shining light on certain suppressed memories and unlocking the boozy night, 'if I can't remember it then I don't have to apologise for it' stuff, to help you remember much of what you have forgotten. The nights out when alcohol severely retarded your memory of the evening can be newly reflected in all their glory."

"Sounds like you're advising against?"

"On the contrary, I think it'll really help you in general. It's just that I'm also preparing you, it comes warts and all."...

...*I roll my eyes back and continue to pace,* "Don't tell me... from across the galaxy, you saw me playing 'Snake' on my mobile, and I was really fucking good at it, so you thought I'd be good enough to command your fleet of battleships to smash alien races up?"

"Not exactly."

"So what then?"...

..."You've missed something big out of this plan. I'm not a killer or a maimer, I'm not even a fighter. What if I don't want to do it?"

"I'm sure you are, deep down inside. But, if not, I can drop you off at any habitable planet or space station that takes your fancy. You can pick an isolated planet, and I'll give you enough supplies and resources to live out your natural life. Or live on a space station amongst alien races, or you can fight for me and live here in paradise. Whichever garden of earthly delights you choose, and I'll protect you and sustain you."...

…"I didn't like fighting him, and I didn't want to kill him. If he'd been some big ugly bruiser, or even someone I hadn't been introduced to, it would have been easier. That said, I knew what I had to do, and I can live with it. It just tastes sour."…

…"You don't need my help. You can always steal another sucker to do your dirty work for you."

"You are very good at it though."

"Being beaten up and occasionally killed. Really good at that."

"But you like killing."

"Avatars or opponents? The first because I'm so bored, I can't think of anything else to do with them. The second lot, I've killed enough of them for you, for many lifetimes. I've paid any debt you may think is due, considering I had little choice when entering the contract."…

The sound continues as 15 starts to talk again. "You are, you were clever, calculated, you didn't leave any clues, you showed no remorse, but something changed, you stopped and disappeared, you fell in love. You met Emily, and she changed you, she cured you, she didn't know this or who you were, but you stopped. You repressed your memories and very successfully I may add. You squeezed them right down into a place that has been very difficult to unlock. You don't remember? I don't care about what you did or didn't do. I just wanted you to be my Champion. You're a dangerous bastard."

"No, that's not me, it's not!" I'm holding my head, wailing, screaming, "You've got the wrong man! You've got the wrong man! I've done nothing!"

"The first two were Sophie and her friend, you slashed their throats in an alley at the back of Frith Street. Sarah was found strangled and then cut open in a bin near Soho Square. Two others, Melanie, strangled with a ligature and disembowelled, found in a graveyard in Wardour Street and Karen, found in a car park with her throat cut and a fork in her eye. I know this, I've always known. That's why I chose you. You're vicious, calculated, dangerous."

"That's not me, I'm not a killer, you've made it up with avatars and shit."

"You dropped straight back into it. You're a killer plain and simple, no morals, no shame, no feeling. Cold-hearted, exactly the sort of Human I needed. Like Pierre, He killed his wife and children and buried them under the muck heap in his farm."

"You've got the wrong man; I'm not like him, I'm not like that. It must have been someone else? I'm no killer."

I'm blubbing now, my head's imploding. I fall to the ground in a ball.

"There's no doubt, I know who you are, in the same way as I knew about Pierre and the Murdering Mormon I'm not wrong, you know that."

"I'm not a serial killer!" I'm in a ball on my haunches shouting, sweating, holding my head.

"Do you remember now..?"

"No."

"Do you remember the screams..?"

"No, fuck off."

"You remember the fear in their faces...?"

"FUCK OFF."

"You watched mercilessly as their lives ebbed away..."

"NO, no."

"You cut their throats."

"Fuck off, fuck off."

"You slashed them."

"FUCK OFF!!"

"Do you remember? You killed them all." The looping sounds of conversations abruptly end at this moment.

There is once again the absolute silence of outer space. I pause and wipe my wet nose down the back of my left arm. Then I look up at 15.

"I do, I fucking do, I fucking remember every fucking second, I can't fucking help it. I couldn't fucking help it, I had to kill them, I fucking had to. I couldn't stop myself. I fucking killed them. You know I did then you allowed me to kill again, I didn't want to kill again." I'm angrily spitting the words out through snot and tears.

"But it was so simple."

"You should have told me."

"You knew."

"You should have told me."

"You know who you are."

"Yes, I fucking know. I've always fucking known. It was pushed down and locked away for years, but the avatars are so easy…"

Now out in the open, I feel calmer, it's all true, I have no remorse.

"I don't want to do this anymore. I want to stop killing. I just want you to let me go. Let me go." I'm still agitated but calmer. I wipe my nose again down my arm and push back my hair, I can breathe again, I take a couple of long deep breaths and try to compose myself. "I just want to go back."

"You can't, they're all dead. Everyone's dead. Those people you were on the train with every morning had no idea they were sitting beside a murderous madman."

I pause, briefly, and replay in my head what 15 has just said. My madness and mania have subsided. I heard that. I listened to what 15 just said, and a lightbulb has gone off, a realisation, something I would never have thought about without all of this being revealed to me. Now I see it all.

"You made this happen! It was you all along. You knew who I was. I didn't, I'd pushed it down, all but forgotten, but you knew." I'm standing up striding towards 15. I get close and crouch down to the flashing light until we are

face to face, centimetres apart. I'm red-faced, angry, spitting, snarling. "You knew where I was, you knew what I was, and you wanted me. You tipped a petrol tanker off a rail bridge onto the train and set it on fire at precisely the right time to be able to get me out of there. You did it, and you call me a murderous bastard! You killed 43 innocent people and injured hundreds more just to get me. You made children motherless and fatherless by your actions so you could abduct me, steal me away from my wife and children. I wasn't due to die, neither were they - you made it happen. You told me you were benign, that you'd always tell me the truth. You're not! You're a liar. A fucking, stinking liar. You're worse than me, I may be a serial killer, but you're a mass murderer! You're as psychotic as me, probably worse."

Now I'm really shouting, I've seen the light,

"YOU'RE A FUCKING MONSTROUS EVIL BAST..."

The lights go out.

I stop breathing, mid mouthful. Just stop, as it started. I'm suddenly in darkness, floating not breathing, I know it's the same as the first time. The pain has gone, but I'm struggling for breath. I'm gasping, desperate to fill my lungs. Even when you want to die, the act of dying makes you want to live, you try to save yourself. I'm not choking, but I'm scrambling with my hands to clear my airways, nothing is blocking them, I know this. I know it's the final way. Pure blackness, asphyxiation. A few more seconds of grasping, scratching, struggling. My hands stop first;

my arms go limp and fall away from my face down to my sides. It doesn't take much longer, another few more seconds only. Although in total darkness, I can just see white flaring, it's in my head, it's the lack of oxygen in my brain building, building...

CHAPTER 67

2,015 Earth years in.

T HE REMAINS LAY THERE on the grey whiteness.
They may have laid there for another thousand Earth years, or they may have laid there for just the blink of an eye.

Some time later, the field collapsed, and they were gone.

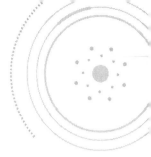

Epilogue

A PALE BLUE LIGHT BLINKS on, and then off, in the grey whiteness.

Some time later, it starts to flash red...

Acknowledgement

N OT HAVING DONE THIS before I've 'leant' on quite a few people for help.

Thanks Mum for all of your help. I wouldn't be here without you (obvs). Love you.

The manuscript was first read by my cousin John Green, because he reads a lot of Sci-Fi. My one question was, 'Have you paid money for worse than this?' Fortunately he answered positively, although he also told me that there was still a lot of work to be done to the script before I could publish it. The second person who read was my eldest sister Paula, both her feedback and that of her husband, Andy, has been invaluable. The book was then read by my other older sister, Alison and my younger brother Mick, again both helped hugely with editing and sorting out plot inaccuracies of which there were many.

Then the other readers; Simon, Jamie, Chris and Jerry. Also Marjorie Torrance for her belief and for putting me in touch with Mark and Lucy Millar who encouraged me and helped with industry contacts.

Finally, my long-time mate and collaborator Garry Staines for designing and illustrating the cover and agreeing to do so for no financial gain!

Printed in Great Britain
by Amazon